Silver Leaf

Annie M. Cole

Copyright © 2012 by Annie M. Cole

ISBN 978-0-7414-7726-2 Paperback
ISBN 978-0-7414-7727-9 eBook
Library of Congress Control Number: 2012941400

Printed in the United States of America

Published August 2012

INFINITY PUBLISHING
1094 New DeHaven Street, Suite 100
West Conshohocken, PA 19428-2713
Toll-free (877) BUY BOOK
Local Phone (610) 941-9999
Fax (610) 941-9959
Info@buybooksontheweb.com
www.buybooksontheweb.com

To my husband, Bubba, the one who holds my heart.

Chapter 1

$\mathcal{G}$reat and awful moments in life are sometimes like ghosts: you don't look for them, and you certainly don't expect them, but suddenly they're just there, staring you in the face.

Landis Blakely McPherson, or "Lannie" as she was known by nearly everyone in the small town of Moss Bay, Alabama, led a well-ordered life. Many envied her spirit and the way she moved through life with a certain sense of grace and purpose, but, just like the lazy current of Bayou Bell, meandering along its undisturbed course, something large was about to plop into the water right in front of her. And, that *something* would forever change the course of her life.

The remnants of sleep still lingered in Lannie's voice as she called out in response to the persistent knock on the door. "I'm coming, I'm coming."

Feeling weary and drained, Lannie unhurriedly tied the cotton robe around her slender waist, rubbed her swollen eyes, and made her way to the door. Peering through the beveled glass of the sidelight, she saw the distressed face of her younger half-sister, Mindy, and her two-year-old niece,

Sadie. Yanking the door open, Lannie called out, "Mindy! What on Earth is the matter?"

"Keep away from me," Mindy snarled. "Here, take her. I can't take it anymore. He's dead and it's all your fault!" Mindy thrust Sadie forward unceremoniously. "She's *his* child! If Cade had left you like I asked him to, he'd be working for my father now and still alive—we'd be a family!" she screamed in frustration, tears streaming down her cheeks. "I can't stand to look at her anymore...either of you!"

Lannie stared blankly at her sister for one horrifying moment as she tried to absorb the information through her foggy mind. The words *she's his child* swirled around in her head. A tremor ran through her, snapping her out of the paralyzing trance. Moving slowly, Lannie lifted Sadie into her arms and stepped inside the house. After placing the little girl on the sofa with a book, she returned to her sister, quietly pulling the door shut behind her.

Whap! Lannie's hand struck hard across Mindy's cheek. "How dare you do this to Sadie!" Whap! "And how dare you do this to me! You make this accusation *now*...now that Cade isn't here to defend himself!"

Mindy stumbled backward, rubbing her inflamed cheek. She turned and fled down the steps toward her car. Yanking the car door open, she pulled out an overnight case and flung it into the shrubbery. The case popped open and the contents spilled out, catching on the branches. In one swift movement, Mindy jumped behind the wheel of her car and sped off.

Solemnly, Lannie watched as a wisp of gray smoke vanished in the air behind her sister's squealing tires. Stepping down the porch steps on trembling legs, she began gathering the scattered items of Sadie's young life. Colorful and delicate pinks and greens, yellows and blues, the colors of innocence and childhood draped across the dew-drenched hedges and over the lawn. A tight knot formed in her throat as she stared at the mocking testament of betrayal in front of her.

Sadie's suitcase was clutched tightly in her hand as Lannie climbed the steps, hovering near the door. With a deep breath she tried to gather her strength to face this new challenge. A profound trembling threatened to overtake her body as she thought of Mindy with Cade.

Mindy had always been selfish, even as a child, boasting often that she'd always gotten what she wanted in life. And it was no secret that what Mindy had wanted in life was Lannie's husband, Cade.

Never taking the infatuation seriously, Lannie assumed most young girls fantasize about older, attractive men. "Mindy is off the chain. You can't believe her," she whispered, reasoning with herself. "This is just like her to draw attention to herself in the middle of a crisis."

Stepping inside the house she glanced at the mantle clock, as was her habit, and noted the time: 9:23 AM. No matter what happened that day, Lannie knew that from that time forward nothing would ever be the same again.

Looking down into Sadie's wide brown eyes, Lannie suddenly saw clearly what she had missed for the past two years: the dimpled cheek, the brown eyes full of wonder. *Why haven't I noticed before?* Swallowing hard, Lannie cleared her throat to stave off the encroaching emotion and grief. The suddenness of her husband's death had taken its toll, but *this* revelation stunned her beyond belief. Sadie was the mirror image of her father, Lannie's husband!

Cade had been one of Moss Bay's most capable fire-fighters. The possibility of injury had always been in the back of Lannie's mind, but the fear had eased over the years in the routine of life. She'd seldom dwelt on the very real danger of his profession. The chance of serious injury had always seemed so remote. It happened, but always to someone else, some other family.

Bitterness intensified as she thought of the accusation against her husband. The fact that he was not here to defend himself against it made it painfully hard to handle, leaving her frustrated and hurt.

Despite Lannie's best efforts to conceal her emotions, Sadie seemed to instinctively know something was wrong. The little girl's soft, pink lips trembled as she fixed her eyes on Lannie.

"Come here, Sadie girl," Lannie cooed, releasing a heavy sigh. Lifting Sadie from the sofa she nuzzled her neck, feeling the child's downy, white-blond hair tickle her cheek. Easing into a comfortable chair, Lannie held the little girl close, embracing her tightly as they experienced the warmth of each other in that bittersweet peace that often follows devastation.

In the weeks that followed her husband's death, when Lannie thought her cup of despair was at its capacity, news of the passing of her beloved friend, Tilda Wheeler, reached her.

Lannie stood near the casket and through tear-swollen eyes quietly observed the descending coffin as it met the hard soil of the grave with a thud. She clenched her small hands in tight fists as she gathered her strength and choked back tears. Tilda Wheeler was now gone forever.

Captain Jake Chamberlain seemed relatively young, maybe thirty or so. But, the lines around his azure blue eyes, accentuated by the weathered tan of his skin, bore the weariness of sleepless nights. Running a roughened hand through his dark brown hair, Jake raised his head to catch a sudden, cooling breeze. Guilt surfaced in the back of his mind as he watched the casket of his aunt, Tilda Wheeler, being lowered into the earth.

Jake had only met his Aunt Tilda once, and that had been at her request a few short weeks ago. He thought back to their conversation that day. Tilda was his dad's oldest sister, and Jake had been surprised to find that she'd kept up with him throughout the years. She astonished him with her knowledge of his affairs; she even knew the name of the ship he captained in Norfolk, Virginia. The repeated question in his mind was, *Why would she leave half of all she owned in this world to me, a virtual stranger?* He'd thought of every possible reason. The only thing that was sure was that Tilda Wheeler wanted him here, in Moss Bay, Alabama, and the sizable estate she'd left to him was proof of it.

As the priest gave his final blessing, Jake lowered his gaze, catching a glimpse of a small, trim woman pausing before the open grave. She wore a simple, sleeveless black dress. Light ash brown hair lifted in the breeze and played around her shoulders, wisps of it catching in the corners of her mouth. He watched her lips mouth a few words, and then she kissed a long stemmed rose and tossed it into the grave. His eyes took in the graceful movements of her hands as they released the flower.

With much curiosity, Jake observed the woman. Her shoulders lifted and fell, as if the weight of the world pressed down upon her. There was an elusiveness about her, yet also something very alluring about the way she carried herself. She turned away from the graveside and headed toward a woman standing at a distance, holding a small child. He watched those same graceful hands reach out and take the child from the arms of the woman. Then slowly, the trio walked toward the cemetery gate. He found he could not pull his attention away from the scene.

One by one, the mourners began leaving. Already they seemed unconcerned about how fleeting and fragile life really was. Muted conversations hovered around the topics of dinner and golf games. For reasons unknown, even to himself, Jake pressed through the crowd, intent on speaking with the intriguing woman in black. But, just as he came into the clearing, he could see that the woman had already walked through the gates of the cemetery. A light rain began to fall as his eyes searched between the wrought iron bars that surrounded the graveyard, seeking just one more glimpse of her before she disappeared.

Chapter 2

Lannie closed her eyes against the dull ache that had been throbbing in her head since she returned home. The lack of sleep mixed with sorrow had left her numb. With trembling hands, she filled the kettle and set it to boil. Wandering over to the front window, she groaned inwardly, not sure what to do anymore. Thankfully, Sadie had succumbed to sleep during the drive home. After dropping off her mother-in-law, Wren, Lannie headed straight home, intent on having a hot cup of tea and a long soak in the tub to relieve the stress of the day.

Wren had been careful to conceal her delight at the news that Sadie could possibly be her granddaughter. Lannie smiled when she thought of Wren's attempt to keep the joy from showing on her face as she explained in detail what had happened and what Mindy had claimed about Cade.

Raindrops began to pelt the hot pavement, sending people scurrying for cover on the somewhat busy neighborhood street of Moss Bay. A car passed, then stopped suddenly and began backing up, pulling up next to the curb.

Footfalls splashed on the steamy sidewalk as an elderly man, clean-cut and distinguished looking, made his way to the door.

Lannie didn't wait for a knock but pulled the door open as the man approached. "May I help you?" she asked cautiously, searching the man's eyes.

"I certainly hope so," the man replied, somewhat out of breath as he wiped down the sleeves of his navy blue jacket. "I'm William Forsyth, Tilda Wheeler's attorney. If you're Landis McPherson, I'd like a word with you if I may."

"Oh!" Lannie responded. "Of course, come in." The tea kettle began a shrill whistle from the kitchen. "Would you like a cup of tea, Mr. Forsyth?" Lannie offered. "I was just about to have one myself."

"I would love a cup of tea on this dreary day. You certainly don't find very many hot tea drinkers this far south anymore, you know. That'll be a real treat." William's smile reached his eyes.

"Well, you happen to have one here. I agree with C. S. Lewis when he said, 'You can't get a book long enough or a cup of tea big enough to suit me.'" The soft syllables of Lannie's South Alabama accent warmed her response. Indicating a chair, she said, "Have a seat, Mr. Forsyth, and please call me Lannie."

Although losing her friend Tilda grieved her terribly, Lannie knew in her heart that Tilda had always looked forward to the day of her homecoming with great anticipation. Her husband had passed away many years ago, and she missed him terribly. She spoke often of the blessed day when she would join him in heaven and how they would be whole again.

Stepping into the kitchen, Lannie poured two cups of tea and arranged several cookies on a tray. She gave a half smile as she recalled Tilda's concern as the years went by that she would be older than her husband in heaven. "If the Lord is truly merciful," she would say, in her breathy voice, "he will see to it that I don't look a day over twenty-nine."

"Here you go, Mr. Forsyth." Lannie placed the tray on the coffee table. "Please, have a cookie."

"Thank you, I believe I will." He reached for a cookie, took a big bite, and said as he chewed, "This shouldn't take much of your time." Pausing, he turned the cookie in his hand. "What are these? They're wonderful!"

"Old fashioned tea cakes."

Sipping his tea, he closed his eyes briefly and said, "Delicious. Thank you. Now," he continued, "as you may well know, Tilda Wheeler had a mind of her own, and she had certain...notions." He gave a brief laugh. "All of the details of her last wishes have been neatly organized. And, I might add, meticulously arranged according to her designs."

Lannie smiled softly as she remembered her friend. She had filled a hollow place in Lannie's heart since she had been a small child. Even now, she could almost hear Tilda's unique and raspy voice describing some wonder she had found. Not much ever escaped Tilda Wheeler's notice. The woman had a gift of perception that rivaled the Prophets'.

William sat his cup down with a clink and reached in his jacket for his glasses. He snapped the briefcase open. "Mrs. Wheeler left you half of the property known as Beauchene." He peered at Lannie over the top of his glasses.

"That really doesn't surprise me," Lannie stated, holding her cup with both hands as she casually took a sip of her tea.

"Tilda loved Beauchene, and she knew I did, too. She knows I'll look after it."

William studied the woman, not quite sure what to make of the casual response to such joyful news, then he remembered the tragic events that had plagued her for the past few months. It was certainly no secret in the small town of Moss Bay that Lannie McPherson's husband, Cade, died on the job after falling through a burned out floor in a house fire. A day after his funeral, her half-sister revealed that she and Cade had had a child together. And now, Lannie was left taking care of the child that her sister had abandoned on her doorstep.

"Beauchene...that means beautiful oak, doesn't it?" William asked, masking the pity he now felt for the young woman.

Lannie nodded, fingering the silver medallion around her slender neck. It was embossed with a silver leaf and had been a gift from Tilda. Smiling warmly, she replied, "Yes, it does. The place is named after the beautiful silver leaf oak that grows in front of the house."

"Yes, I remember that tree, quite beautiful. I don't believe I've ever seen another one like it." William paused. "Well, since you knew Tilda so well, it probably won't surprise you to learn that you're to share the estate with her nephew, Captain Jake Chamberlain."

Lannie lifted her brow. "The Yankee?"

William chuckled before reaching for his tea. *Well, that got a response out of her*, he thought. "One and the same, but from what I understand he won't be around much. He's a captain on a cargo vessel out of Mobile Bay." Sensing some apprehension, he added, "I've met the man, and he seems like a fine fellow. And, I might add, he's not at all upset to learn he's to share the property with you. In fact, I got the sense he was glad that someone would be on the property. He's away so much of the time."

Putting the cup to her lips, she took a slow pull of the tea, showing mild interest.

"Of course, as you remember, Tilda's house is actually two separate apartments. Since her house in Mobile was her primary residence, and she hasn't been at Beauchene for the past several years, I'm sure there will be some condition issues with the property, but the house remains divided."

Lannie smiled. "Yes, I remember. Her sister Bess lived on the south side of the house, and she lived on the north side. I always thought of them as the good witch of the north and the wicked witch of the south." Lannie gave a weak smile, and then began to rub her temples, seeking some relief from the stress of it all. The pounding in her head seemed to ease a little, allowing her to think more clearly.

William frowned at the mention of the name Bess. "Yes, I remember Bess quite well. She once called me a stinking polecat and tried to chase me away with a broom!" A deep frown gathered at his brow, and then he smirked. "I've never understood why some people have such an aversion to people of my profession."

Lannie hid a grin behind her cup, thinking how much she liked this man, William Forsyth, and for some odd reason, she trusted him.

Closing the briefcase with a snap, William added softly, "I'm terribly sorry for your recent losses, Mrs. McPherson. And I do appreciate you taking the time in your grief to see me today. Later, you may have questions about the thirty-three acres and how they are to be divided. The house and all of the outbuildings are clearly marked on the map I'm leaving with you. Mr. Chamberlain also has a copy. The property begins at the edge of Bell Forest to the south and east with a wide swath of bay front to the west." He tapped the papers lightly. "It's all in here. But, should you need me for anything, just call or drop by. I'll be happy to assist you in any way whatsoever." Seeking to put her mind at ease, he added, "The little bit I know of Jake Chamberlain, he seems an honorable man. And, knowing Tilda, she never would have made an arrangement like this if she didn't trust the man."

The leaves of the silver leaf tree were fresh and alive, their growth no doubt brought on by the endless spring rains, as Lannie, armed with a quilt, cleaning supplies, and Sadie, stepped up to the house. The roses were in bloom, and even in the heat of the day they were still the same soft shade of pink Lannie remembered from happier times. Tilda's elusive laughter drifted through her mind as they walked along the wide porch. Inspecting the damage time had wrought on the house, she ran a hand lightly around the window frame. The heady scent of roses mixed with vetiver wafted up, filling her head with old memories of the only home she'd ever really known.

Stepping into the entry hall, shafts of light spilled across the wooden floors from the transom above the door, just as it had in countless days before. But, in the growing silence it was obvious that so much life had seeped from its rooms in Tilda's absence. A lump formed in Lannie's throat as she peered into each room, rooms she had always believed were somehow magical because they housed the wisest woman Lannie had ever known.

Tilda's wisdom had been a simple wisdom. She held complete trust in God and in His providence and saw His mighty hand at work in nearly everything around her. But that never stopped her from helping Him out at every opportunity, especially when it came to what she thought was best for those she loved.

Now, as Lannie glanced around, the house seemed soulless. Pockets of leftover debris cluttered the darkened corners. Soon after Tilda's funeral, unknown relatives had descended on the place like vultures, hungrily picking over choice items, never realizing what Lannie knew to be true…that the real treasure here had been Tilda Wheeler.

After making a pallet on the floor for Sadie, Lannie reached for the broom and dust pan and began clearing away the clutter and sweeping out the cobwebs from around the window sills. Intent on giving the house a thorough cleaning before she moved in and her fellow new owner arrived, she set to work. Tilda would have expected no less from her. Helping out a neighbor was simply the right thing to do. Tilda always said, "Do the next right thing that lies before you," and she meant it.

Wiping her forehead with the back of her arm, Lannie paused in her work to check on Sadie. She smiled, seeing the little girl content to play with her doll and tea set. Sadie raised a tiny cup up as if offering it to some imaginary friend. "Well, aren't you just the perfect hostess," Lannie said, patting Sadie's white head. Scrubbing the house from top to bottom felt good. Her muscles ached and her back was sore, but oh, how good it felt to release some energy to a task! Pretty soon, the moving truck would arrive, and they'd begin the transition to their new home and their new life.

That night, the first night in their new home, Lannie enjoyed a good soak in a fragrant tub, then she relaxed across the bed. She was grateful that Sadie had once again succumbed to sleep so quickly. She seemed to be adjusting nicely to the new surroundings. The soft sounds of crickets mixed with the orchestra of tree frogs soothed her through the open window. She stared at Sadie's tiny body curled into a ball in the middle of the bed. Gentle, light breaths moved the hair around her tiny face in a rhythmic pattern. As if hypnotized by the sight, Lannie hugged a pillow close to her and slipped into a deep, restful sleep.

Chapter 3

The simple, two-story, Creole-styled home resembled houses Jake had seen on his many trips to the West Indies. Slowing his truck, he stuck his head out of the window, inhaling the soft summer breeze. An earthy smell permeated the air as he passed beneath an old brick archway leaning precariously against a giant oak. The vine-covered arch rose above the dirt road, connecting with the remnants of a brick column, its outline clearly defined by the covering of green undergrowth. Like so many structures in that part of the world, it didn't take long for the encroaching forest to reclaim her territory. Thick vines and saplings grew around the entrance, as if on a race to reach the top.

Partially blocking the road was a rusty old gate with a trail of vines clinging to its bars. Grass grew between the ruts that meandered over the flat land toward the house in the distance. A smile tugged at the corners of his lips as he caught sight of a clothesline beside the house, sheets flapping and snapping in the breeze like the sails of an ancient ship. *It's been a long time since I've seen a clothesline,* he thought. *This is like stepping back in time.* Already he'd envisioned the little old lady who would be his new neighbor, the widow McPherson. He'd been told by

William Forsyth that Mrs. McPherson had been Tilda's best friend and that she would be occupying her apartment by the time he returned from the sea. And, from the look of it, she had settled nicely into her new home.

The truck tilted and dipped into a rut as he drove through a sparse stretch of maritime forest, and he momentarily lost sight of the house. Swarms of gnats swirled just above the road as he bumped onto the worn-out wooden planks of a bridge. He noticed the swamp-like surroundings: trees rubbed smooth by time and murky water produced eerie sculptures on the olive green surface. Once across the bayou, the road opened up into a clearing, giving Jake a clear view of what was to be his new home. The dirt road ended in front of the old house, which faced the bay. He rolled to a stop underneath a huge, silver-leafed tree that stood proudly in front of the house, spreading her canopy of shade over the yard.

The house was rectangular in shape, slightly elevated off the ground with a low hanging roof extending over a wide porch. Timeworn metal followed the slope of the roofline, faded silver and rusted by countless washes of rain. In places, the house seemed to be peeling off her white clothes, showing her brown skin underneath. A faded, white-trimmed screen door hung slightly askew in the center of the house. Flanked on either side of the front door were two sets of tall and narrow French doors, evenly spaced. Although the house was old, it showed signs of great care and seemed to be in good shape—immaculate, in fact.

A pink rose bush rambled across a portion of a rusted, wrought iron fence, spilling out into the yard and filling the air with its scent. Jake stared at the house. A long moment passed before he opened the truck door and stepped out. The soft ground gave slightly under his boots, and he welcomed the feel of it. Too long had he been at sea without the pleasure of the good earth underneath his feet. Inhaling, he breathed in the scent of earth and grass.

Even a casual observation told him that someone had loved the place well. Sweet shrubs in full crimson bloom surrounded a small shallow pool tucked into a corner near the porch. It flashed with goldfish swimming languidly in circles. It looked as if the occupants of the home had stepped out of a previous century. Not even a power line could be seen.

He took a deep breath as he looked around, filling his lungs with salty air, satisfied that his new home was located near his beloved sea. He lifted his hand to shield his eyes from the glaring sun, scanning the property as he looked toward the source of the fresh salty air. "You're out there, just beyond the bay. I can feel you," Jake said under his breath.

The home had everything Jake had ever wanted in a place. The land he now owned came complete with a branch of Bayou Bell running across a corner of the land, a good stand of maritime forest outlining the edge of the property, and bayfront footage. Preferring natural and secluded settings, he was pleased to find that privacy was not going to be an issue. He'd been informed, and the information had been given with much local pride, that the forest surrounding the perimeter of his property was Bell Forest. And he was also told that no finer people could be found in all of Moss Bay than his new neighbors. Making a mental note, he planned to pay a visit to his neighbors at his first opportunity.

The iron-gate squeaked on its hinges as Jake stepped into the yard and made his way up the stone path. An old wooden rocker caught his eye as he mounted the steps. The cane seat of the old rocker was worn and tearing away from the frame in places. Glancing over his shoulder, he noticed the view one would have from that position. Beyond the great silver leaf tree, an expanse of grass swayed gently toward the bay. Tall trees stood proudly, their trunks partially obscuring the view of the water in the distance. A path was noticeable in the grass leading toward the bay.

Turning, he yanked on the screen door, loosening it from the frame. It seemed to protest the intrusion. With key in hand he turned the knob, surprised to find it unlocked. Glancing around the shadowed entry hall, he was struck by the tidiness of everything. Wood floors gleamed softly, reflecting shafts of light angling in from the transom above the door. The white beadboard lining the walls gave the small room a feeling of clean spaciousness. A narrow table with a lamp and a small vase of roses sat next to the staircase that hugged the left wall. The entry hall was simple but inviting and smelled of heady roses and something else he couldn't identify.

Two doors were visible in the entry hall and faced each other, one on the left and one on the right. Propped against the door on the left, near the foot of the stairs, was a broom with a note wrapped and tied around the handle. Releasing the note he read, "Welcome to Beauchene, Mr. Chamberlain. May you find all the joy and happiness left by the previous owner, Mrs. Matilda Wheeler." The note was simply signed, "Your neighbor, Lannie McPherson."

Well, what about that? I guess that's what you call good ol' Southern hospitality. I sure hope the old woman can cook as well as she can clean. Jake pictured an elderly woman pulling out a freshly baked pie from the oven. He glanced at the door across from his and smiled. *This may be like coming home.*

It was a day to try any woman's strength of mind. Lannie slid into the kitchen chair and looked across the table into the sweet face of her two-year-old niece, Sadie. Warm brown eyes stared back at her with an uncertain expression that matched hers. Tufts of white blonde hair stuck out from Sadie's tiny pigtails set high on her head. A crooked finger hooked her pert little nose as she sucked rapidly on her thumb.

The new surroundings would take some getting used to for Sadie. *So many changes for the little girl can't be good*, Lannie thought. But, she knew that moving to Beauchene had been for the best. Peace had already crept into the corners of the home, and Lannie intended to see to it that Sadie had every chance for a good life.

Pushing aside the mass of notes and sympathy cards from friends and coworkers of her late husband, Lannie sipped her tea as she thought about Cade. She'd always marveled at the charm and popularity of her fireman husband. The small town of Moss Bay had loved Cade McPherson as though he could do no wrong. She'd felt that way herself, once, until the knock on her door that forever changed her life.

With much effort, she pushed the destructive thoughts away and focused her attention once again on Sadie. She knew full well that no amount of mulling over the past would change a single thing. Still, the scene of her husband with her sister played over and over in her mind like a despised tune that gets stuck in your head.

"Well, Miss Sadie, what's it gonna be for lunch? Fried chicken...or maybe, fried chicken." Lannie said, with enthusiasm she certainly didn't feel. Every good Southerner knows that fried chicken cures whatever ails you. Throw in a chocolate pie, and you're back on your feet in no time. Well-meaning church members had supplied plenty of both, more food than she could possibly eat. The freezer held three or more chicken casseroles, one ham, two pound cakes, and a Key lime pie. "Remind me to make meatloaf the next time I'm called to send a meal to a grieving family," she teased lightheartedly. Popping the chocolate pie in the oven, she reached over and pulled the toddler out of the highchair and into her lap.

Sadie rested her head on Lannie's shoulder, letting out a shuddering sigh that seemed to push up from deep inside her tiny body. Compassion filled Lannie as she held the little girl tightly, pressing her nose into baby-soft hair. Never in her life had she felt the unspeakable sweetness of a child pressed against her body, needing the comfort she provided.

"Come on, Sadie. After we eat, we're going shopping. You need your very own bed just like a big girl. No more having to make do around here. You'll have your very own room."

By evening, a sense of order had fallen over the household. Lannie purchased all of the items she thought a toddler might need to be properly cared for at her favorite secondhand furniture and linen store. But even with her hands busy, her mind swam with the sting of betrayal. *Will I ever stop thinking about it?* It had been particularly hard given the fact that Lannie and Cade had never been able to have children of their own, as much as they'd wanted them.

"No sense crying about all that now," she said to herself for the hundredth time. Blowing hair out of her eyes, she concentrated on the task before her. The challenge of putting together a child's bed was nothing compared to the challenge of tamping down the urge to head straight to the cemetery and stomp on her husband's grave.

As Lannie turned the last screw, she looked around, noticing a few left over parts scattered on the bedroom floor. Standing, she pressed down on the frame and began to shake it vigorously just to make sure it was stable enough to hold the toddler. With no small amount of self-will, she stopped shaking the bed. Gathering some measure of self-control, she collected the freshly washed linens and made Sadie's bed. With a deep breath she reigned in her emotions, turned, and was surprised to find Sadie, wide-eyed and watching her, nervously sucking her thumb.

Lowering her voice, Lannie forced a smile. "Well, Miss Sadie, I do believe that should hold you. I love these vintage sheets; they're so soft and pretty. Now, how about a nice warm bath? Then, I'll nestle you down into your new bed, and we'll read a story. How does that sound?" Draping a blanket over her shoulder, she reached down and picked up the little girl. Sadie turned her face into the blanket and rubbed the satin edging between her fingers, letting out a soft sigh.

After the bath and story, Sadie was tucked in tight for the night. Lannie turned off the lamp and eased out of the room, leaving the door slightly ajar. Feeling the need to have some familiar ritual to keep her mind in order, she made her way to the kitchen and began heating up a kettle for tea. Her stomach tightened as the thought of her sister and her husband producing a baby together assaulted her mind once more. *What kind of a coldhearted person could live with a lie like that...treating his daughter like a niece?* A shrill whistle sounded from the kettle, dragging her attention back to the task at hand. She pulled out a tea bag. *What kind of a mother tosses away her child like last year's fashions? Maybe it's all a lie. Maybe Mindy saw an opportunity to get rid of her child. Is she really so stupid that she fails to realize that she could get a Social Security check for Sadie? If, in fact, Cade is the father.* Images of Mindy as a child flashed before her mind. How many times had she berated her little sister for her wasteful lifestyle? To Mindy, everything was expendable, disposable, and could be easily replaced. Only now, what was expendable was a precious, innocent child.

Dipping the tea bag absentmindedly, Lannie's lips moved in a silent, pleading prayer. "Lord, You've got to help me get through all this." She chewed worriedly at her bottom lip with her teeth. "I don't know what to do or how to do it. And I need more money if I'm going to pay off all those final expenses."

A knock sounded on the door. Looking across the room at the mantle clock, she noticed it was half past 7:00 PM. Outside, the sky was muted and tinged with pink. *Must be the Methodist Mafia,* Lannie thought, remembering her father-in-law and how he loved to tease his wife about the ladies circle. A woman had called earlier, letting her know they'd be dropping by with food. Lannie shook her head as she wondered again who could possibly think of eating at such times, much less after having their whole world collapse in on them. Smoothing her hair behind her ear, Lannie forced a smile and opened the door.

Chapter 4

The whirring sound of cicadas seemed to come straight out of the Alabama dirt in a shimmering wave of heat before slowly fading into the air. Unaccustomed to the heat and humidity, Jake tugged on his collar, hoping to catch a slight breeze through the screen door. He stood in the sweltering entry hall, waiting for the Widow McPherson to answer the door.

As the door opened, Jake drew his head back sharply, taken completely off guard by the sight before him. He held his breath, looking down into a young woman's face. And not just *any* face—it was the face of the woman from the cemetery! Silky, light ash brown hair with highlights the color of moonlight fell across her shoulders. Translucent gray eyes stared up at him as a faint whiff of perfume drifted past on the warm evening air.

"May I help you?" she drawled, in the soft consonants Jake was still finding hard to get used to.

Smiling, he extended his hand. "I'm Jake Chamberlain, and I live next door." Jake swallowed hard as the breath caught in his throat. He was baffled over the response his body was having to the petite woman.

They stood for a moment, immersed in the sounds of the cicadas rising again in the evening heat. Then, suddenly, realization hit. Lannie's muddled mind formed the words on her tongue. "Oh! You're the Yankee that will be living next door."

"That'd be me." Jake smiled, finding it somewhat amusing that he'd been referred to as the "Yankee" by nearly everyone he'd met since arriving in the small town of Moss Bay, even though he was from Cape Charles, Virginia. "I wanted to thank Mrs. McPherson personally for cleaning my place. That was a thoughtful thing to do. Is she home?"

"I'm sorry. I've had a rather hard day, and I've forgotten my manners." She extended her small hand. "I'm Lannie McPherson, your neighbor."

Lannie's eyes held a measure of distrust. *Understandable,* Jake thought. *I am, after all, a stranger.* Jake backed away from the door, but his eyes never left her face. "I just wanted to introduce myself and say thank you for your kindness," he said, giving a warm and reassuring smile. He felt he'd better put some space between them. He told himself he didn't want to frighten her. But, the truth was that he was a little frightened by his reaction to her. *She's just a woman, and women are all alike. She can be forced from my mind at will just like all the others,* he reasoned.

"I thought I'd walk the property before the rain moves in. Kinda … acquaint myself with the surroundings." His heart pounded in his chest, even as he put distance between them.

"Oh sure, and you're welcome, Mr. Chamberlain. I'm happy to have you as a neighbor. Enjoy your walk."

"Jake."

"Jake. And please, call me Lannie. Mrs. McPherson is my mother-in-law."

"I'll remember that," Jake said with a half grin as he stepped away.

Lannie watched as the screen door slapped behind him. He strode across the porch with a heavy step and down the front steps into the yard. There was a very commanding presence about him. He was tall with broad shoulders and a lean, angular jaw. His dark brown hair, slightly curled at the collar, was neat but relaxed in style. Bright blue eyes, wrinkled at the corners and set in a rugged face, gave him an air of authority. He carried himself as if on a mission. "Huh," Lannie said under her breath, before dismissing her thoughts. She shrugged and slowly closed the door.

Before Jake had gotten very far, a car came into view. As it approached the house, a white trail of dust rose behind its wheels. He waited, not sure if his friend Cornelius had decided to arrive a day earlier than expected. The car came to a stop in front of the house and out stepped three ladies, each carrying a covered dish, chattering in hushed tones and wearing somber expressions.

"That poor, poor girl," a heavyset lady remarked, shaking her head before looking up into Jake's raised eyebrows, "and so young, too." The woman's eyes were kind and held a genuine compassion that seemed to radiate from deep within. "How is she holding up?" The old woman climbed the steps slowly, pausing briefly on each one as she caught her breath. She looked over her shoulder at Jake, waiting for an answer.

"Um…I'm sorry, ma'am, but I seem to be at a loss?" Jake cocked his head, waiting for a reply.

The woman looked baffled. "Why, I'm talking about Lannie! She recently lost her husband *and* her best friend inside of a month! Her husband was killed in the line of duty fighting a fire several weeks ago, and Tilda, the owner of this very house, died not far behind. Such devastating losses to all of us; they were both fine people. Cade was a true hero." Heaving a heavy sigh, she slowly made her way to the door to join the other women gathered there. "Is this the right door?"

"Yes. Go inside the entry-hall; it's the first door on the right." Jake was shocked. He'd never imagined Lannie had lost her husband so recently. *What she must be going through.* He remembered back to when he had first seen Lannie at the cemetery and the small child she'd held in her arms. *How tragic for them.*

The hot evening air was stifling. Dust hung motionless over the ground, waiting for a breeze to chase it across the green fields. Restless now and uneasy, Jake headed toward the sea. As he approached, he caught sight of a structure, half hidden in the humid haze. An overgrowth of weeds and brambles partially hid the small cottage. Cutting his way through the thicket, he noticed the cottage was missing a porch. A door, sagging on its hinges, stood ajar.

Grasping the sides of the door frame, he pulled himself up, lowering his head as he entered the run-down dwelling. Squinting, he waited for his eyes to adjust to the dim light as he looked around. He noticed the room was small and sparsely furnished. A wooden table sat at an angle in front of a fireplace. A rocking chair, much in need of repair, faced the window. On the floor was a pallet of straw, dirty and flattened. A scattering of empty beer bottles surrounded it.

The close proximity to the bay and the secluded nature of the place made it an attractive hideout for anyone seeking a little privacy. The remnants of several fires in the old fireplace told of many nights spent in the cozy hideaway.

Back outside, Jake surveyed the grounds, looking for signs of a road or path. "They must've walked up from the beach," he mumbled under his breath.

A car door slammed near the main house. Jake walked around the cottage to get a clearer view. Wiping his brow with his shirt sleeve, he watched as the visiting ladies returned to their car and disappeared down the road.

He shook his head sympathetically, knowing all too well what Lannie was going through. Not a day went by that some thought of his deceased wife had not haunted him. His emotions ran deep. So deep at times that he half believed he'd somehow caused his wife's untimely death. His mind traveled back over the events of that horrific day. Could he have done something to prevent it?

Jake let out a deep breath. He'd learned that that kind of thinking did no good at all and sapped a man's strength and ability to function. He'd vowed never to let a woman rely on him again. His love, his passion, would always be the sea. And that, Jake surmised, made him an unworthy and unfit husband for anyone.

His gaze swept the house in the distance. *What a beautiful old place.* The wind picked up, swirling the gray haze around as the leaves of the silver leaf tree trembled. A translucent, watery figure appeared on the porch, or was it a remnant of dust or heat rising from the boards? Narrowing his eyes, he watched as the vision slowly lost shape and vanished from sight.

"Stop your daydreaming, young man, and get to work!" The sharp words rang out behind Jake, bringing him around in one quick motion.

There in front of him stood a smallish monk, bent with age and leaning heavily on a cane. The voice was bold, but the body seemed frail.

"It's a pity," the monk said, gingerly watching his steps as he made his way closer to Jake. "No respect these days."

He stopped to catch his breath, gesturing with his cane toward the cottage. "Poor misguided souls. I pray for the hooligans. You know, that's one thing everybody is powerless against: prayer."

Jake eyed the monk suspiciously. "They say that the perpetrator always returns to the scene of the crime. Is that true of you, Brother?" Jake asked, masking a grin.

A mischievous twinkle shone in the old monk's eyes. "Ah, back in the day, my boy, I assure you I was a much worse scoundrel than these poor fellows. But, like I always say, it's not how you start; it's how you finish."

A grin spread across Jake's face as he quickly covered the distance between them, extending his hand. "I'm Jake Chamberlain, Tilda Wheeler's nephew."

"Oh I know all about you, my boy. Tilda was a treasured friend. She chose me to hear her confessions over the years, you know." He lifted his bushy white eyebrows. "Why she chose me, I'll never know. I told her many times that that was the responsibility of her new priest and that I was in retirement. But she would have none of that. She told me we'd gone much too far to turn back now." He shrugged. "We all have our crosses to bear. Now, I hear confessions from the Sisters over at Sacred Mercy." His face held a pained expression. "I must say that I have to agree with what Bishop Sheen said on the matter. He said that hearing nuns' confessions was like being stoned to death by popcorn! Now Tilda on the other hand…oh never mind, never mind." He shook his head, dismissing the comment on the tip of his tongue. "The point is that I happen to know all about you." The glint returned to the old monk's eyes, making Jake feel suddenly uncomfortable. "I'm Ignatius, Brother Ignatius. And I'm pleased to finally put a face with the name. Now tell me, my boy, has that high-spirited little Lannie moved in yet?" The monk snickered, waiting for an answer with childlike eagerness.

"Yes. I've only just met her, but she seems to have settled in." He watched the monk with interest, not at all sure why he was so amused. "I understand she's recently lost her husband. Does she have a child?" Jake shifted his stance and crossed his arms. Reading people had always been his strong suit, but this particular fellow proved hard to get a handle on.

"Yes...I do believe she does. I do believe she does." With that said, the old monk chuckled and turned away, walking near the shoreline. He waved over his head. "Goodbye, goodbye."

Was that a smirk on his face? Jake scanned the surroundings, looking for some sign of a vehicle. *Where did he come from, and, more importantly, where is he going? This jungle heat has me seeing things.* Just then he remembered the monastery he'd passed on his way to Beauchene.

The sun was a shimmering ball of red hanging low over Mobile Bay as Jake pulled his attention away from the shoreline. The monk had disappeared from view. "This place promises to be anything but boring," he said, as he headed up the path toward the house.

Mellow light filtered from the windows of the old home, forming shafts of warm gold on the porch floor. Jake remembered the weeks that had followed his wife's passing, and he paused on the steps, lost in thought.

The tiny figure of a little girl appeared in the tall, open French door. She pressed her face against the screen, flattening her nose as she peered at him.

Something strange and unfamiliar tore at his heart as she continued to stare at him with longing in her eyes. Jake tried to ignore the tight knot curled in the pit of his stomach. Then a movement from inside the room caught his attention. He looked up as Lannie came into view. In one swift, fluid motion, he watched as she lifted the little girl into her arms and hugged her tightly. Pulling back, Lannie brushed a stray lock from the little girl's cheek. He noticed again the delicate and graceful way she moved her hands as she spoke in soft, loving tones to the child. The scene filled Jake with desire, for what, he wasn't quite sure. Oh, he had women if he wanted them. And children…well, he'd never even considered the possibility. For one, he was never around. The nature of his chosen profession required that he travel the seas for months at a time. Only recently, since working out of Mobile, did he settle his schedule into a one month out, one month in, rotation. The adjustment proved to be difficult.

"What is wrong with me?" He yanked open the screen door. "Blast this heat!"

Jake believed firmly that women were much too needy to be able to cope with long periods of time alone. Of that, he was certain. After all, hadn't his wife proven that? His thoughts turned to his gentle wife, Belinda. She needed him, and he wasn't there for her. Oh how she would wait for him to return; and she'd never leave his side once he made it to shore. Seldom did he have a private moment while he was home. Belinda clung to him as if he were a lifeline. Guilt struck swift and painful as he recalled the feeling of relief he'd had the morning he left for sea. That proved to be the final time he would ever see his wife again. Shortly after his departure, she'd taken her own life.

Emptiness gnawed at him as he reached the door to his apartment. Then suddenly, Lannie's door opened across the hall and she called out to him, "Jake, sorry to bother you, but the Methodist Mafia brought in enough food to feed an army.

It smells wonderful. There's even hot homemade bread with sweet butter and…."

Before she could finish, Sadie darted out and crossed the hall to Jake. With outstretched arms, she craned her head way back to look up at him. Quickly, Lannie crossed the floor and snatched up Sadie. "Sorry, she acts like she's escaped from prison. I promise…I don't beat her," she joked. "By the way, this is Sadie." Lannie smoothed the hair away from Sadie's eyes and smiled. "Anyway, as I was saying, I was wondering if you'd like to have some dinner."

Jake smiled nervously. "I appreciate the invitation, but I'm expecting someone." *I hope she gets the message.* This woman made him nervous and being nervous around a woman was not good, nor something he was used to. Jake was used to having women chase after him. Every woman he'd ever known seemed to want exclusive rights to his company. He'd learned to be firm and honest at first contact, that way there would be no misunderstandings. He waited for the typical reaction of disappointment.

"Oh that's perfect!" Lannie exclaimed, delighted. She reached inside her door and pulled out a large wicker picnic basket. "I have packed enough for you and your date. There's even chocolate cake. And what girl doesn't love chocolate? She'll love you for it!" She handed the basket to him and smiled. "You can just put the basket next to my door when you're finished with it." As she turned, she called over her shoulder, "Enjoy!"

"Uh…thank you." More than a little confused, Jake stepped inside his apartment, placed the basket on the table, and scratched his head. "I must not be her type."

Chapter 5

*L*annie had slept late, snuggling deeper into the comforter, still hovering in that space where pain is absent and dreams are a blessed relief.

Opening her eyes, she was startled to find two wide, brown eyes staring at her, inches from her face. "Good morning, Sadie," Lannie whispered sweetly. "Did you rest well?" Yawning, Lannie reached over and smoothed the hair away from Sadie's eyes.

The toddler continued to stare as she placed her thumb in her mouth and began vigorously sucking. She watched Lannie's face as if she were observing some great mystery.

Dragging a leg across the sheets, Lannie dropped one foot to the floor as a shrill voice invaded the room from the yard outside.

"River Adams," Lannie grumbled, before letting her head fall back and hit the pillow again. She'd been reading in the living room the night before when she heard Jake's date leave, so she knew it couldn't be that woman. That woman had been quiet, barely making a sound except for an occasional low and throaty laugh. But no one on God's green earth had quite the same shrill and whining voice as her cousin, River.

Sure, River was beautiful. Probably the most beautiful person Lannie had ever seen; no one would ever dispute that fact. Her stunning indigo blue eyes, thick coffee-colored hair, and well-proportioned frame made her the envy of nearly every female east of the Mississippi. River and her sister, Mary Grace, were thought to be the most beautiful women in all of South Alabama. Lannie and her cousins owed their unique appearance to their mothers, the Dupree sisters, and their Creole heritage. But nothing—not beauty, not money, not refinement, not anything—could ever make up for the simple fact that River Adams was the most annoying person Lannie had ever encountered.

"Why me, Lord, haven't I suffered enough?"

Pushing up from the bed, she waited to hear a knock on the door. After a long moment, she looked at Sadie and asked, "Do you think she went away? Wait here, I'll check it out."

Curious, she tiptoed to the French door just in time to see her neighbor, Jake, lean into River and kiss her.

"Unbelievable," Lannie whispered, as she turned from the window and smiled. "At least she's not here to see me." Pleased she stepped back into the bedroom and called to Sadie, "Sadie, my girl, I think this is going to be a great day after all!"

After breakfast and a much needed cup of coffee, Lannie poured Sadie's bath. Moments later, the little girl emerged pink and flushed and ready to face the day.

With every intent to avoid her cousin, Lannie eased to the front window just to make sure River was nowhere in sight. As she was scoping out the area, she saw her mother-in-law, Wren, pulling up into the yard.

Lannie smiled. She loved her mother-in-law. It broke her heart when she thought about how lonely Wren must be. She'd lost her husband several years ago to illness and now she'd also lost Cade, her only son. The only bright spot for Wren was Sadie. She'd watched her mother-in-law contain her excitement over the news that Sadie was probably her granddaughter. Lannie knew she was overjoyed, but out of concern for her Wren had kept her emotions in check.

"I hope I'm not intruding," Wren called from the doorway, after a brief knock.

Locking doors was never high on Lannie's list of priorities. That was something she needed to work on now that Sadie was part of her life. It was obvious the little girl had a fondness for wandering.

"Oh, not at all! We're up. Come on in, I'll pour you a cup of coffee."

Lannie worked for her mother-in-law at her antique shop, Keepers of the Past. Her job was to find valuable and salvageable pieces and restore them, which just so happened to be Lannie's passion.

Working with her mother-in-law had proved to be sheer pleasure for Lannie. Wren simply radiated goodness and that made her attractive to nearly everyone who ever entered her store. She was a pretty woman, but it was more than that: she had a kind spirit. Her laughing, dark eyes sparkled from deep within her soul.

With the loss of Cade, Lannie was even more aware of Wren's desperate need to have something to hang on to, some reason to get up in the morning and go on. She faced the same sorrow and understood her need to be needed.

"I thought I'd tackle refinishing the buffet today," Lannie said, tucking her hair behind her ear as she poured Wren's coffee. "Of course, as soon as I can I'm going back over to the Parker place to do some more salvaging."

Wren's face lit up. "Want me to take Sadie to town? We could shop for some new clothes. Give you time to get your work done."

"Oh, would you? I have that piece sold to Mrs. Otis. She's willing to pay extra if I can have it done before Friday. That's when her sister comes to visit."

Wren pushed her dark brown hair away from her face. "Well, we'll just have to bring back some chocolate cheesecake for you, won't we, Sadie?" She lifted Sadie from the floor and propped her on her hip. "Don't kill yourself over that piece, Lannie, I mean it. I know how you get when you get in your "zone." And for heaven's sake, lock that shop door while you're working in there. Anybody can come in on you, and you'd never know it."

"Yeah, yeah, I hear you." She waved off Wren's concern. "Did I tell you that they're scheduled to tear down the old Parker place in a few months? There's still a lot of value out there, and I want to get out all I can. You should see the newel posts; they have beautifully carved wheat sheaves on them. Jeb Parker's ancestors were bakers, but he doesn't want any of it. Can you believe that? He said for me to help myself, and I intend to." Lannie gave Wren a quizzical look. "Imagine having a piece of your family's heritage and not wanting it."

"Some people just don't know the value of things, Lannie. You of all people should know that."

Lannie tapped her lips with her forefinger. "I was thinking…"

"Oh no, Sadie, I've seen *that* look before. Let's get out of here before she puts us to work digging around in that old house." Wren kissed Lannie's cheek. "Take your time. If you're not here when we get back, I'll put Sadie to bed. But don't stay too long after dark. You know how it worries me."

Lannie twisted her lips to hide her smile. "Have fun you two—and don't forget the chocolate cheesecake!"

Darkness had fallen and still there was no sign of Lannie. Wren wrung her hands in a nervous fashion, thinking of what she must do. Lannie's cell phone was on the kitchen counter along with her purse, but, it was not unusual for Lannie to venture off without those items. She'd seen her do it countless times before and especially when her thoughts were absorbed with some old homeplace.

Sadie was fast asleep after the long day of shopping. Wren hated to disturb her, but she was just about to wake her and go in search of Lannie when she heard a door shut in the hall. *He's home!* Wren thought. Without a minute's hesitation, she went across the hall and rapped on Jake's door.

Jake's frame filled the doorway. Looking down, he saw a tiny, distraught woman gazing up at him with pleading eyes. "Can I help you?" He watched the woman with interest, waiting for a reply.

"Yes you can. It's my daughter-in-law, Lannie."

"Lannie? What's the matter?" Concern swept over him as his eyes searched the woman's face.

"She should be home by now. She's out at the old Parker place, working. Sometimes she gets carried away and works past dark, but it's not safe, and I'm worried." Wren's eyes filled with tears. "She and Sadie are all that I have left in the world. I don't want anything to happen to her. Unsavory types of people prowl around abandoned homesites. She could be in danger."

Jake grabbed the keys off the table. "Is Sadie with her?" he asked, anxiously.

"No, no, I've got her. She's asleep."

"How do I get there?" He kept his voice calm and low, not wishing to upset the woman more than necessary. He knew from seeing the damage at the cottage down by the bay that her words were true; unsavory types did, in fact, look for unoccupied places.

"Get back on the main road. Zane's Trace connects to the main road, but only one way, west toward the bay. The cotton is low, so you should be able to see the house off to the right. There's an old gated-off entrance, a lot like this entrance, just drive through it, and you'll come to the house. There's no power out there, so you'd better take a flashlight."

Driving through the gate at the Parker place, Jake caught a glimpse of a shadow moving just beyond the trees. As he approached, he saw it was Lannie. Slamming the truck in park, he stepped out, more than a little aggravated. His imagination had kicked in on the drive over, and he'd thought of every possible thing that could have happen to her. *What kinda crazy woman prowls around an old abandoned house at night?*

Lannie looked up as she heard the slam of a door. Recognizing the truck, she realized it was Jake. Walking toward him she asked excitedly, "Have you ever seen such a sight?"

"No, I haven't," he replied, annoyance seeping into his tone. "What in the…what are you doing, Lannie?" He'd been sent to rescue her not threaten her. But oh, the temptation was certainly there, especially since she seemed to be oblivious of the stupidity of her actions.

"Sometimes, when the moon is high and soft like this, I like to wander around and just admire an old place. I guess I have an inordinate affection for old things and everything around them. Come and see." She motioned him toward the back of the house. "Look what I've found! I've been struggling with this thing for hours, flipping it over and over again trying to get it to my SUV. Will you help me?"

Jake narrowed his eyes. "What is it?"

"It's the back of a wooden bench. Look at how smooth and weathered and worn it is," she said breathlessly, wiping the dirt away. "It says, 'Friend, there is welcome here for thee, look 'round and all God's glory see, pause and rest and think and pray, then go in peace upon thy way.'"

The sheer joy on Lannie's face in the moonlight caused Jake to forget all the harsh things he had planned to say. He lifted the wood with ease, walked to the SUV, and slid it into place. "Is this it?" he called over his shoulder.

"No, there are a few more things I need to get from the house. Just a couple of newel posts. I'll come back later with a few more tools for the bigger stuff. I'm not leaving that soapstone farm sink or all that cypress flooring for the demolition crew. Those boards have been polished smooth by the feet of countless caretakers of this old place. You just don't walk off and leave something like that."

Flipping on the flashlight, Jake followed Lannie up the creaking steps and into the darkened house. "Aren't you afraid of ghosts?" he asked, as he shined the light around the room, making the shadows dance eerily upon the wall.

"Old abandoned houses inspire me to do what I do. I'm drawn to them for some odd reason. I don't know why. I guess it's the emptiness. They're alone, abandoned, forgotten, and I find that appealing."

"So, the apparent loneliness draws you in?" Looking around, Jake was trying hard to understand the appeal.

"The sadness draws me, I think. It moves me. And I feel it, keenly. In some way I think it's terribly romantic. When I work in a place like this I can sometimes hear the sounds of life gone by: the slap of a screen door or the voice of a child. It's touching. I've always been attracted to old homesites, even as a little girl, the kind of places that have daffodils growing in a line where a sidewalk used to be."

More than a little intrigued, Jake asked, "So, you're never frightened?"

"Of ghosts you mean? No. But that's not to say that this place isn't haunted. There is said to be the ghost of a girl here who threw herself from a window on the second floor during a long and drawn-out dinner party. If you've ever been to a big fancy dinner party, I'm sure you can understand."

Contemplating her words, he tugged at his earlobe and twisted his lips to conceal his smile. The mood had lightened considerably. "So tell me, do you want me to dismantle this house for you and haul it out of here tonight?" he teased.

Ignoring his comment, she said, "Shine your light on that wall. Have you ever seen such a beautiful shade of blue-green?"

"Yep, I have. It's called 'ghost-infestation green.' I think Sherwin Williams carries it."

Lannie cut her eyes to Jake. "Funny. The newel posts are at the bottom of the stairs. If you don't mind, get those, and I'll get a chip of this paint, then we'd better head back. Wren is probably worried sick. She likes for me to be home before the streetlights come on. I'm guessing she sent you."

"You guessed right."

Lannie responded with a low chuckle of amusement. "Sorry, my mother-in-law is a worrier. I hope she didn't interrupt one of your...dates."

Jake watched her thoughtfully. "No, as a matter of fact, I don't have a date tonight."

Lannie controlled her amusement only slightly. "River must be slipping."

"Come again?"

A beam from his flashlight flooded her with light. "I bet I can guess how you met," Lannie ventured, as she took out a small knife from her pocket and began scraping the wall for paint chips. "It was at the bank. You went in to open an account, and *Kathy* helped you set up an online checking account." Placing the paint chips on a piece of old newspaper, she went back to the wall for more. "That's when you began to wonder why it's taking so long to open an account. By this time, Kathy has stepped out of the office several times, delaying the process. Then suddenly, an incredibly beautiful woman steps into the room and asks if this is where you sign up for online checking." She cut her eyes back to Jake, who was standing near the stairs. "How am I doing so far?"

Rubbing his face with his hand, he narrowed his eyes, pausing a moment as he watched her. "That's…about the size of it."

"River and I are cousins. But don't feel so bad, Captain. You've been handled by a pro. She has the predatory skills of a cat. Of the women in my family, she's the most developed in the art of scheming. Kathy is her partner in crime, and she called River once she 'qualified' you. You must be single and have a sizable account. The fact that you're handsome, well, that's just icing on the cake."

He looked at her carefully and spoke distinctly. "So…how do *you* rank in the family lineup?"

With a start of surprise, Lannie tilted her head. "By the grace of God alone, Captain, I'm nothing like my family members—with the exception of Ma Tess, my grandmother." She fingered the small medallion around her neck, turned, and gathered her things. "I'll follow you home. Just let me grab this one piece."

With an arm full, Jake made his way toward the truck. He glanced back at Lannie, shining the flashlight in her direction as he watched her work a small table backward, one side at a time, as she moved it to the SUV. "Hold up, I'll get that for you."

Suddenly, a table leg collapsed, sending her tumbling to the ground. Her leg hit something sharp and blood oozed from the cut, dripping onto the dust. Jake ran toward her and, swoosh, she was lifted off the ground and placed carefully on the tailgate of the SUV.

Half startled, half relieved, Lannie leaned back on her hands as Jake examined her leg. Pain shot through her leg and everything was getting fuzzy. She winced as Jake slowly turned her ankle. Leaning further back, she clasped one hand to her eyes. "I get sick at the sight of blood," she informed him. Jake's slow and deliberate movements comforted her. His warm and woodsy sent had a calming effect on her, and she was grateful for it.

He propped up the flashlight so he could have a better look. "You're not afraid of ghosts or night stalkers, but you're afraid of a little blood. Go figure."

She shifted slightly at the feel of his fingers pressing her skin. "Funny."

"You're not going to faint are you," he asked, noticing the sudden whiteness around her lips.

"I wish I could, then I wouldn't have to sit here and be humiliated." She groaned. "Is it bad?"

His focus was on her leg as he replied, "It's not too deep, and I don't think you'll need stitches. If you'll stay put, I'll grab the first aid kit and fix you right up."

Busy staring up at the sky, concentrating on not fainting, she didn't hear everything Jake had said. As he began walking off she called to him. "Where are you going?"

"To cancel MedFlight," he replied sarcastically, grinning at her over his shoulder.

As he came back with the supplies, his gaze ran over her, and it was obvious he was masking a grin. She thought of what she must look like. Hurrying to the site while it was still daylight, she'd grabbed a pair of old, faded, and torn jeans and yanked on an Alabama Dirt Shirt, a T-shirt Telie had given to her that had been dyed in North Alabama red clay.

"This is going to sting," Jake said, as he poured a fair amount of alcohol over her wound.

Wincing, she tried to distract herself. "Why is a ship called she?" The question was random, but it was all she could think of in her discomfort.

"Because it takes an experienced man to handle her correctly," he said, never looking up from his task.

"Ha! Well, I know plenty of men who should stick with boats instead of taking on a real woman."

"Or *any* woman! And I agree with that statement completely." Wiping away the excess alcohol from her leg, he paused and inhaled. "After I wrap it, you'll need to keep it dry for a few days. If you need me, I'm just across the hall. I'll take care of whatever you need." He spoke in declarative sentences as he tended her leg.

"How will I…I mean, I've got to have a bath."

His laugh seemed to rumble low in his chest. "Like I said, I'll take care of whatever you need."

The look of shock on her face was too much for him and he added, "I'll wrap your leg so water can't get in. If you need help beyond that, you just let me know."

A flush of embarrassment came over her face as Jake's smile widened. She dropped her eyes. "I think I can manage, but thanks for the offer…so helpful and all."

"I do what I can," he replied, snapping the first aid kit shut.

Chapter 6

An ivy and lichen-covered stone wall about chest high surrounded the property of Beauchene on three sides, leaving the west side open to the bay. Here and there, the roots of massive oaks heaved up the wall in places, making it lean. Seemingly, the only thing keeping it from tumbling over was the tight weave of ivy covering the face of the stone.

Jake stopped along the path and squatted down to rub a patch of thick green moss covering the ground. "Amazing," he said out loud. "Can you believe this, Cornelius? This stuff is like carpet."

Cornelius nodded. "Sure looks like you've landed in the garden of Eden."

Jake looked up, seeing his friend's eyes fixed straight ahead. He followed their path to the shore. "That's not Eve, my friend, that's my neighbor, Lannie McPherson, and her daughter, Sadie. She's recently lost her husband."

Cornelius smiled. "Neighbor is it? Well now, just how far away does the young lady live from you?"

Jake looked sheepish. "We actually live under the same roof, only on separate sides."

Cornelius raised an eyebrow. "The devil you say? Now how have you managed that?"

Jake shrugged. "It was all my aunt's doings." He stood up, slapping his hands together to loosen the dirt. "Lannie is a nice girl…and, I might add, not in the least bit interested in me."

"Go on with you. You mean to say there's a woman alive who is immune to your charms? Well, I'll be." He looked back at the figures wading near the shore. The sun danced in Lannie's hair and sparkled on the water at her feet. She was a vision of loveliness. He scratched his head and said, "I've got to meet this one. Make the introductions."

A ship's horn blew in the distance, close enough that Jake could feel the effects of it vibrate through him. He took a deep breath. "Ah…that's music to my ears."

As Jake and Cornelius stepped onto the narrow beach, Sadie looked up and ran toward Jake, dropping sea shells along the way. She stopped in front of him and held her hands high in the air until he swooped down and caught her up in his arms.

"Cornelius, this is Sadie. Sadie, Cornelius."

"Pleased to make your acquaintance, young lady." He shook her tiny hand. "I'm glad to see that your powers over women are still intact, Captain. You had me worried there for a minute."

"Yes, well, I do seem to hold this one's interest. But, her mother is a different matter altogether."

Lannie walked up to the men, smiling. "Sadie seems to like you, Jake. It must be your aftershave. What is it, Old Spice?" she teased.

"What else would a seaman wear?" He jostled Sadie causing her to giggle. "Lannie, I'd like for you to meet my friend, Cornelius Longcrier. Cornelius, my neighbor, Lannie McPherson."

Lannie extended her graceful hand. Both men seemed enthralled with the simple movement. "Tell me, Mr. Longcrier, are you a seaman as well? You have the look of one."

The man's face split with a rakish grin as he met her warm hand. "All of my life, ma'am. I guess it shows, huh?"

"Well, that's something to be proud of Mr...."

"Cornelius. Please ma'am, call me Cornelius."

Jake stood amazed. Cornelius was a hardened man, up in years and not one to be easily swept away by the opposite sex, but he was almost drooling over this girl.

Lannie brightened. "Cornelius. Are you from up north, too?"

"No, ma'am. Jake and I are both from Cape Charles, Virginia."

"Um, Cornelius, around here Virginia is considered a northern state," Jake said, widening his eyes.

Cornelius stared at his friend as if to assess the seriousness of his comment. "I didn't know that."

"So now you know. Just don't tell any of General Lee's descendants. They get a might touchy over it." Jake handed Sadie back to Lannie.

"We're not as backward as Jake makes us out to be, Cornelius. It's your accent that throws everybody off. Most Southerners are known by their accent, but, you two seem to be missing yours."

"I suppose you're right. We sail with so many people from different parts of the world that it makes it hard to hang on to one particular form of speech." Cornelius smiled. "But, if I stay in this heat much longer, I'm liable to have a heatstroke. That'll slow my words down considerably."

"Anybody who's ever experienced a South Alabama summer knows when you're not in the water, you're in the oven," Lannie said softly. "It was nice meeting you, Cornelius. I hope we'll see you again, soon."

"I certainly hope so, too," Cornelius replied, smiling.

"By the way, Lannie," Jake said, leaning close and out of earshot of Cornelius, who was already making his way up the path. "I was wondering if you and I might do some trading. I have a proposition for you."

"Oh? What have you got in mind?"

"That old cottage," he motioned with his head toward an overgrown patch of brush near the edge of the beach. According to the map it belongs to you. I want to trade out the use of it. I'd like to fix it up for Cornelius, to give him a place to stay when we're in town. In exchange, you're welcome to the barn. I've noticed some of your stuff is already being stored there."

She moistened her lips. "I have a proposition for you, too."

He slipped his hands into his jeans pockets. "I'm listening."

"I'll furnish and decorate the cottage after you repair it and get the plumbing fixed. Occasionally, I may need your help loading and unloading certain heavy pieces in and out of the barn. And, from time to time, I need help connecting my trailer to the SUV. So the deal is, Cornelius may live in the cottage rent free in exchange for the use of your barn and for your help."

He considered her as she stood before him motionless with her head held high, staring him straight in the eye. He rubbed his mouth. "Fair enough."

"Great! I'll get started collecting a few things for the cottage. If you need someone to clear away all of that brush, our neighbor, Michael Christenberry, will be happy to help. He owns a landscaping company near here, and he'll do a good job. His wife, Telie, won't let him demolish everything in sight. He'll respect the land and leave as many trees as possible."

"Thanks, I'll keep him in mind." Jake took in the sight she made with the sun bathing her in light from behind, silhouetting her small form as her cotton skirt flapped in the breeze. He smiled, thinking of what a natural beauty she was, but she seemed so much more than a pretty face. "So, I take it you're fond of nature."

"I've decided to live with nature rather than try to bend it to my will, as much as possible that is." She tucked her windblown hair behind her ear and hiked Sadie up higher on her hip.

"So, what if I told you I found a hornet's nest in the barn?"

Lannie's eyes grew wide, then narrowed. "Smoke it out! Sadie will be in there with me, and I just won't have her in harm's way."

Jake tried to conceal his smile. "What about nature?"

"Protecting your young is about as natural as you can get, Captain."

Chapter 7

The Old Red Brick Café was especially inviting. An open gate with softly glowing gaslights illuminated the way to the outside entry. The walled courtyard contained intimate spaces, with splashing fountains and warm candlelight flickering in glass mason jars on the tables. Under the gentle breeze, a distinctive Creole feeling permeated the atmosphere as a small band began playing a lively tune. That's when he noticed her. Seated near the fountain, Jake watched as Lannie swayed in time to the rhythmic music. With her face glowing in the candlelight, the wind flirted with her hair. He smiled as he watched it dance softly across her shoulders. She was beautiful. Her bare shoulders, lightly tanned, caught the warm light and reflected it, shimmering. The light green dress she wore glistened under the moon. He was transfixed. She was by far the loveliest thing he'd seen that day. And, unlike most women, she seemed completely unaware of the power of her natural beauty.

River joined him at the table. "I can't believe it. You just can't seem to get away from all that swamp music anymore. I mean, give me a break already!"

"I like it. It's uplifting and kind of festive." He took a gulp of his Coke.

The waitress came and took their order and stepped away after gathering the menus.

"These gas lanterns around the courtyard really enhance the old world feel, don't they?" Jake was trying hard to keep his attention away from the table near the fountain. He'd noticed that the table was set for two. As he glanced up again, he saw the stout frame of his chief steward, Cornelius, pulling out a chair to be seated at Lannie's table.

Jake sat back and folded his arms, looking squarely at the other table. A grin began to form on his whisker-shadowed face, his teeth gleaming white against the tan of his skin.

"Why are you grinning like that?" River asked, turning her head to glance over her shoulder. Rolling her eyes, she replied, "Don't tell me…you know Lannie."

Jake sat up. "Know her? We're practically living together."

"Whaaaat!" River shrieked, causing every head in the establishment to turn in their direction.

Jake started to speak but was interrupted by Cornelius, waving heartily, saying, "Captain! Join us!" He gestured to the empty chairs at his table.

"Come on, River, let's join my friends. Lannie lives in the apartment next door to me, and Cornelius is a friend." He stood to assist River from her chair.

River sat as if stunned for a moment but quickly recovered. There was no way she was letting this fine catch of a man out of her sight. She knew Jake had money and lots of it. Her best friend was a teller at the local bank and was more than happy to share that little bit of information; the fact that he was handsome just added to an already perfect setup. "Of course, it's been too long since I've seen my cousin."

"Cousin? You and Lannie are cousins?" Now it was Jake's turn to pretend. A smile touched his lips. He knew it was only a matter of time before he cut her loose. Spending time with a woman he didn't trust was not something he relished, no matter how beautiful. Eventually he planned to let her go just like all the rest.

River crossed the room, swaying provocatively around the tables until she reached Lannie. "Hello, Lannie," River said, forcing a smile. She eased into a seat, flipping her coffee-colored hair over her shoulder.

"Hello, River. Jake would you mind making the introductions?" Lannie asked, as she casually sipped her drink.

"Sure. Cornelius, this is River Adams; she's Lannie's cousin."

"Well, I'm mighty pleased to meet you, River. I'm glad you and Captain have joined us." Cornelius laughed nervously as his attention went from one gorgeous creature to the other; he was obviously overjoyed with his tablemates.

Jake observed, "I certainly should have figured out you two were related. You seem so much alike, and the resemblance is uncanny. Such rare beauty is hard to find; I should've known."

Lannie smiled, but her smile didn't quite reach her sparkling eyes. Taking a small bite of cheesecake, she savored the taste and then looked up. "Cornelius and I were just discussing life at sea. So tell me, Captain, are seamen as superstitious as I've always been told?" She touched a napkin to her lips.

After signaling the waitress to bring their order, Jake leaned forward in his chair. "Right alongside the most modern technology is that age-old maritime tradition. It's as ancient as seafaring itself." Jake's face ignited with pure passion as he settled his elbows on the table, hands clasped together. "I guess it has more to do with how sailors cope with danger and uncertainty. They try to control their environment since so much of their success and survival are linked to things they can't control, like the weather."

Lannie nodded once, understanding the feelings completely. She pressed, "So, give some examples of things a sailor will do to ward off trouble."

Jake looked at Cornelius and smiled. "We had this one guy who pierced his entire body numerous times. He wore gold earrings—four of them in each ear. And, those were only the ones we could see. Tattoos and piercings are said to ward off evil spirits."

Cornelius piped in, "Don't forget the things you shouldn't do, like whistling and eating bananas. Whistling is forbidden on a ship, hence the expression 'Whistling up a storm.' I'm not sure about the significance of bananas, but I never serve them on board. Some of the guys would get pretty nasty about it if I served up a good ol' banana pudding."

Jake nodded, chewing his food. Swallowing, he added, "And my personal favorite: women onboard ship can make the sea angry. But, interestingly enough, there's a way to counter this effect. Having a naked woman onboard a ship will calm the waters. This is the reason for the naked figureheads."

Lannie choked slightly on her tea. "Okay, so no bananas onboard ship, it spells disaster." A pink blush crept up her slender neck. "So, I'm guessing most seamen are not men of faith." Lannie waited for an answer, looking first to Jake, then Cornelius.

Jake waved his fork toward Cornelius as he finished chewing. "At times, we're the only two believers onboard. Although...another man who professes to be a Christian has recently joined us. He's my first mate. Still, we're clearly in the minority."

Lannie studied him thoughtfully, then, realizing she was staring at him, quickly turned her attention to her plate.

River, seeing the attention Lannie was giving to Jake, decided to pick a fight. "Not to change the subject, but Lannie, I was wondering if you've ever forgiven me for breaking your favorite white cups. You know, the ones belonging to Ma Tess." River ran her hand along her throat, displaying a sparking square-cut diamond on her right hand. She meant to provoke Lannie. She knew what had happened the last time she broached the subject, and she was hoping for a repeat performance.

The diamond ring River so proudly displayed had belonged to Ma Tess and was supposed to go to Lannie, as the eldest granddaughter. But Lannie's mother, the eldest daughter, gifted it to River instead, because she assumed River would appreciate it far more than would her daughter.

"Of course I've forgiven you, River." Lannie took a casual sip of her tea. "I understand that when you threw my cups in one of your fits of uncontrolled rage, you didn't realize the value of what you destroyed."

Jake assessed the situation and made a move to diffuse the tension before further damage could be done. "There's no sense in hyperventilating over all this girls. Let's just go pick up another set of cups. Problem solved." The smirk on Jake's face proved he was satisfied with his solution. But soon, he would see the folly of his assumption.

Lannie quietly placed her cup on the table and looked directly into Jake's eyes. "Let me explain something to you, Captain," Lannie said, in a calm and controlled tone, as if speaking to a child. "Some things in life just can't be replaced. I'll tell you this: when I stir my coffee each morning, it makes me happy to use the remaining shallow white cup that once belonged to Ma Tess. That attachment runs clear through me...to my good ol' Louisiana Creole roots! You just can't pick up another."

Jake held her eyes a long moment. "I stand corrected."

Struggling for composure, River decided to retreat to the restroom where she could let out a scream. "If you'll excuse me, I need to go to the powder room." River got up and left the table.

Leaning forward with her elbows on the table, Lannie bent her head and whispered low to Jake, "And Captain, if you *ever* compare *me* with *her* again, I'll storm your ship pulling a wagon load of bananas and whistling Dixie the whole way...fully clothed!"

Cornelius choked back a laugh, pretending to cough, and then excused himself.

With everyone else gone, Lannie was left under the scrutiny of Jake's bold and somewhat amused stare. He seemed to always dominate the scene around him with an air of command.

Trying hard to keep her mind off him, she turned her attention away and began listening to the soft and alluring sounds of the band. Her heart fell into a normal rhythm again as her temper subsided. She took a deep breath and risked a glance at him.

He studied her with a slight smirk on his lips. "You really need to do something about that temper of yours, Lannie. I think you scared poor old Cornelius."

The color flew to Lannie's face, and her eyes fell from his gaze. She hadn't meant to make a scene; she'd simply had enough of River and the Captain. "I'll go and apologize to him. Placing her napkin on the table, she murmured a quiet apology, slid from her chair, and brushed past him, leaving only a hint of her fragrance behind.

River approached the table, thankful that Lannie and Cornelius had finally gone. Jake sat leaning back in his seat and let out a breath, turning a dinner knife from side to side, lost in thought. River had mistakenly thought Lannie and her boyish ways could give her no competition in her efforts to capture Jake. But, she had not counted on this battle of wills between them to draw attention away from her physical charms. She had no intention of leaving Jake with a favorable opinion of her cousin, at least not if she could help it.

"Oh Jake, I'm so sorry about all of that drama with Lannie. I hope it hasn't ruined our evening." River slid into the chair and reached for his hand across the table. "I guess I should have warned you about her." She covered his hand with her own and squeezed. "Lannie is just…backward. She is nothing like the rest of her family. Her own mother can't even stand to be in the same room with her." As if to prove her point, she showed Jake the diamond on her finger. "This ring belonged to my great-grandmother, Leta. She left it to the oldest daughter, Ma Tess, with instructions that the ring should be passed down to the oldest granddaughter, which was Lannie's mother, Hettie, and then to the oldest great-granddaughter, which is Lannie." River tilted her hand under the candlelight, admiring the sparkle of fire from the ring.

Jake turned and raised an eyebrow at her.

She shrugged innocently. "Hettie gave it to me because she knows that I have an appreciation for the finer things in life. The only thing Lannie appreciates is curbside trash day on Thursdays so she can scrounge around in others people's cast-offs looking for 'treasures'"

Jake frowned heavily. "You're not saying that you have a complete and total disregard of the wishes of your deceased great-grandmother, are you? You're not so callous and unfeeling as to flaunt the very ring under the nose of the rightful owner, are you?" Jake won a private battle by not smiling at the shocked look on River's face. He kept his expression stern.

"Well, before Lannie got so riled up over those stupid cups I was planning on giving the ring to her tonight. It rightfully belongs to her. Even though I am Hettie's favorite niece, she had absolutely no business giving it to me. Hettie and I share a special relationship, but right is right and that's just how it is. I don't think I can even sleep another night knowing that I have something that belongs to another." Satisfied with her explanation, River smiled sweetly into Jake's eyes.

He gently picked up her hand and kissed it. "I couldn't bear the thought of you having a sleepless night. I'll take the ring and make sure Lannie gets it. You have my word."

Chapter 8

The rain pounded down upon Beauchene as thunder crashed, shaking the house. With each flash of lightning, the treetops were visible, thrashing against the darkened sky. The night was fierce and the wind howled around the corners in a low, mournful wail.

Jake looked up from his papers and tilted his head as a loud cry came from across the hall. From his position near the front French doors, he saw a light reflecting off the wet boards of the porch. He turned his head, listening again to Sadie's muffled cries. He tossed the papers aside and pushed up from the chair.

After knocking on Lannie's door, Jake waited: no response. He decided to put more effort into the knock so as to be heard over the storm and the wails coming from Sadie, so he pounded out a steady, loud beat, vibrating the door.

Lannie snatched open the door, and it swung back swiftly hitting the wall with a bang. Her expression was one of frustrated anger as she glared at Jake. She shifted the wailing little girl from one hip to the other. "As you can *plainly* see, Jake, I'm a little busy right now. What do you want?" Her words came out in a rush.

Jake knew in an instant what needed to be done. But, seeing the wild look of desperation in Lannie's eyes, he also knew that great caution needed to be exercised. He approached her calmly, as you would a cornered animal. The tone of her words was enough for him to guess she'd reached a snapping point. Immediately, his manner changed from one of curiosity to that of helpfulness. He held his hands up in front of him. "I'm only here to help, if I can," Jake spoke low and comforting, giving her a reassuring smile.

Upon hearing Jake's voice, Sadie snapped her head around and, with quick catches of breath, stopped crying. Stretching out her arms, she reached for Jake.

Lannie was visibly stunned as Jake lifted Sadie from her arms. Though no words passed from her lips, she felt that what Sadie had done was pure mutiny. She turned her back on them and walked into the living room, collapsing onto a chair. Pressing her forehead into her fisted hands she hit a mother lode of frustration and grief and began to weep softy.

"Hey now, there is no reason for all that. See, Sadie is just fine; she's just frightened of the storm, that's all." Jake looked perplexed. "Lots of children are afraid of storms, I hear. Is this something new for her?" He patted Sadie's back gently, reassuringly.

"I…I wouldn't know," she cried, the tears now streaming unchecked down her flushed cheeks. Rocking her head back and forth she continued, "I just don't know."

Easing onto the sofa, Jake grunted as he stretched out first one leg and then the other. The couch was made for a lady and a small one at that. He held Sadie in that awkward way a man holds a child when he's not used to it. Pushing her up higher on his chest, he continued to try and make sense of what Lannie was telling him. Understanding what was going on in the situation was proving difficult. "You mean she has never been this upset before?"

"I mean...*I don't know*...I don't know if she cries during storms, or if she hates raisins, or if she's had her immunizations, or if she's allergic to strawberries...and I don't know if it's normal for a two year old not to talk!" Frustration poured out in the form of tears as she struggled to keep from screaming through the overwhelming hopelessness of it all.

He sat there quietly for a moment, assessing the situation. Sadie was fast asleep against his chest. Gently, he placed her down on the sofa and covered her tiny form with a quilt he pulled from the back of the couch.

"I need more of an explanation than that, Lannie. I don't understand what you're telling me." He fought to keep the annoyance out of his voice, his own frustration now mounting.

Inhaling deeply, Lannie let out a ragged breath. "Sadie is the product of an affair between my late husband and my younger half-sister, Mindy. I didn't find out about her until after Cade's death." She rubbed her temples. "My sister came to me distraught and angry over the fact that Cade wouldn't leave me and marry her." Lannie dipped her head and continued calmly. "She blames me for his death, saying that if Cade had left me and taken a job with her father, he would still be alive and they'd be a family." Quickly, she brushed at her eyes and then glanced up to find Jake watching her. "So, that's the reason why I don't know anything about Sadie, or about being a mother, or about anything having to do with children."

Jake carefully considered her words, stroking his mouth with his finger and thumb. He paused, watching her doubtfully. "What you expect me to believe is that you didn't have a clue that your husband cheated on you."

Lannie's face burned at the truth of his insinuation. As much as she wanted to lash out a denial, she couldn't. The truth of it stung. For a long time, she'd held on to a thin hope that maybe, just maybe, she was wrong and Cade McPherson was the innocent man he'd always portrayed himself to be. The lump in her throat tightened. Swallowing hard, she said, "I suspected. I just didn't want to believe it. Cade began acting strangely. Sometimes I'd find him staring at me with a look of pain, or pity, in his eyes. But, I didn't question him. I guess I didn't really want to know. The news of Sadie was a complete surprise, though." The translucent gray eyes pooled with unshed tears. "I loved my husband. I'm not a martyr, Jake. I just haven't figured out how to stop loving him. If he was here, right now, I would beat him half to death for doing this to me, but I'd still love him."

Jake's penetrating eyes bore into hers. He winced suddenly as he straightened his leg. "So, your sister left Sadie for you to care for because she belonged to your husband."

A loud peel of thunder shook the house as lightning flashed white in the room. Jake glanced down at Sadie's still form, reassured that the noise of the storm had gone unnoticed. Gently, he pulled the quilt over her tiny feet.

The tender gesture touched something deep inside Lannie. "Yes, and I'll fight my sister and anybody else who tries to take her from me. I'll go to jail...I don't care...but *nobody* will take her from me without a fight. I promise you that!"

"Ah...." Jake smiled, nodding once. "You *are* a mother after all." He got up and crossed the room to look out the window. "It looks like the wind just ran out of breath. Do you get a lot of storms like this around here?"

"All the time. This area is famous for its storms. It has something to do with the warm bay waters, I think."

Jake looked back on the apartment. How different it was from his simple place—"charming" was the word that came to mind. The walls were pearl gray and most of the furniture was a clean, soft white. Tall white shutters, a pair on each French door, swung open against the wall. A chest, painted light gray, sat between the French doors and held a glass lamp filled with shells. A stack of books, artfully displayed, with such titles as *The Shabby Chic Life, The Art of Restoration,* and *What's So Amazing about Grace* sat on top of the chest. The sofa, covered in white cloth, sat opposite two pickled wooden chairs with wide, curving arms. A broad yellow-and-white checkered pattern covered the cushions of the chair Lannie sat in with her feet curled up in the overstuffed upholstery. An oval rug in muted yellow, green, and gray covered the space beneath the coffee table. The room was cheerful, even on a dark and rainy night.

Jake's eyes fell to Lannie. He looked at her with wonder and a little admiration. *She seems so small and fragile, but she's filled with fight and spirit. What an unusual combination.* "I think it's time for me to go. Lead the way, and I'll take Sadie to bed."

Covering a yawn, Lannie got up and went to Sadie's room and turned down the covers. Jake walked in and placed Sadie down on the sheet as Lannie tucked the covers in around her. A small frown touched Lannie's brow as she turned and looked up at him sheepishly. The feeling of helplessness was not something Lannie was accustomed to, and she was somewhat embarrassed. "I'm...uh...sorry for the little meltdown. Thank you for helping me."

Jake hid his grin as he walked toward the door. "Not a problem. Goodnight, Lannie."

"Night, Jake."

He fumbled in his pants pocket a moment before turning around. "Oh, I almost forgot. I have something that belongs to you."

Lannie stared at his open hand. There, shining against velvet in a small box, was the platinum diamond ring that had once belonged to her great-grandmother. Lannie gasped, "How did you get that...wait, do I want to know?"

Jake laughed. "Would you believe that River had a change of heart and wanted you, the rightful owner, to have it?"

"No."

Jake looked down until the sparking gray eyes came to meet his. Amused at her blunt honesty, he said, smiling, "Then I guess I just bring out the best in people."

Chapter 9

$\mathcal{M}$orning broke with vibrant hues across the eastern sky. The very air seemed fresh with a clean mist. A wash of green faded into pale blue as the Beauchene property stretched toward the bay, joining with it in a magnificent blending of earth and water.

Lannie stood alone on the porch, bathed and warmed in the fresh light of the rising sun. On mornings like these, she missed her husband the most. Her arms hugged her waist as she thought of Cade. She could almost feel his strong arms around her. His embrace was nothing but a memory and getting more distant each day. *How do you stop missing someone, even when they've hurt you?*

A soft breeze stirred the fragrance from the roses, filling the air with sweetness. Taking the hand clippers and a basket from the small table near the door, Lannie stepped from the porch and out into the yard. She pulled the baby monitor from the back pocket of her jeans and clipped it on the handle of the basket. *Sadie will sleep late today*, she thought, as she bent to inhale the heady pink blooms.

The cool morning faded into the bright light of day as the heat began to rise. Looking around, Lannie noticed she had ventured near the barn in her quest to fill her basket with fresh cuttings of Tilda's flowers. As she bent to snip a wildflower blooming against the barn wall, a movement caught her eye. Jumping back, she placed her hand across her chest to still her rapidly beating heart. She eased back and circled the barn, hanging the basket over a fence post. She pushed the barn door open and entered, returning shortly with a hoe.

Jake had noticed Lannie gathering flowers around the yard earlier that morning. He stood at the kitchen sink, admiring the view as he sipped his coffee. Her loose-fitting blouse snapped in the fitful breeze like the sails on a ship. The wind, he decided, liked playing with her hair, for it lifted and swirled it around her shoulders. He saw the arch of her brow as she contemplated each choice for cutting and the way she worried her lower lip with her teeth. Then suddenly, she jumped back and began running around to the side of the barn, emerging moments later with a hoe. *That can only mean one thing.* Slamming the cup down on the counter, his feet seemed to move of their own volition, and he soon stood behind her, snatching the raised hoe out of her hand.

"You're on my land now, Lannie. I decide what lives and what dies," he said, with laughter in his voice.

Lannie twisted her lips as she listened to Jake's command. "It's a rattlesnake, Jake. I can't live with a rattlesnake around here. It doesn't know the boundary lines, and it might just slink over onto my property."

"Let's see what we've got here." Jake took the hoe and pulled the tall grass back, exposing the snake. "A rattlesnake, is it? It's a rat snake, Lannie, a farmer's friend. Because of this fat guy, we don't have rats crawling all over our house. You really should thank him."

She could feel his nearness in every fiber of her being. The manly soap scent of him invaded her senses. She wanted to do something, to say something, but she couldn't. Not when his blue eyes bore into hers with that infuriating smirk on his handsome face. She had an overwhelming urge to slap his face, but her thoughts were interrupted by the ringing of his cell phone.

Jake handed the hoe to Lannie with a warning in his eyes as he pulled his phone from his pocket. "This is Jake." There was a long pause. "Um-hmm. Okay...thanks."

Snapping the phone shut, Jake looked out toward the bay. He was silent for a second, then in response to Lannie's questioning stare, he said, "It's Cornelius. He's in the hospital. How do I get there?"

"Let me get Sadie up, and I'll go with you."

Majestic live oaks provided the classic Southern frame for the drive into Moss Bay. Spanish moss swayed in the trees as they passed through an alley of oaks on the country road leading into town.

"Are those pecan trees?" Jake asked, as they passed through a row of trees stretching out into the distance in single file.

"A *peecan* is what you take with you when you go fishing with your daddy. Those are *puhcan* trees.

"I see...thanks for the lesson. I'm sure that will be the first of many." He cut his eyes to her.

"Happy to help."

After dropping Sadie off at Wren's house, Lannie got back into the truck. "Why don't you let me drive?" She looked at Jake, waiting for an answer. "I'll drive you straight to the front door of the hospital."

"I've got it, Lannie."

"I'm an excellent driver…just in case you have some concerns for your truck."

He looked at her as her soft gray eyes lifted to meet his. A sweet, exotic fragrance clung to her, hanging on the air inside his truck. "I've never known a woman who could handle this truck or much of anything else for that matter." *Did I just say that out loud? I must really be stressed,* he thought, not sure which was more stressful, Cornelius in the hospital or Lannie inside his truck.

"Oh, is that right?" Lannie gave a half-laugh. "Well, you obviously haven't known very many women."

Now it was Jake's turn to laugh. After a period of silence, he said softly, "Listen, Lannie…"

She turned to look at him, waving her graceful hand in the air. "I know, I know. It's okay. You didn't mean it."

"Oh I meant it; I just usually have the good manners not to say it."

Lannie looked at him incredulously. Biting back a comment, she pointed sharply down the road. "Head straight until *I* tell you to turn." She glanced briefly at Jake; his mood was impossible to read. She kept her comments to a minimum. *If Cornelius wasn't sick, I'd give that man a piece of my mind.* "Take the next right," she said, waving to a street lined on each side with a row of hot pink crepe myrtles. "Follow this around and you'll be at the entrance."

Cornelius's eyes fluttered open. Seeing Jake's strong frame towering over him, he smiled. "Don't get your hopes up, Captain. I'm not dead yet!"

"I guess this means more of that disgusting shepherd's pie, doesn't it?" Jake smiled, revealing a rare and dazzling smile that made Lannie's knees weak. Oh, she hated how her body responded to the infuriating man.

"If you rushed down here to see me die, couldn't you at least have brought that pretty little neighbor along?" Cornelius smirked. "Give me something to look at besides your ugly mug before I leave this world."

Lannie stepped close to the bed and smiled sweetly at Cornelius.

"Oh! I must surely be a goner. I'm seein' angels!" Cornelius reached for Lannie's hand, giving it a squeeze.

The doctor came in, extending his hand first to Jake, then to Lannie. "I'm Dr. Cane. I assume you're Captain Chamberlain?" The bald, round-faced doctor peered at them over the top of his glasses.

"Yes, we spoke on the phone." Jake motioned toward Lannie. "And this is Lannie McPherson."

Nodding, Dr. Cane looked down at his chart. "We're going to run some tests to determine if there is blockage. I suspect there is. We'll know something by the end of the day." He placed the chart under his arm and asked, "Do you have any questions?"

Jake folded his arms across his chest. "If there is block-age, when will you schedule the procedure?"

"That depends."

Jake looked back at Cornelius and gave a crooked smile. "I was hoping to get out to sea before he gets back on his feet." Jake turned and winked at the doctor.

The doctor relaxed visibly and answered, "Depending on what the tests show, we should be able to schedule the procedure for tomorrow morning. I'm kind of like a circuit riding doctor; I'm only here once a month. I spend the rest of my time in Mobile." He smiled, giving them a reassuring nod. "We'll know something soon. As a matter of fact, I see your ride coming now, Mr. Longcrier."

After they wheeled Cornelius from the room, Jake plopped down into a chair, resting his elbows on his knees. He ran a frustrated hand through his dark brown hair and let out a breath.

Lannie leaned against the window, closed her eyes, and silently prayed.

"You're tired. Here, sit down and rest." Jake got up, motioning to the seat.

Lannie saw a spark of compassion in his eyes. She dismissed his comment. "I'm just praying, Jake. I'm not tired."

"I hope He hears you," he whispered, moving to the chair on the far side of the room.

"He always hears us. Maybe God's presence among us is more involved than we think. I honestly don't think I could've survived these past few months without knowing that." She sat down in the chair, curling her legs under her.

Jake got up and left the room without comment.

Doesn't that man ever explain anything to anyone? Lannie rolled her eyes. *He just walks off without a word.*

A few minutes later, he came back into the room and handed her a Sprite. "Sorry, they're fresh out of raspberry tea."

"Thank you. This is more than fine." Lannie sipped the drink, wondering for the hundredth time if she would ever figure him out.

A pretty, black-haired nurse sashayed into the room, cradling a cup of coffee in her hands. Following closely on her heels was a skinny blonde, wearing a vicious shade of red lipstick. Lannie recognized the women instantly as Kara Stone and Milly Harrington.

"Here you go, Mr. Chamberlain." Kara handed the coffee to Jake. "I made this fresh, just for you." She tossed her raven curls coyly, and her large black eyes scanned his face.

"Thank you, ladies." Jake took a long pull of the coffee. "Perfect."

Kara beamed. "I'm glad you like it."

Milly wandered over to his chair. "Can I get you a blanket, pillow, anything?"

"Maybe later, girls," he held up the coffee. "This is all I need for now, thank you."

With disappointment showing on her face, Kara turned and saw Lannie curled in the chair.

"Oh, hello, Lannie, I didn't see you there." A concerned look crinkled her brow. "I've been so worried about you. How have you been?"

It was obvious that Kara now had a reason for staying in the room, and that pleased her.

"I'm fine, Kara. But, thanks for asking." Lannie worked to keep the annoyance from her voice. Fake people drove her crazy.

"Bless your heart. I've been meaning to come see you. You've been on my mind so much lately." Kara moved to the chair, bending down to give Lannie a tight hug. "I can't imagine how you've endured everything. Especially what your very own sister did to you, dropping that child off on your doorstep like that." Kara turned and wiggled her finger in Jake's direction. "Are you two related?"

Months of grief and tension had built beneath Lannie's calm demeanor. She was in no mood for games, especially from two starry-eyed, simple-witted dingbats. "No, we're neighbors."

Milly piped in, "Aren't you living out at the Wheeler place?"

"Yes," she turned to Jake and smiled, "we are."

The look of shock on the girls' faces was priceless. Jake was enjoying himself immensely, sipping his coffee to hide his grin as he watched the scene play out before him.

"Tell me, Kara, are you and Taylor still engaged?" Lannie's tone was soft and appealing, no hint of the anger that was smoldering just beneath the placid surface.

"Oh my goodness, I don't even know anymore. Pastor Thad requires six months counseling before he'll marry us. That's three months longer than he requires for anybody else," she whined. "Taylor is just not interested. So, I guess it's all up in the air, and I'm still a single girl." Tilting her head to the side, she smiled, satisfied that her message had been relayed effectively.

Kara turned her ring, hiding the diamond in the palm of her hand, and quickly changed the subject. "I've wondered how you've been doing, Lannie, now that you're a mother. All those new responsibilities, I bet you never have a free minute anymore. You just look so worn out."

"Oh, I've managed. I have some pretty good help." Something in Lannie snapped, like a dry twig under a heavy boot. But before she could put Miss Kara in her place, Wren walked in, holding Sadie's hand.

The moment Sadie saw Jake, she let go of Wren's hand and flew into his outstretched arms.

A smile of satisfaction crossed Lannie's face. "Ah...here is my heavy burden now."

"How cute," Kara said with a weak smile, as she watched Jake cuddle with Sadie. "Well, we'll see you later, Mr. Chamberlain. Let us know if you need anything at all." Without hesitation, the girls left the room.

"What was that all about?" Jake asked, as Sadie snuggled in his lap.

"Take my chair, Wren," Lannie said, as she moved to sit on the bed. "I go to church with those girls. Every time I see Kara, I'm reminded of why I love my pastor. Kara and her 'fiancé' have been living together for the past two years, and she was teaching a class for young women at church. Kara's father told the pastor about her living arrangements, so Pastor Thad asked her to step down as teacher and enroll in a beginner's class called Christianity 101." A laugh bubbled up within her and spilled out, filling the room with the music of it. "You've got to meet that guy. You'd love him."

"I'd love to...when?" Jake stared directly into her eyes, waiting for an answer.

Regaining her composure, she said, "Uh, I don't know…"

"How about Sunday? I've been looking for a church to attend." He turned his attention to Wren. "Do you go to church there, too?" Jake asked, shifting Sadie into a more comfortable position on his leg.

"No, I go to a church across town. But interestingly, I've been invited to visit by one of my customers. A very handsome customer, I might add." Wren winked at Jake.

Curious now, Lannie asked, "So, do I know this handsome customer?"

"Don't think so. Anyway, Jake, where did you attend church in Cape Charles? Are you Catholic like Tilda?"

He finished off the rest of his coffee and placed his cup on the floor beside him. "No, I wasn't brought up in church. I guess it was a blessing to have been thrown on a ship with Cornelius at a young age. You might say he's my spiritual father. He pointed and directed me to the Savior and never gave up on me. He told me bluntly and without apology the passage of scripture that says, 'I am the way, the truth, and the life, and no man comes to the Father except by Me.' You don't just casually walk away from a statement like that." Jake was quiet for a moment, and then said, "I owe that man my life."

Dr. Cane stuck his head in the door. "The test went well. He has a blockage in an artery. The procedure will be first thing in the morning."

"Thank you, doctor," Jake said, as he lifted Sadie, holding her close as he stood to shake the doctor's hand. "I appreciate all you've done."

After Cornelius was settled in for the night, Lannie and Wren took Sadie home. Jake relaxed in the chair and said a silent prayer.

Chapter 10

The slamming of a door drew Lannie's attention away from preparing Sadie's lunch. It was the screen door to the entry hall. *Could Jake be home so soon?* She had gotten a call from him earlier saying that the procedure had gone well and that Cornelius was resting.

Wiping her hands on a dishcloth, she stepped from the kitchen just as a light knock sounded on the door.

"Who is it?" Lannie called, a sudden dread rising in her throat.

"Pitney."

Lannie was stunned, unable to answer. Her mind raced with a thousand confused thoughts as she tried to think of what to do. Her heart pounded in her chest, and her hands began to sweat. With shaking fingers, she reached for the doorknob, slowly turning it. Easing the door open, she raised her eyes to meet the eyes of her husband's best friend, Shane Pitney.

Even in her wildest imagination she'd never considered the possibility of Shane coming to her door. It would be too much like seeing Cade, and the pain of it would be almost unbearable. A soft light shone from the transom above the front door, spilling into the hallway and outlining his profile in a glow that made him seem even more warm and approachable than he usually was. His gold-flecked hair, slightly disheveled, gave him an innocent look that somehow calmed her.

"Hi Lannie," Shane said, just above a whisper.

"Hello, Shane."

It was a long moment before they realized they were just standing there. Clearing her throat, Lannie said, "Come in, Shane. I was just making Sadie's lunch. Can I offer you a peanut butter and jelly sandwich?"

Shane held his hand out, "No, thank you."

"Well, how about some lemonade then?"

"Now that sounds good."

As they stepped into the kitchen, Sadie smiled from her highchair, offering Shane an apple slice from her messy tray.

He smiled. "No thank you, Sadie, your mom is making a glass of lemonade for me." As the word "mom" left Shane's mouth he cringed, regretting his choice of words. Keeping his eyes lowered, he waited for a rebuke. When none came, he looked up into Lannie's clear, gray eyes. She handed him a glass, then turned and busily began preparing the sandwich for Sadie, cutting it into small pieces.

"Here you go, Miss Sadie, just the way you like it."

Shane pursed his lips thoughtfully, regarding the scene before him. Sadie seemed happy, swinging her feet as she nibbled on her sandwich. The kitchen was painted buttery yellow with white cabinets. Gossamer yellow-and-white checkered curtains tempered the abundant light from the kitchen window. The well-worn farm table, nicked from years of use, was solid and strong underneath his arms. Crayons, paper, and small teacups peppered the surface of the table, bringing a smile to his face. A long moment passed without a word.

"All right, Sadie, finish up with that last bite. It's naptime. Tell Mr. Pitney goodbye." Wiping off Sadie's mouth and hands with a damp cloth, Lannie picked her up and left the room. A moment later, she returned, saying, "Would you like to sit outside on the porch?" Her gray eyes moved slowly to meet his as a cold, tight feeling began to form in the pit of her stomach.

"That's fine." Shane followed her outside, taking the rocking chair and giving her the swing. He took a labored breath, leaning forward in the chair with his elbows on his knees. He began tapping his fingers together. "I need to tell you something, Lannie. Something I feel Cade wants me to tell you."

She leaned forward on the swing with her arms clenching her stomach. "Go ahead."

Shane's apprehension was apparent. He glanced at Lannie as he weighed his words. "Cade was terrified of losing you. So terrified, in fact, that for the last two and a half years, he's lived with the secret of Sadie. He had been blackmailed by Mindy; she wanted Cade to marry her, but he refused. He loved you."

Wearily, Lannie nodded, wondering vaguely why she wasn't surprised by what she was hearing. Some part of her had known that there had been another, but Mindy? Well, that thought had never occurred to her until the day Mindy revealed it.

Shane continued, "Mindy had been after Cade for years. Even on your wedding day, she came into our dressing room at church begging Cade not to marry you." Shane's lips turned up slightly in the corners. "Cade turned her around, popped her bottom, and told her to run on."

Lannie's lips quivered at the memory of seeing Cade do that very thing repeatedly over the years. Mindy seemed to always place herself in Cade's path, and a good-natured smack on Mindy's behind always seemed to do the trick. Neither she nor Cade had taken much notice of the infatuation, chalking it up youth and immaturity.

"One morning, Cade came to the fire station visibly shaken. I thought someone had died. There was no consoling him. He told me what had happened."

"Stop!" Lannie held her hands over her ears. "I can't hear any more of this, Shane. I really don't think I can hear this." She began to choke back tears, her lips trembling.

"I have to tell you, Lannie. Cade won't let me rest until I do." His eyes pleaded with her.

Lannie nodded her consent, placing a hand on her forehead; she wished for the world she was hearing anything but this.

"It happened one night while you were out at some homeplace. Cade said he'd told you to be back before dark. When he got home, he saw a woman he thought was you in the bedroom, dressed only in a towel with her hair wet from the shower. He grabbed her from behind and began kissing her shoulders. That's when Mindy turned around in his arms and began feverishly responding to him. Once he realized it was Mindy, he said he should have stopped, but he didn't...and that was his fatal mistake. He let his desire overrule his heart. He hated himself for being so weak. He let passion ignite and the fire consumed him. That was the real fire that took his life, Lannie, over two years ago. He'd never cheated on you, not until that one moment. He loved you so much he was willing to do anything to keep you. But, the guilt was wearing on him. He'd even made an appointment with Pastor Thad to confess and get counsel on what he needed to do. He wanted forgiveness…from God and from you. Above all, he wanted to keep his marriage together, and he was terrified that once you found out, you'd leave him."

"What about Sadie?" Lannie asked, sniffling.

"Cade saw his sin every time he looked at the little girl. He took care of her physical needs, but he wouldn't let her near his heart." Shane stopped, as if remembering. "This one time he asked me if I thought Mindy might let him have full custody of Sadie. He said he'd be willing to pay whatever it took to have her. I'm not sure why he asked, but I told him the truth. I said that Sadie was Mindy's connection to him, and there was no way she would ever give that up. I don't know what he was thinking, but he must've been thinking about bringing Sadie home to you. He always said that it wasn't fair that someone like you couldn't have a child. He said you'd be the perfect mother of his children."

At the last sentence, tears fell into her lap as she expressed all the sorrow she felt in her heart. Shane got up and sat beside her on the swing. He wrapped his arms around her, letting her cry until all that remained were a few jerking gasps.

At that moment, Jake pulled into the yard. Squinting through the glare of the sun on his windshield, he looked up and saw a man embracing Lannie on the porch swing. The sight caused him to swallow hard. He looked away, grabbed his coffee cup from the holder, and got out of the truck. Annoyed at his reaction, he slammed the truck door and made a wide circle around to the back entrance. Once inside, he tossed his keys on the counter and headed straight for the shower, intent on scrubbing off the hospital smell and the sight of Lannie entwined with some guy on the porch swing.

Moments later, rubbing his head with a towel, Jake stepped into the kitchen. Pulling open the refrigerator door, he heard a car door slam, then voices. Looking out the French door he saw his date, Heather, talking to the man that had been with Lannie. The man was leaving, jiggling his car keys as he briefly spoke with her before getting into his car.

He walked to the bedroom, grabbed a T-shirt off the bed, and yanked it on as a light tap sounded on his door.

"Well, looks like I got here just in time," Heather said, ducking underneath his arm to enter the apartment. "And for the record, it's not my habit to meet a man at his apartment. I usually require a pickup."

Jake's brow creased. "Who was that man I saw you talking to?"

"Jealous?" she teased. Seeing his mood darken, she quickly added, "That's Shane Pitney. He was best friends with Cade, Lannie's husband." She had his full attention now, so she continued with her story. "I'm not surprised to see him here, though. He's so much like Cade. He even looks like him. Lannie probably asked him over. I'm sure she's getting lonely for a man."

"Come on, I need a few things from town." Jake slid his keys off the counter, barely suppressing a growl.

Lannie plopped down onto the soft couch she had arranged on the second floor of the house. The entire top floor had been a complete surprise to her. She'd never ventured into that part of the house, assuming Tilda's relatives had swiped it clean as they had all the others rooms. After her discovery, she'd gathered a few supplies and set to work cleaning and arranging the small space. The room was filled with a plethora of antiques and one small, overstuffed couch. From her vantage point, once night fell, you could gaze out through the window into the star-filled night sky hanging quietly over the bay. Downstairs, Wren's sweet, muffled voice could be heard singing a child's tune as she bathed Sadie. Thankfully, her mother-in-law had dropped by not long after Shane's visit. Lannie needed some time to absorb all that Shane had revealed to her, and sharing it with Wren helped. Still, she felt emotionally drained.

Looking around, Lannie decided that the heavy mahogany pieces went well in the room, giving it a decidedly masculine feel. A massive and simply carved four-poster bed dominated much of the room. Mosquito netting hung from the canopy frame and was draped back at the posts. The rich mahogany glowed with the sheen of oil rubbed over it. One small table, stacked with books, was placed near the couch facing the windows.

She was rather pleased with herself. The room blushed softly in the fading evening light. Crickets and cicadas sang out from the grounds below through the open windows. Sheer white curtains lifted in the breeze, filling with sweet summer air. She wondered briefly if Jake knew about the room. If he did, he'd never mentioned it. Gathering her supplies, she headed back downstairs.

Dinner had come and gone. Wren was reading Sadie a bedtime story when Lannie stuck her head in the door to Sadie's room. "I left my book upstairs, I'm going to get it then come back and take a long soak in the tub."

"Okay, we're just going to read one more story."

Lannie climbed the stairs into the darkened room. Through the billowing curtains, a faint beam from the window provided enough light to see by.

As she reached the corner of the couch, a strong masculine arm grabbed her, pulling her across his lap. She knew it was Jake by the scent of his pipe tobacco. She meant to protest, she meant to pull away, until she felt the warmth of Jake's breath on her face and the gentle way his hand slid behind her head as he drew her near his lips.

Bending down, his lips moved across hers softly, tenderly. His hand smoothed the hair away from her eyes before it moved to cup her face. He spoke softly and gently against her lips, then his hand slid to her neck as he kissed her forehead, then her cheek, before capturing her lips again. At the sound of Heather's voice from below, his lips stilled.

The scent of the woman in his arms filled Jake's senses. "Lannie," he whispered against her lips. For one brief moment their eyes locked together as their pulses quickened. His lips hung from hers, reluctant to let go.

Lannie suddenly jerked back. Heat crept up from her neck and ignited on her cheeks. She rolled off his lap in one quick motion as the medallion around her neck caught on a button from his shirt and snapped. She snatched the book from the table and fled the room, passing Heather at the top of the stairs.

Heather looked at Lannie curiously as they passed.

"I forgot my book," Lannie said calmly, holding it up for inspection. "Good night."

Chapter 11

ake walked around the house toward the back porch as Heather's car lights flashed through the trees. He'd had every intention of entertaining a date for the evening, but he suddenly found his thoughts too troubled to enjoy company.

He gazed at the muted yellow light coming from Lannie's kitchen window. An occasional shadow would cross, then, as he neared, he saw her standing at the sink rinsing a dish. Her hands moved gracefully as if she were conducting some magnificent piece of music. Mesmerized with the fluid motion of her hands and carried along with her soft humming, Jake found himself fascinated by the tranquil scene.

The gentle and soft night with the sound of a single cricket from a shrub near the window added to the sense of well-being. Peace enveloped him for the moment like a warm blanket. He glanced up at the low-hanging moon near the treetops, puzzled at his strange feelings. Turning his attention once more to the window, he watched Lannie's small figure move with grace and ease as she tidied her kitchen.

Annie M. Cole ~

Jake toyed with his glass for a moment, tilting it slightly in his hand before he moved to knock on her back door.

"Hey," Lannie whispered, as she opened the screen door, wiping her hands on a kitchen towel. "Sadie is asleep," she pointed with her finger at a window facing the back porch then placed it over her lips. "That's her bedroom window." Stepping outside, she gently shut the screen door behind her.

"Can we talk?" Jake asked in a low, husky voice.

"Sure, let's step over to your side of the porch, away from Sadie's window. If she hears you out here, she'll come running."

Jake eyed the newly upholstered sofa and chairs he'd added to the back porch. "I've been meaning to break in this furniture. I like a cushy place to plop down at the end of a day. Antiques aren't the most comfortable things to sit on, you know?"

Taking a seat, Lannie said, "Yeah, I did notice you don't appreciate the finer things in life."

Jake smiled rather sheepishly. Taking a lighter from his pocket, he lit the citronella candle on the table. Reaching over, he lifted the lid on a small, ornate wooden box and took out a pipe. "Do you mind?" he asked, gesturing with the pipe.

"Not at all. I happen to love the smell of a pipe. I followed a man through a tobacco shop once just to breathe in the heady scent from his pipe. My husband used to..."

"I guess in some ways men are all alike." His hand with the pipe cradled in it pointed up toward the sky. "That's a beautiful moon over those trees."

She turned to look directly over the trees, noticing the pale, soft moon. "I love the night," she sighed. "I think I even prefer it to the day, really. I like to grab a quilt and lie out under the stars. It's soothing, and the air is cooler, easier to breathe."

Jake thrust the pipe into his mouth and lit it; it illuminated his features slightly as he puffed it to life. "About that...incident, Lannie, I'm...sorry for the mistaken identity."

She waved off his concern. "Don't worry about it. I've forgotten it. You know," she said, changing the subject, "I'm finding there's a certain pattern to living out here. It's like a rhythm you get into, and it's not based on the clock. It's based more on the comings and goings of the sun, the moon, and the sea. I like it...very much."

Clenching the stem with his teeth, he tamped the embers into the bowl of his pipe with his thumb. He continued to study her, amused by her quick, dismissive response to his apology and her deep musings. She was nothing like River. In fact, she was nothing like any woman he'd ever met before. "Would you like some tea or something?"

"No, thank you. I just had some."

Taking the pipe out of his mouth, he asked, "Tell me something. What is the significance of the silver leaf tree? Aunt Tilda mentioned it several times in the letter she left to me."

She looked at him uncertainly, not knowing whether she should confide in him the secrets of the tree. Those stories were sacred to her, something only Tilda and Lannie shared. "What letter?"

"William Forsyth gave me a letter from Tilda the same day he handed me a map of the place."

Lannie was curious now, and Jake held her full attention. "Oh? Well, what did she say?"

Jake shrugged. "Something about considering the way of the silver leaf and learning her secrets. There's more, I'll have to get the letter and read it sometime. I can't remember exactly." A breeze stirred and once again he captured the faintness of her scent. "What is that haunting fragrance you wear?"

Lannie smiled. "It's called 'Landis'—that's my given name. Madeline Warren, a friend of mine, created it especially for me. She expresses what a person means to her through fragrance. I only wear the body crème; is it too much?"

"No. In fact, it's just right. Your friend nailed you. It's very...appealing."

"Thank you." A light breeze rippled through her cotton shirt, playing with her hair. Smoothing it behind her ear, she titled her head. "I think we may have a visitor."

The screen door creaked on its hinges. In the pale light of the porch the tiny figure of Sadie cautiously approached. Neither Jake nor Lannie acted as if they'd noticed her, and they continued talking.

From his peripheral vision, Jake watched as the form moved toward him. Stopping in front of his chair, after a pause, she gently climbed up one leg at a time, then inched her way next to him.

In one easy movement, Jake placed his arm around the tiny shoulders. Sadie remained still, listening to the low tones of their conversation until her eyes grew heavy, and she dropped her head against him.

Looking down at the little girl resting against him, something stirred in Jake. *What courage it must've taken for her to approach me*, he thought. Then his thoughts turned to his heavenly Father. He wondered, at times, if He felt the same way when His children came to Him.

Lately, Jake's image of himself wasn't a pleasant one. The cutting truth was that he'd stubbornly guarded his privacy and certain sins he'd refused to deal with. The portrait he saw of himself caused him more than a little distress. "By the way…I just want you to know that when I have company, they won't ever be spending the night."

"I know how to tend to my own knitting, Jake. What you do or don't do is none of my concern."

"Still, for Sadie's sake, I won't set that kind of example."

Lannie raised an eyebrow. "You claim to be a man of God. If that's true, then He's the only one you should be concerned about. What He thinks matters, not what I think, or what Sadie thinks, or anyone else. I always try to remember that I live my life for an audience of one. I really don't care what others think of me. Being a captain, I'm sure you know that you lead by example."

It was true, and the truth of her words shot straight through to his heart. Jake knew he had shoved God to the sidelines lately. Appearance seemed to matter more than the truth, and he didn't quite know when things began to shift. Other things had crowded his life and pushed out the only relationship that really mattered. After the death of his wife, Jake just seemed to stop growing spiritually. In fact, he seemed to be going backward. With a determined effort, he would fix that problem.

Lannie had to admit, if only to herself, that the times she'd spent in Jake's company were the most pleasurable moments she'd spent with anyone. It was as if a part of her came alive, a part long dormant beneath the heavy weight of mourning. She didn't want to think about the fact that she'd allowed Jake to kiss her without even a small objection. In fact, she hadn't struggled at all. Her face flamed. Taking a deep breath, she said, "The story of the silver leaf tree...it might not be as interesting as you suppose."

"Let me be the judge of that." He casually drew on his pipe.

Smoothing her hair behind her ears and adjusting herself in her chair, she began her story. "When I was a little girl, Tilda and I met one day while I was digging through her roadside toss outs." She was a little embarrassed at her own admission, but she continued, "I wandered all over in those days, looking for treasures that I could drag back to my home." Lannie looked wistfully at her hands, remembering. "Tilda asked me if I wanted to see a living treasure, growing in her front yard. I jumped at the chance. She took me to the silver leaf tree. We tilted our heads up as the sunshine filtered through the leaves, turning them bright silver. It was beautiful and seemed so magical. She said that the silver leaf tree was not native to the area, but that it survives, in fact thrives, here. And do you know why?" Lannie raised her brows, looking directly into his blue eyes. "All because of an underground stream of life-giving water. Tilda said, 'Like the silver leaf tree, we too need the life-giving water of God's word and His Spirit, which is taken up into our souls just like the roots of the tree suck up fresh water. If you do that, you can survive anything in this old world.' She gave me hope, something I'd never really had before. After that, my little purple bike found its way down that dirt road for many summers. I've always considered this place home. It's where I'm the happiest."

"And your parents...where are they?"

"My father is out there somewhere." She waved her graceful hand. "But, he's never been in my life. He left my mother once she decided to have me. I was told by Mother that my father didn't want children and that once she decided to keep me, it was over between them." Lannie got up. "I'm going to get my tea; my throat suddenly went dry." A moment later, she came back to her seat, sipping iced tea. "Look, I know you only asked a simple question and didn't expect to hear all about my unfortunate childhood."

"What about your mother?" Jake ventured, letting her know that he very much wanted to hear about her life.

"Hettie is…well, just Hettie. I'm grateful to her for giving me life, but we've never really bonded. I think she still blames me for her stretch marks." Lannie gave a soft laugh. "My mother is preoccupied with acquiring things. And to acquire what she wants, she has to find a certain type of man to supply her wants—a filthy rich one, to be quite honest about it. The women in my family all have this disease, and they spare no expense to see that they stay attractive enough to land the money."

Placing his pipe in the ashtray, he ran a hand through his hair as he sighed. "I'm beginning to understand River a little more. So, where did *you* come from, and how have you survived in this family?"

"I'm a lot like my grandmother, Ma Tess. She produced three girls, and all of them are exquisitely beautiful. River and her sister, Mary Grace, take after my mother and her sisters, but none have inherited the strength of character of Ma Tess. I've survived by what Tilda and Ma Tess taught me. Tilda told me that just like the silver leaf, I'm different and not native to my surroundings. But, by reaching down deep, I can tap into a spring of life-giving water, and that can make all the difference. Ma Tess taught me to appreciate the simple things in life and to find pleasure in everyday common things. Both women were women of enormous faith in God."

Jake folded his hand around Sadie's little form nestled against him. "God has certainly watched after you, Lannie. You're a blessed woman."

The sky bled pink and red as misty shafts of morning light fell between the trees. Jake, Lannie, and Sadie bumped along the sand and gravel road heading for church.

Seated with her back to the passenger door, Lannie kept an eye on Sadie, who was fastened tightly in a car seat behind Jake's seat. Jake glanced at her before turning his attention back to the road. A fresh, natural beauty radiated from Lannie. Hair streaked the color of moonlight fell softly around her face and shoulders. The simple white dress she wore brought out the bright gray of her eyes.

"You know the saying, 'Red sky in the morning, sailors take warning?' He glanced toward the sky, then looked back at Lannie. "Guess we're in for it again." He rubbed his chin with his fingers. "Why haven't you been to church in a while?"

The question caught Lannie off guard. "Would you believe I'm practicing quiet attentiveness before God?"

He raised an eyebrow, looking at her suspiciously. "So, what you're saying is that you're so heavenly minded you're no earthly good?"

Lannie laughed out loud. "Exactly." But something in his eyes made her want to just spit out the truth. "I got tired of people whispering behind their hands whenever they saw me in town. I'm even avoiding the grocery store during certain hours these days. This will be the first time I've been back to church since Cade died. I planned on going back as soon as things settled down and people got bored with the news of my life, but honestly, I just didn't have the strength to deal with it. I'm stronger now."

Jake nodded. "I think I understand. You needed to sit with your grief and kinda explore it before exposing yourself to the opinions of others."

Lannie smiled. "Yeah, that's pretty much it."

"So…have all those turbulent thoughts found calm waters at Beauchene?"

"Beauchene is like medicine to my soul. The place has always helped me put things in order in my mind. I now believe I know what needs to be done for our lives. For a long time, I've been confused about what direction to take. I'm not confused anymore."

His brow furrowed as he watched the mischievous glint in her eyes. Something nagged at him. He was missing something, that was true, but what? "I'd say it's high time you got yourself back to church. Something tells me you didn't get enough discipline as a child." His face broke into a soft, lazy smile.

Lannie turned away, disturbed by the thrilling warmth that ran through her as she watched his face spread into a warm smile, but not before the sudden blush had been detected.

By the time they pulled into a parking space, people had already gathered on the steps of the church to stare. Large drops of water began to fall hard and angry, chasing the gawkers inside. Jake's strong hand reached over and squeezed Lannie's arm. "Nothing like a little spray of water to get rid of pests."

They waited in the cab of the truck, and after a few minutes the rain stopped. Lannie's frown gradually softened, turning into a smile. "Come on, Captain, let's do this thing."

Jake got out and lifted Sadie from the car seat, then followed Lannie as she lead the way through the doors of the church. Stomping his wet feet on the doormat, he looked around the foyer, noticing all the curious stares of onlookers as they made their way through the crowd and into the sanctuary.

An audible gasp sounded from a pew as they passed. Without looking, Lannie knew the gasp had come from her cousin, River; the Adams family had occupied the same pew for over twenty years.

Jake stopped and allowed Lannie to enter the pew, then sat down in a seat near the aisle, adjusting Sadie on his lap.

"Jake!" River said in a loud whisper from the aisle. "Why didn't you tell me you were a church-going man? You could've come with me." River mockingly eyed Sadie, assuming Jake was uncomfortable holding the child.

The answer was slow in coming. "You didn't ask."

River looked put out. There was no way she was going to let him sit there with Lannie. "Do you mind if I sit with you?"

A long pause ensued before Jake spoke again. "Whatever makes you happy, River. By all means, sit." River was creating a scene, and it annoyed him.

River wedged herself between Jake and Lannie, smiling triumphantly over her shoulder at her cousin. "Do you mind taking your…child? I'm sure Jake would appreciate it."

"Not at all," Lannie replied, reaching around River to collect Sadie.

Jake laughed softly as Sadie clung to him. The humor in his eyes was infectious and Lannie smirked. "Whatever makes you happy, Sadie, by all means," she said, repeating Jake's words as she let go of her.

"I've got to hand it to you, Lannie. You've trained that child well. Tell me, have you taught her to say "Daddy" yet?" River asked, glaring at Lannie with pure loathing.

Lannie blinked in surprise. "I hadn't thought of that. What a perfectly wonderful idea."

An amused smile twisted Jake's lips as he overheard the low-toned conversation. He pulled a hymnal from the holder and began flipping through the pages. "If you two are finished, service is about to start. And, the Lord knows you both need to hear it."

Pastor Thad finished his sermon and was calling the congregation to its feet for the last song, "It is Well with My Soul." At the first notes, Jake raised his gaze in wonder at the simple wooden cross displayed on the high wall behind the pulpit. *Of all the songs, it had to be that one, Lord. Thank you for thinking of me.*

Making a last announcement, Pastor Thad encouraged everyone to stay and enjoy the church picnic. "Now that the Lord has seen fit to clear the rain away, we can enjoy our scheduled dinner outside on the church grounds. Please stay and fellowship with us, won't you?"

Lannie turned to Jake. He stood in the aisle waiting for the girls to make their exit. River moved next to him and began pulling him toward the back of the church. A broad-shouldered man passed them, running his hand through his light brown hair as he focused his attention on Lannie. As he reached her, he wrapped his arms around her in a tight embrace. "I was just about to come get you. I've had enough of your solitude, Lannie. I'm glad you've come back."

Lannie wrapped her arms around him, sagging wearily against his chest. "I know, Michael. It's just taken me a while." She turned her head and noticed Jake standing nearby, watching her with keen interest. "Michael, come here, there's someone I want you to meet."

Jake straightened as the man drew near, noticing the confident manner and strong look about him. His muscular build and weathered skin told him he was an outdoorsman, and a man accustomed to physical labor.

"Jake, I'd like for you to meet a friend of mine, Michael Christenberry. Michael, Jake Chamberlain."

Jake stuck out his hand. "Pleased to meet you," he said, confidently grasping Michael's hand in a firm shake.

"Same here," Michael said, pumping Jake's hand. "I understand you're my new neighbor."

"Oh?" Jake raised his brow, waiting for an explanation.

"Yes, our properties touch near the bay. We live at Bell Forest."

"Where is your wife, Michael?" Lannie asked, looking around the church. "I seldom see the two of you apart."

Michael threw his head back and laughed. "Please, Lannie, leave me some dignity, will you? Not everyone in Moss Bay needs to know how that woman controls me. Telie is helping with dinner. She'll be thrilled to see you! In fact, she's the one who insisted that we pay you a little visit...drag you back to the land of the living."

Jake smiled slowly at his thoughts, not sure why he was relieved to know the man was happily married.

River interrupted. "Michael, why don't you and Telie take Lannie home after dinner? I'm sure Jake won't mind giving me a ride home. I can't stay for dinner, and I rode with my sister, Mary Grace. She never misses these things, you know." She turned her sapphire blue eyes up at Jake. Not waiting for an answer, River rushed on. "I'm sure Telie will want to spend some time with Lannie and her...child."

"Sadie," Jake offered. "The child has a name, and it's Sadie." Mocking azure blue eyes gazed back at her.

"Oh, of course, Sadie. Now that's all settled."

"That will certainly tickle Telie," Michael added, extending his hand once again to Jake. "Jake, it's been a pleasure. Call on me anytime. Let me know if you need help on the property. I'd be happy to do whatever you need. Lannie has my number."

"I appreciate that, Michael. And, you'll hear from me."

Chapter 12

𝒯he rain had cleared out, leaving behind a humid heat that no one seemed to mind. Crisp tablecloths stirred in the breeze as women arranged their dishes on long tables under the sun-dappled trees. Children played and men talked as they waited for the call to dinner.

June Meyers raised her chin and peered down her nose at the little blonde girl standing in front of her. The wide straw brim of her hat lifted in the breeze as she stared in confusion at the child's outstretched arms.

Never before had such a thing happened. *Children don't come to me. There must be some mistake. She couldn't possibly want me. She must think I'm someone else.*

Glancing up, she looked around, her hat shading her eyes from the glare of the noon sun. June searched the faces, trying to find anyone who looked as if they were missing a child. Seeing no one, she dropped her gaze to the little girl, whose tiny hands continued to stretch toward her.

The warmth of the little girl's brown eyes drew June to her; they radiated a tender, caring warmth. June smiled in response, in spite of herself, noticing for the first time the gentleness of her expression. She welcomed it, like you'd welcome a soft summer rain after a long dry spell.

She hesitated. She didn't want to pick up the child and then have her scream and cry once she realized a stranger held her. She was, after all, in the churchyard surrounded by her friends. What would they think?

After a long, agonizing moment, June relented and reached down to slowly lift the little girl off the ground. Awkwardly she held her against her white linen suit.

June was a striking woman in appearance. Smooth salt-and-pepper hair impeccably pulled into a tight chignon accented her dark, almond-shaped eyes. Tall, thin, and regal, June Meyers was anything but matronly. The years since her husband's death had been especially hard. Childlessness had always been a very real part of their marriage, and she'd accepted it, but at this particular time of her life she felt even more alone surrounded by all of her friends with their stories of children and grandchildren.

It was no secret that June Meyers was a handful, but the people of Moss Bay accepted June and her outspoken ways as one would tolerate an eccentric old aunt. She spoke her mind freely and never apologized for it. Very few people ever earned her respect, but, once they did, she was loyal to them for life.

Risking a glance at the child in her arms, June cut her eyes, seeing those same brown eyes that had melted her heart moments before. Without warning, the little girl leaned into June and gently pressed her lips against her powdered cheek.

"Sadie!" called a frantic voice from across the chur-chyard. June looked up to see a pretty young woman fast approaching. As she neared, she realized it was Lannie.

"So, Sadie is it? Well, Sadie, it looks like we're in trouble." Bracing for the impact, June gave a weak smile. "This little one must belong to you." Sadie held on tightly to June's neck as she tried to release her to Lannie.

"Yes, thank you. You must think I'm a terrible mother." Lannie wiped tears of relief away from her eyes as she pulled Sadie to her. "It's just...it's just," she choked as the tears caught in her throat.

June patted Lannie's arm. "No harm done. In fact, this little girl just made my day."

Lannie sniffled. "You must think I'm awful, losing my child like that."

Realization hit June as she remembered the circumstances surrounding Lannie and her deceased husband, Cade. "Not at all, dear. As a matter of fact, I was just thinking what a wonderful mother this child must have for her to be able to show such love and affection to a stranger."

Lannie smiled, letting out a grateful sigh. "Thank you, June. I needed to hear that. I'm new at this motherhood business, and I'm not at all sure I'm doing it right. I never realized how quickly a child can make a break for it and be gone from your sight in an instant."

June looked up, shielding her eyes from the sun with her hand. "Is that Telie over there waving at us?"

Turning around, Lannie smiled. "Yes," she said, waving back, signaling that she'd found Sadie. "Telie and Michael have been searching everywhere for her. I told them that Sadie has a mind of her own. She picks her own friends."

June beamed. "Is that so? Well, I'm honored to be counted among the many."

"Among the few," Lannie corrected. "So far, not counting me or her grandmother, Sadie has chosen to befriend only two, you and Jake Chamberlain."

June turned sharply, giving Lannie a questioning look. "You mean that good-looking Yankee captain belonging to Tilda Wheeler?"

"One and the same."

"Oh my, I do feel honored. I had the pleasure of meeting him in town a few days ago. He helped me with my grocery bags. Heather was with him. Are they dating?"

"Jake has several girls, and she is one of them."

"Oh...I see. He seems like a nice young man." June stated, with a clear question in her voice.

"He is, June, one of the finest."

Michael's truck bounced over the rough dirt road leading to Beauchene. Lannie, Sadie, and Telie sat quietly as they passed through the gate. In the distance, the outline of the silver leaf tree shimmered in the afternoon light.

"What a magical place," Telie whispered. "I've never ventured this way before."

Michael reached in his shirt for a cigar. "My dear Telie, is it not enough for you to worry me to death with all of your wanderings to the south and east of Bell Forest? Let's leave the north end to Lannie, how 'bout it?" His teeth clamped down firmly on the cigar. "I don't suppose it ever occurred to you that you just can't go around like you did before you were expecting," he said around the cigar. "I'm surprised your guardian angel hasn't collapsed from overwork and exhaustion. I'm near it myself."

Telie rolled her eyes, speaking over her shoulder to Lannie. "Michael thinks I should stay in bed, flat on my back, until the baby comes."

Lannie laughed, pushing Michael with her hand. "That's worse than letting her get exercise! You need counseling, Michael."

Michael threw up his hands. "Hold up, I'm clearly outnumbered. Where's Jake? There's gotta be a man around here somewhere."

"Oh, he's around. I see his truck parked near the barn. But, he's probably entertaining." She let the insinuation hang in the air.

Michael narrowed his eyes but didn't respond to her statement. "What's it like living so close to a bachelor, Lannie? Does he *entertain* a lot? I've heard a lot of stories about seamen." Concern seeped into his voice.

"Oddly enough, he's a very good neighbor. He minds his own business and works around the property, mostly. But he's also protective of Sadie. He watches over the place, and I like having him around."

Michael and Telie exchanged glances.

Unmindful of what passed between them, Lannie continued, "The other night when the storm hit so hard, Sadie was inconsolable. I was worried that her cries were keeping him up. He came to check on her, and the minute he picked her up she stopped crying." Lannie glanced at Sadie. "Yes, you're a traitor, Sadie," she said, in a singsong voice. "And now everyone in Moss Bay thinks I beat you unmercifully and you'll do anything to escape me. You've formed alliances with Jake Chamberlain *and* June Meyers!"

Telie gathered her honey-wheat hair in her hands, pulling it off her shoulders and securing it with a band as she laughed. "Sadie just may have won the two greatest allies to be had around here. Sounds like this Jake is someone you need to have in your corner."

Michael cleared his throat. He cocked an eye, watching Telie closely. "You just make sure I'm the only one in *your* corner...got that!"

Telie playfully swatted his arm. "Can you believe this, Lannie? Michael is jealous of his pregnant wife."

"I think it's wonderful," Lannie said, as they neared the house. Her eyes fastened on the tall figure that strode from the shadows of the porch. *Is he waiting for us?* He wore jeans, topsiders, and a white button-down shirt with rolled-up sleeves. On trembling limbs and with a rapidly thumping heartbeat, she hopped out of the truck. She stepped around the back of the truck to lift Sadie from the car seat, but Jake was already there, holding Sadie high in his arms. The night Jake had mistakenly kissed her seared its memory on her mind. Tearing her eyes away from the line of his shadowed jaw, she began smoothing her dress, not sure what to do with her hands *or* her thoughts.

Rolling down the truck window, Michael stuck his elbow out and called to Jake, "Telie and I want to have you over for dinner, sometime. What works for you?"

Jake leaned in. "Any time you say. I've always had to rely heavily on the charity of others when it comes to meals. I'm not much of a cook. In fact, if it wasn't for Cornelius and the months I'm at sea, I'd starve to death."

"Have you met my wife?" Michael asked, leaning back in his seat so they could exchange a handshake.

"No, I haven't." Jake smiled warmly as he extended his hand. "Jake Chamberlain."

"Nice to meet you, Jake, I'm Telie." Her eyes dropped behind him. "What is that strange plant behind you, Jake?" Telie asked, the click of her seatbelt sounding as she opened the truck door on her way to investigate.

"Oh no, here we go, "Michael murmured. "Looks like I'm gonna be here for a while. I've seen that look before, and it always means trouble."

"That works for me. I'd like to show you a little project I'm working on down by the bay. It's a guest house; we call it the sea cottage…if you have the time that is." Jake handed Sadie over to Lannie, playfully rubbing her head.

Michael motioned with his head toward his wife. "She's already looking around for a shovel. Something tells me you're going to be missing some of your yard here shortly."

Jake laughed. "In this jungle, it won't take long for anything to grow back, I assure you. She can have all she wants."

As the men neared the sea cottage, Michael noticed a dense, tangled hedge of briars almost covering the walls and roof. Weeds sprouted where once a garden grew along a broken stone path leading to the door. The front porch was nonexistent.

"I'll be leaving in a few days—out to sea—and there are a few things that need to be settled before I leave. I'll be gone a month or so this time, and I'd like to have some work done while I'm gone." Jake glanced about in frustration. "It doesn't look like it, I know, but I've cut away half of the brush already."

Michael reached into his shirt for a cigar, then searched his pocket for a match before remembering he'd given up smoking and only chewed on stogies these days. "What stays and what goes?"

"Take it all out, except the trees and the plants that are valuable. I can't tell what's what. As you can see, the place needs a porch. I've got a drawing of what I'd like inside. If you know anyone who can build, I trust you to hire them. Lannie has a lot of confidence in you, and that's good enough for me."

"Don't worry, I'll handle it. We'll get started tomorrow. I'll have my helper, Joe, with me. He can work on the garden while I get started on the big stuff that needs clearing. I'll put a call in to Josiah. He's one of the best carpenters we have around here. He works for a friend of mine, Samuel Warren."

"Great. I'll be ready to help you get started first thing in the morning."

Michael paused, then turned his blue-green eyes to meet Jake's straight on. "Anything else you need me to do for you while you're away?"

Jake peered at him closely. "If you don't mind, keep a check on the place for me. Make sure the girls are doing okay. I worry about them way out here by themselves. I don't want it known around town that I'm going to be away."

Michael read the intent of his words and nodded. "Will do."

The heat of the summer day bore down on their shoulders as the men walked around the cottage. Lannie turned from watching them to observe Telie examining a vetiver plant with childlike wonder.

"Okay, I've got to know. What is this stuff?" Telie ran her fingers along the stiff blade.

"Vetiver. It has probably been in the United States ever since the French occupied Louisiana. It makes a wonderful perfume. As a matter of fact, it's advertised as the original scent of New Orleans. It's also known to be deeply relaxing for anyone suffering from stress. The oil is used in many perfumes and fragrances."

More than a little curious, Telie set to work clearing away debris from around the base of the plant with her hands so she could get a better look at it. "Where is the oil, in the leaves?"

"In the roots; it's called 'the oil of tranquility.' Tilda used to add it to my bath when I'd come out here all covered in dirt from digging around in my treasure piles. I've never felt more relaxed in my life than when I was out here. She kept me sedated with the stuff. Even now I like nothing better than a good ol' afternoon nap. I keep a bowl of dried vetiver root on a table in the entry hall so that that is the first thing you smell when you enter the house."

Telie turned and stared at Lannie for a long, indecisive moment. "What does the oil smell like, lemongrass?"

"It's more exotic than that. It's very unique and kind of masculine."

"Madeline *needs* this. How can I get my hands on this stuff? She could use it for her soaps and creams. She's starting a new men's line." Telie's hands worked the dirt around the plant, digging into the rich soil.

"You can also use it in sachets and pop it in your drawers and closets; it protects clothing from mildew and pests. Bugs seem to absolutely hate it. It's as necessary to have vetiver down here as it is to have iced tea."

Telie was overjoyed with her discovery. "Can I *please* have some? Don't make me come back after dark and steal it from your yard. I've already repented of my thieving ways, and I'd sure hate to backslide. The monks over at the monastery would sure give me a fit. Brother Raphael can always tell when I've been up to something. They'd probably twist my ear and make me clean toilets with a toothbrush if they ever found out I'd been rustling plants again."

"Get all you want; we're overrun with the stuff. Only let me do the digging. I don't want Michael fussing at you. The guy needs to relax. Is he always so overprotective? No wait." She threw her hand up. "Never mind, I remember that about him." She shook her head. "There's a shovel in the barn and an empty bucket; I'll go get them. Will you stay here and watch Sadie?"

Chapter 13

Annie turned her head at the sound of a car coming down the road. Visitors were rare at Beauchene, and every car drew attention. She craned her neck, standing on her tiptoes in an effort to see through the cracks in the barn wall. She nearly groaned. "Pauline."

The darkened stall made it hard to locate the shovel, but she finally saw it leaning against a post beside an empty beer bottle. The property had been covered in beer bottles. She and Jake had collected no fewer than a hundred in their recent cleanup efforts.

Grabbing the handle of the shovel with one hand and the bottle with the other, Lannie pushed the barn door wide with her foot. She had known it was only a matter of time before Pauline paid her a visit. Armed with all she needed to fight the woman, she set her jaw and strode toward her with determined steps.

Lannie had felt Pauline's eyes on her during church service. She was one of the main reasons she'd kept her distance from church for so long. She knew she would take Cade's death like some kind of sign—Pauline was always on the lookout for signs and wonders. Most people ignored her, giving her a wide berth because, frankly, everybody was scared to death of her. She had a way of looking at a person like she was conjuring up a curse.

From their vantage point at the back of the cottage, Jake and Michael watched with mild curiosity as Lannie walked out of the barn holding a beer bottle and a shovel. She walked straight over to the tawny-haired, skinny woman with a purposeful stride.

The woman was standing next to Telie, who had gotten up, slapping the dirt from her hands. Her arms were folded and the displeased look on her face was visible, even from a distance.

Pauline began pointing an accusing finger at Lannie and, if her body language was any indication, shouted vicious words. Telie moved near Lannie and squarely faced the woman as if to say, "You'll have to come through me first!"

Jake made a move to intervene, but Michael stopped him. "Lannie can handle this woman. We all know her; she's from church. But Lannie needs to be the one to put her in her place. If we interfere, she'll only come back when we're gone."

Reluctantly, Jake stopped, crossed his arms, and leaned against a tree. But he never took his eyes off the woman in front of Lannie.

Lannie calmly caressed the bottle in her hand with one thumb, running it up and down the neck as the woman railed against her. Lannie's face remained serene. Seemingly angry and full of rage, the woman turned around and headed straight to her car, calling out a threat before climbing into the driver's seat. She cranked the engine, tearing a wide circle in the field in her hasty departure.

Telie held out her hand, giving Lannie a high five.

The men walked up the path, looking first to Lannie, then to Telie, noticing the smiles of satisfaction on their faces.

"What was that all about?" Jake asked, looking down the road where the woman had made her quick exit.

"If you can believe it, she came all the way out here to tell me how the devil is after me." A brief moment passed, then she continued in a low tone so Sadie wouldn't overhear her. "She said that the devil took my husband and Tilda, and next he'll take Sadie. Then I got a sermon on the evils of alkeehol." She looked down at Sadie, who was content to dig in the dirt with a stick.

Jake narrowed his eyes. A muscle twitched in his cheek. "She sounds like a pleasant person; sorry I missed meeting her."

"I think the beer bottle set her off," Telie added softly.

Lannie smiled. "Yep, works like a charm. Sometimes you have to be bold in your choices if you want a change. I just can't live in peace with a person like that haunting me." Lannie turned to Jake. "How long were you standing down there watching us?"

"Long enough to be envious of a beer bottle," he replied, taking the bottle out of her hand. "I must admit, it was hard watching that little scene play out. Michael stopped me from coming over. He said that you could handle her; but…that woman looked like she could kill you."

"If looks could kill, I'd be with the Lord right now. But that's the only way I know to get rid of her. Nothing repels Pauline like alcohol. It's like kryptonite to superman."

Telie grinned. "Or vetiver to an annoying pest."

"Exactly." Lannie smiled, brushing a strand of wispy hair from her face.

Jake tossed the bottle in the air, flipping it before he caught it again. He paused for a moment, staring down at Lannie with those penetrating blue eyes. His voice was so low she barely caught his words. "If *anyone* ever threatens you or Sadie again, they'll have to answer to me. And I don't care who they are."

Lannie was silent, unable to respond to the words she thought she heard.

Michael heard a few words and read the body language. Smiling, he thought, *This is my kind of guy.* "I'll be along in the morning, Jake," Michael said, gripping his hand in a firm shake. The captain had gained Michael's respect, which was not something easily done. Placing an arm around his wife, he whispered in her ear, "I'll have Joe get those plants for you tomorrow. Come on, let's go home."

Rain hit the old glass on the window beside Lannie's bed as she sat up with a start. Her hair was soaked with sweat, and her heart pounded fiercely in her chest. She'd had another dream of Cade. This time she dreamt they were divorced and separated by many miles. It was a terrible dream. But the worst of it was that there was no longer anybody to tell her dreams to. It was Cade who had listened in the night as she shared her deepest thoughts. It was Cade who held her close when her own family pushed her away. It was always Cade, and now all she wanted was her husband.

Sliding her feet off the bed, she tiptoed across the wooden floor. Lifting her robe from the back of the door, she tied it loosely around her waist and stepped into her slippers. She headed out to the porch swing for some night air.

Lannie remained on the swing for some time, sitting with her knees pulled up to her chin like a bewildered child, barely able to gather her wits.

"I don't know where my husband is," she said aloud into the damp night. Nothing but dripping water responded to her words. She wished more than anything that she knew where he was. Did he have time to make peace with God?" She dabbed her eyes with the sleeve of her robe. Suddenly, the faint smell of Cade passed in front of her, all warm and spicy and familiar. Did it come from the fibers of her robe and the many embraces they'd shared? She didn't know what it all meant, but in that smell, that Cade smell, was the truth of it. She loved him, even though he had betrayed her. How much more would God love him and forgive him if he only asked?

Wet gravel crunched and water splashed under the wheels of Jake's truck as he pulled up to the house. Crossing the yard, he dodged the rain as his boots hit the steps in quick succession. He caught sight of a slight movement in the dark, turned, and saw Lannie huddled on the porch swing.

"Hey," he whispered, low and hoarse.

Lannie's gray eyes peered up at him, but her chin never moved from her knees. "Hey."

"Are you all right?" he asked, concern seeping into his voice as he watched her still, small frame.

"Bad dream."

"Oh," he said, nodding once. "You wanna talk about it?"

"It's late, and I'm sure you're tired and ready to go to sleep."

"I'm..." he fished in his pocket for his house key, "about to make a cup of Earl Grey tea. Want some?"

She lifted her head from her knees. "Sure, if it's not too much trouble."

"I'll be right back." The swing vibrated slightly from his heavy steps.

Moments later, Lannie had her hands curled around a warm cup of tea. Sipping it, she explained, "It's always the same dream. Cade is gone far away and can't get back to me. Only this time we were divorced. Is that normal? Should I be concerned that maybe I'm losing it?"

Lannie's low, velvety voice stirred something strange in Jake's heart, but he didn't have time to explore his thoughts. He sat transfixed as she slid her daintily slippered feet to the floor and pushed the swing to a slow movement. The satin robe shimmered in the darkness. "Cade was the most intimate person in your world, Lannie, and all of a sudden he's not there anymore. How can you not be affected by it? He was your husband...your feelings are very normal."

Lannie searched the swaying wet branches of the silver leaf tree as it sifted raindrops down to the ground. "I guess some things never die away, do they?"

"Some things never should," he said, in a hoarse whisper.

"Sometimes...for a moment...I think I hear his voice. I turn my head, trying to tune into whatever I'm hearing, then I lose it. What do you think he's trying to say to me? Or do you think I'm going crazy?"

"Maybe what he's saying is that love endures, even in the pain of poor choices. And, that's no whisper in the air."

After absorbing his words for a long, silent moment, Lannie finally stood. "Thank you for listening and...for this." She held up the teacup. "I believe I can sleep now." Smiling warmly down at him, she patted his cheek with her soft hand as she passed, leaving a wisp of her fragrance behind. "If you ever have a nightmare, I'm just across the hall. Don't hesitate to come knocking."

Once inside, Lannie peered in to check on Sadie. After assuring herself that the little girl was sound asleep, she shrugged off the robe and hung it on the door hook before returning to bed. The rain had passed, so she pushed open the window. A fresh, rain-washed, sea wind flowed in. Shivering slightly in the light cotton gown, she jumped into bed, pulling up the soft duvet cover and snuggling down deep into the bed until a restful sleep found her.

It was a long time before Jake could sleep that night. He sat staring at the silver leaf tree as thoughts and strange feelings swam around in his head.

Morning arrived with a sound of a buzzing chainsaw. Lannie woke with a start. Rubbing her eyes, she leaned over, pulling the sheer curtains back to look out the window. "Is that Sadie?" she said out loud. Scooting off the bed, Lannie peered closely at the trio standing near the fish pond. It was Sadie all right, and Wren had her by the hand. Telie was standing next to them with her arms folded across her chest. All three seemed to have their attention fixed on the sea cottage.

"What time is it?" Turning, she noticed her bedroom door had been shut. She hurried to take a shower and dress. A short time later, she emerged wearing jeans and an old, white cotton shirt. Her hair was pulled back at the base of her neck and loosely clasped. After pouring a cup of strong coffee from the pot, she eased out the door to join the rest of the crowd watching the work commencing at the sea cottage.

Wren turned at the slap of the screen door. "Look who is awake, Sadie," Wren whispered excitedly to the little girl. Sadie let go of her hand and ran across the yard to greet Lannie.

Seeing Sadie run toward her both shocked and thrilled Lannie, and reaching down, she gathered her into her arms and squeezed, kissing her soft cheek. "Good morning, sweet Sadie. Are you keeping this bunch straight out here?"

"Oh, she certainly is," Wren responded. "We don't dare let go of her hand, or she'll be back down there with the men, hauling off brush."

"A girl after my own heart," Telie said, looking with longing as Michael, Jake, and Joe cleared away the overgrowth from years of neglect. She wanted to be down there so badly her hands itched. The sea cottage could actually be seen now, and the sweeping metal roof line gleamed in the sun. "I hope they don't murder that gorgeous crepe myrtle by pruning it too severely. See those long branches? You need to prune them a certain way, or they'll hang over with full blooms and break off during heavy rains," Telie stated nervously. She had the look of a caged panther.

"Go tell them, too. That cottage is mine, and I give you permission to oversee the landscaping. Come on, we'll go tell them to stop the massacre."

The girls approached the guest house cautiously, feeling the noise of two chainsaws reverberate through them. Jake and Michael were at opposite sides of the same massive tree, cutting away the lower branches that had grown out of control, almost swallowing the cottage whole. Joe was raking up the fallen limbs as fast as they were falling. Upon seeing the girls, Jake killed the motor of his chainsaw. Michael looked up curiously, and then followed Jake's eyes down to the girls. He stopped the motor of his chain saw and stepped carefully down the ladder.

"What, no lemonade?" Jake asked, grinning as soon as he said it. "Can you believe that guys? They come all the way down here empty handed."

"Don't worry, we're planning a nice lunch for y'all. A break now would only slow progress," Telie remarked.

Michael wiped the sweat from his brow with the back of his arm. "What'd I tell you, Jake, she's ruthless. You're lucky she's expecting, or she'd be down here showing us all up."

Running his hand across his forehead, Jake said, "I don't doubt that one bit. She's got a wild look in her eye. I've seen that look on a few pirates right before they take your ship!"

Michael threw his head back and laughed.

Jake added, "I've gotta tell you though, when I first got a look at Joe here I had my doubts."

Joe stopped raking and looked up at Jake at the mention of his name. He was more than a little in awe of the captain; Jake's profession had captured the young man's imagination to no small degree.

Jake lifted the camouflaged cap off of Joe's head and turned it around, pressing it back on his head securely. "If a man still hasn't figured out that his cap has a brim on it to shade his eyes, not the back of his head, I thought I could do without him," Jake said to Michael, laughing. "But I was wrong. Joe's been a big help. He's a hard worker."

Joe beamed. Never before had he been accused of being a hard worker, but when he was in the presence of the captain, it was like a switch flipped on inside of him. He wanted to give whatever he was doing his best effort.

Telie spoke low to her husband. "If I'd done that to Joe, he would've sulked for a week!"

Michael bent near to Telie and whispered in her ear, "You're not a sea captain...you're the pirate who has captured my heart."

Telie's golden-brown eyes lifted to her husband, and she smiled. It was as if no one else was around witnessing the love that flowed between them.

"You get used to it," Joe supplied, tossing his head in Michael's direction. "I usually find a shady spot and wait it out...been going on for over a year now."

"Sounds like a good idea." Jake moved to a clearing under a tree, with Sadie in step right behind him.

After a brief kiss, Michael and Telie joined Lannie and Wren to look over the progress. Telie pointed out trees that should stay and ones that should go.

Very few things ever distracted Lannie when she was working on a restoration project, but the sight of Jake tying Sadie's shoe caused her to pause. Such tenderness seemed oddly out of place in the rough and handsome captain.

Sadie picked her own friends; that was certain. No one in three counties would have been brave enough to approach June Meyers, or the captain, for that matter. Lannie smiled before turning her attention back to the work.

Jake hoisted Sadie to his shoulders and stepped near the cottage. "This place is older than I first thought. Look at this. What is that stuff under the brick?"

"That's *bousillage,* a mixture of clay, moss, and hair. It insulates well, too. This low-lying land around here is damp. Most of our houses are raised above the ground like this cottage to give cross ventilation. Those front and rear casement windows allow breezes to flow through," Michael said, pointing to the front of the house. "This place used to be the slave overseer's cabin. It was built better than the slave cabins, so it's lasted longer."

"Ah…a look back in time to when human beings were forcefully held as property—what a reflection," Jake said sarcastically. "I'm not sure I want to restore that kind of image."

Michael ran a hand over the exposed bousillage from the missing bricks. "A bad reflection, that's certainly true, but one we've got to own and learn from. Just as a plantation house tells a story, so too does a slave cabin. We don't ever need to forget the lives that once lived before us and what they endured."

Michael's stock just shot up in Jake's estimation of the man. Narrowing his eyes, he looked at Lannie and asked, "If you'll permit me, I'd like to have Michael add the porch back, but make it a little wider this time. The roof seems intact, but I'd feel better if we can shore it up, extend it, *and* paint it." Jake glanced overhead. "Why would anybody paint a ceiling that odd shade of blue? They did the same thing up at the big house."

Telie explained through soft laughter, "That's called haint blue. Haints can't cross water, so you paint the ceiling blue to fool them and keep them from crossing into your house." Lannie's smile widened at Jake's quizzical expression. "You don't want to have a haint in your house; you could be influenced."

He cocked his head to the side. "What the heck is a haint?"

Everyone laughed at once. Lannie explained, "A haint is a spirit, a ghost. But Tilda said that the only ghost we have in our house is the Holy Ghost. She kept it that color to keep away bees, wasps, and spiders. They're fooled into thinking the ceiling is actually the sky, or so they say."

Shaking his head, he said, "The chamber of commerce should pass out a manual on this kinda stuff."

Chapter 14

An eerie white mist clung to the ground as its creeping fingers came up from the low-lying marshes. Circling around massive trees and swallowing everything in sight, it swirled and parted around Lannie's feet as she walked the grounds. A flock of pearl-gray bald heads bobbed behind her as she made her rounds, showing the guinea fowl the perimeters of the property. Establishing boundaries with guineas was not an easy thing to do because they were wild by nature. But they had room to roam and plenty to eat, so Lannie expected that they'd settle into their new environment quickly.

"You've lost your mind," River called out, as she reclined in a chair on the back porch, fanning herself with a magazine. "What are those fat, gray things following you?"

Lannie stopped. "Look, River, there's not a person within shouting distance around here. If you don't make yourself scarce, I'll do it for you. There's no sense in anybody being harassed on their own property."

River kept on talking. "What is that annoying noise they're making, that ch-chee-chee-chee sound?"

"They call out their warning at anything new or, in your case, unusual. It takes a while for the guineas to learn what's threatening and what is normal in a place."

"Well, they better get used to me, then. I plan on being a familiar sight around here." River crossed her legs and began casually swinging her foot.

"In case you haven't noticed, Jake's not here."

"I know, but he's coming here with Cornelius." The smug look on River's face made Lannie roll her eyes. Just then, they heard Jake's truck coming down the road. As he pulled up, the guineas fled in all directions.

Cornelius got out of the truck first, then Jake. Slamming the truck doors, one after the other, both men looked in the direction of the barn where the odd birds scattered.

Adjusting the blue baseball cap on his head, Jake asked, "What are those?"

"Those are guineas, and they hate snakes and will kill any they come across. You wouldn't let me kill the snake the other day, so I got something that will do the job for me. They also eat ticks and spiders. Not to mention they can peck the aphids off your roses without leaving a mark!"

Jake eyed her suspiciously, not sure he should believe all the claims that she was making.

She almost lost her train of thought as he turned those blasted eyes of his on her; she was finding it difficult to keep up her head of steam over the whole snake issue. "I want them in my flowerbed and around the woodpile. I spotted another rattlesnake over there just this morning."

"I told you, Lannie, that's a rat snake, a farmer's friend. It's probably the same snake. He *won't* hurt you."

"I know he won't hurt me because he won't be around long. I've got my own farmer's friend. They call these birds a farmer's watch dog because they warn you when anything threatening is in sight. You should've heard them squawk when they got a look at River."

Cornelius covered his laugh. He was beginning to think that the captain had met his match in the girl, whether he'd admit it or not. Clearing his throat, he spoke up, "Now Lannie, is that any way to welcome a man home who's snatched his life back from the jaws of death?"

She stepped into Cornelius's waiting arms. "I prayed for you, Cornelius. I knew the Lord wasn't finished with a salty old dog like you."

"I felt those prayers, too, Lannie girl. I certainly did."

Jake turned to speak with River, and they walked in the house without a word, leaving Cornelius alone with Lannie.

"You all set?" Cornelius asked in a low voice, bending near Lannie's ear.

"As ready as I'll ever be."

Jake and River came out of the house and walked down the porch steps, heading for the barn. "I'm going to fix that mower for you before I leave, Lannie. I've noticed you like to keep the grass really short around the house. Our lawn has more bald spots than Cornelius's head."

"Well, if there's a snake around, I want to see it. There's nothing worse than a snake in the grass, hiding and ready to strike. No offense, River."

"Why don't you go play mother for a while, Lannie. I'm sure your husband's baby needs you." River forced a smile before slipping her hand through Jake's arm.

"By the way, where is Sadie?" Jake halted his steps, waiting for a reply.

"She's spending the night with Wren."

He nodded. Changing the subject, he asked, "I sent a man out to put in a central heat and air conditioning unit. Have you seen him?" Jake unconsciously rubbed his jaw as he looked around.

"Yeah, I've seen him. I sent him down to the sea cottage." Wiping a piece of imaginary fluff from her shirt, Lannie tried not to make eye contact with him.

Jake turned to her with a question in his eyes.

"That's him coming up the path," she said, nodding in the man's direction.

Jake went out to meet him. Once they were in a conversation, Lannie began walking toward the barn. His eyes fastened on her as the man began relating his encounter with Lannie.

"She wouldn't let me near the place, Mr. Chamberlain. She said that there was no way I was cutting up *her* house, and that she'd handle you when you got home. She ordered me to stay put down at the cottage until you returned."

Even as he watched her go, he couldn't believe the sheer boldness of the girl. No one *ever* put a stop to his orders, at least, not until now.

Lannie paused before going into the barn. She felt eyes on her and glanced back over her shoulder toward the two men. She was startled to find the piercing blue eyes locked on her with a stern intensity. She returned his stare with a defiant glare of her own and then stepped into the barn.

"You're telling me that you let a small slip of a girl stop you from doing your contracted job?" Jake's brow furrowed in aggravation.

"She threw a hissy fit, Mr. Chamberlain." The man held his hands up in a helpless gesture. "What was I supposed to do?"

"You're supposed to do as I say and complete the job. Now, I own this side of the house. You're to begin here. I'll try and reason with the woman over her side of the house. I'll let you know how that works out. I'm paying you by the job and not by the hour, so I suggest you get your men and get started. When you finish the job, your pay will be waiting for you at Christenberry's Landscaping Company. See Michael Christenberry if you have any issues; he's handling my affairs while I'm away."

The man was only slightly more afraid of Mr. Chamberlain than he was of the girl. "Yes, sir, we won't let that girl scare us away from now on. We'll do the job."

With a final nod, Jake walked toward the barn, intent on having a little discussion with Mrs. McPherson.

"Jake! Where are you going?" River cried, uneasy that Lannie had once again beaten her for his attention.

"I'll be back in a minute. I've just got to clear something up."

The musty smell of straw enveloped Jake as he stepped into the dimly lit barn. Looking around, he spied Lannie shooing a guinea fowl from a stall. She looked up as he crossed the barn. The scowl on her face made him uncomfortable under her scrutiny. Then a smile tugged at his lips as he observed her, and he met her defiant stance with an amused grin. *That poor guy,* he thought. *He never had a chance.* A shaft of evening light caught in her eyes, revealing the depth of her annoyance. They were the same seething gray the sea turns before a storm. He grabbed an old ladder-back chair and spun it around, straddling it as he casually laid his arms across the top. He faced her now, eye to eye.

Lannie placed her hands on her hips as she stared into his eyes. "You've taken it upon yourself to install heating and cooling in my house! Did it ever occur to you to ask permission before assuming it would be okay with me? I compromised on the dryer, but I draw the line on this!"

Jake leaned forward until her wide, sparkling gray eyes met the sternness of his blue ones. "You are being unreasonable, Lannie. We live in the modern era of convenience. And hasn't it been nice having a dryer so you don't have to hang out clothes?"

"I'd have to sacrifice too much for convenience, and I'm not willing. Besides, hanging out laundry is good for me; all that sunshine and fresh air nourishes you. That's what's wrong with people today! They need more fresh air and hard work! I guarantee that half of the country wouldn't be on antidepressants if more of them did their laundry and washed their dishes!" she stated firmly. Her eyebrows dropped dangerously low. "And you didn't even ask. What am I supposed to say to that?"

"Thank you?"

The gray eyes narrowed and grew a shade darker. She began to look around for something to hurl at him. Jake drew back and twisted his lips to keep from smiling. He intended to diffuse the situation before it got out of hand.

"Who can live in these swamps without air conditioning, Lannie?" Jake was trying to reason with her, but she clearly was not seeing his side of the issue.

"You'll freeze me out! There will be only one control, and according to that man, it'll be in *your* apartment!"

"You can always put on more clothes," he reasoned.

"Or you can just take off your clothes!" she countered.

Lifting an eyebrow, he smirked as he reached for the top button of his shirt. "Anything to keep peace between us." He was obviously having way too much fun with the argument.

Lannie's face flushed deep crimson. "Keep your shirt on, Yankee. By the way, you already have an air conditioner, a window unit."

His eyes met hers, and he tried his best to look stern. "Yes, I do have an air conditioner. Probably the first one ever made. It freezes up, quits working, and then spits ice at me!" This woman had him with just a look; the last thing he wanted was for her to know how easy it would be for her to bring him to heel. He steeled himself against the power of the soft curve of her upturned lips as she began to smile.

This time Lannie couldn't hold back her grin. "Maybe I am taking this a little too far. I mean, when a man can't even sit in his own house peacefully without being spat upon, well something just *has* to be done about that!"

He knew she was laughing at him, and he didn't care. The adorable way her nose crinkled as she twisted her lips made him want to grab her face in his hands and kiss her. "There's only so much a body can take."

"This is true," Lannie replied, becoming serious again.

Jake loved stirring her blood to the point at which sparks began to fly, but he thought it wise to try and calm the situation. Lannie could be unpredictable; he tried another approach. "Do you really want Sadie to grow up in a primitive environment? When she goes to school, the poor girl will freeze to death because she'll not be used to modern conveniences. They'll tease her, and no one will ever want to spend the night with her because they'll be so miserable! Think of Sadie, Lannie. What harm is a little comfort for her sake?" He rocked forward in the chair, balancing it on two legs as he waited for her response.

Lannie worried her bottom lip with her teeth as she considered his words. The last thing she wanted was for Sadie to be ridiculed at school. She remembered hearing gossip about her friend, Madeline, and how she had never fit in because her home life had been so different. She didn't want that for Sadie. "I see your point. I, uh…guess I got a little carried away with the simplistic lifestyle out here. I want Sadie to have a normal childhood and every chance at a good life."

Relaxing his shoulders, Jake softened his face; he was relieved he'd finally gotten through to her. "That's understandable. Tell you what: I'll make sure the guys hide the vents discreetly in the floor. You won't even notice them after a while, and I'll buy some vintage looking covers to match the wood. It'll look good, and you'll be able to close them off if it gets too cold."

"Just promise me that you won't install recessed lighting anywhere in the house. I'll make sure you have the best old iron chandelier I can find if you promise not to use track or recessed lighting on your side of the house."

"Deal, but the dishwasher stays…period!"

"Deal, but I want a free hand with the upstairs room."

"Alright, I'll agree to that."

Lannie raised her finger. "Another thing while we're discussing this. Keep your little girlfriends out of the upstairs."

"All but one," he stated flatly. At Lannie's glare, he explained, "Sadie and I plan on stargazing up there. I've ordered a telescope just for her. That is…if you don't mind."

"Oh, of course not." Feeling somewhat embarrassed, Lannie smoothed her hair behind her ears and gave a shy smile.

River's shrill voice sounded from the doorway. "What is taking so long in here?" Stunned for a moment, River could do nothing more than stare at Lannie. She watched as Lannie ran a hand over her hair, smiling. She could plainly see that her cousin was flirting.

"We were just…discussing things." Lannie turned to Jake, her voice was silky smooth. "Weren't we, Jake?"

When Lannie turned her translucent eyes on him and spoke in her soft, fluid voice, he nearly shivered. He knew he was being played, but he was enjoying it. "Yes, we certainly were."

River walked toward them, regarding her cousin with sharp, cold eyes and a smirk on her lips. Her eyes roamed over Lannie, lingering on the Kool-Aid stain covering her sleeve. A gray guinea feather stuck out of her shirt pocket. "Well now, aren't you just the perfect little picture of motherhood. I guess that's one way to get a baby: have your husband make one for you."

Something inside of Lannie snapped. But before she could lash out, Jake's chair scraped the wood floor as he stood up, glaring at River.

Lannie quickly made her exit, leaving River to face Jake alone.

River smiled up at Jake. "That Lannie, she has always been jealous of me. If she thinks I'm interested in someone, she tries her best to steal him away from me. It's obvious she's envious of my...well, you know...advantages." She tossed her coffee-colored hair over her shoulder. "She's so boyish and all. I was always surprised when she landed a date and shocked when she convinced Cade to marry her. She was such a wild child."

Jake smiled at her stiffly. "Oh, I can certainly understand her appeal. Lannie is unrestrained, changeable, and seemingly indestructible—and, just like the sea, always beautiful."

"Yes, well you just don't know her like I do. She likes nothing more than to mix it up with all of those Cajuns and Creoles down at the wharf. I've even seen her dance with a few old, disgusting fishermen while her husband looked on!"

Jake paused as he buttoned his shirt. He faced her, leaning into her until she was forced to sit in the wooden chair behind her. He propped a booted foot on the seat of the chair and, bracing an arm across his knee, moved forward until he was inches from her face. "That young girl, with all her unconventional ways, could give lessons on how to be a true woman. There is no guile or false pretense with Lannie. You never have to worry about being tricked, or played, or used with *her*. Not everyone, and you should know this, is without deceit."

The realization suddenly hit River that Jake was talking about her! Her mind began to conjure an excuse for her deception. "You can't blame a girl for going after what she wants, can you, Jake?" Smiling seductively, she ran a hand over his chest. "You were just too tempting to pass up without trying to win you."

Stepping away, he answered over his shoulder, "Blame you? I certainly do."

Chapter 15

It was a calm morning; the water was glassy smooth, and the cry of seagulls sounded overhead. As Lannie walked behind Cornelius, she grew quiet and thoughtful, replaying the long goodbye she'd said to Sadie and Wren only an hour earlier. Now, as she looked up at the enormous ship, she felt a tightness in her throat. Second thoughts began to assault her from every side. *Am I doing the right thing? Think about the money,* she told herself. *In just a few short weeks, I'll have enough to pay off Cade's funeral expenses, and we'll be home free. How hard can this be? And besides, Sadie is in good hands, and Cornelius is with me.* Inhaling deeply, she nodded. "I can do this."

Cornelius looked around. "Did you say something, L. B.?"

Lannie looked confused for a moment before she understood. "Oh no, I just talk to myself sometimes."

The name L. B. had been Cornelius' idea, and one he was proud to have thought of. At first he thought of using her maiden name, Blakely, but then he settled on L. B., nothing fancy, just plain ol' L. B.

"Now remember," he reminded her, "you're to act like a boy. That means no more of this." He waved his hands in a delicate fashion until someone from the shipyard whistled at him.

"Got it," Lannie said, twisting her lips to keep from smiling. The angry look Cornelius cast over his shoulder in the direction of the whistler caused a giggle to bubble up and spill out unchecked.

"And for Pete's sake, stop that! Guys *never* giggle! Just keep a low profile and stay in the kitchen with me. You'll mop, clean, do laundry, and fix the night lunches for the men on watch, but there's no need for you to be around the crew." He eyed her up and down. "Keep your cap pulled down low over your eyes and your hair stuffed inside it. And, whatever you do, don't forget to rub that stuff on your face each morning and cover your lips with it. The clothes are perfect, and the dirtier they get, the better. Watch your speech, and cover up your neck so no one will notice the missing Adam's apple. Do just like we practiced." Placing her seabag on the dock, he turned around to look at her. "You'll have to take it from here. The guys will get suspicious if I carry your bag on board." He saw uncertainty in her eyes. "All those hard-core party sailors have been washed out of the industry. There are laws in place now to handle the wild ones. And one thing every American mariner knows is that you don't want to do anything to risk your license or documentation, particularly with alcohol-related offenses. But, if anyone finds out you're a woman, well so be it. There are women in the Merchant Marine same as men. I'll take responsibility if Captain finds out, but he shouldn't. Your position is…uh, well, one of the lowest on board, and his is the highest. Your paths shouldn't cross."

A little miffed at being ranked, Lannie asked, "So what *does* a captain do anyway?"

"He stays cleaner and makes more money doing less physical labor than the rest of us." Cornelius laughed at his own humor. "Captain is responsible for the welfare of the whole crew, and the decisions he makes affect us all. But you don't worry about that; Captain knows the art of seamanship. He has the hands and the heart of a sailor. You're safe with him at the helm."

Walking on board, Cornelius continued to talk over his shoulder. "Going to sea is a life changing experience. Like anything else, you always remember your first time. Something is new only once."

"And you said we're going to South America?" she asked, trying hard to keep up with his long strides and look boyish all at the same time.

"They still call this the 'romance run.' In the old days, you'd be in port for a long time, but not anymore. Those days are gone. With improved technology, it only takes a few hours to load and discharge cargo. I doubt we'll be in port long enough on any of our stops to leave the ship. I'd rather you stay aboard."

Creasing her brow, she asked, "But what if I get cagey? I mean, that's a very real possibility with me. I don't like being cooped up for a long time."

"We run a set schedule between uninteresting ports. But if you see that you've just got to get off the ship for a while, I'll take you in at one of the nicer ports."

"Are there any dangerous men on board?"

He stopped and turned around to face her. "It's required that every crew have at least one sociopath to keep things interesting. Ours happens to be a guy named Buzz. But you won't have a thing to worry about with him. I told him that you have a special gift and can call up spiders from the cracks in the walls. Buzz is terrified of spiders, and he'll leave you alone."

Lannie smiled. "You told the guy I was some kind of spider whisperer?"

"Yep." He turned back around and kept walking.

They headed down the long, gray steel surface of the weather deck, maneuvering around a maze of pipes, holding containers, and vents. Walking up three decks, they approached an open door marked "Master." Cornelius knocked.

The black leather chair spun around and hard, blue eyes bore into hers. Her face flamed red beneath the light coating of camouflage tan on her skin, and her breath caught in her throat. *He certainly wears his position well*, she thought, as her timid gaze took in the whole of him. She could see no recognition in his eyes. He observed her with something akin to...pity?

Jake's stern features softened as he stared at the sight before him. When a smile tugged at the corners of his mouth, he quickly caught it and asked a question. "May I have your papers, son?"

"L. B. is my new assistant, Captain." Cornelius took the papers from her hand and gave them to Jake.

Jake briefly scanned the documents before a man entered and interrupted by holding out a clipboard for his quick perusal. Signing off on the clipboard, he handed it back with instructions to proceed. With a nod to Cornelius, he remarked, "It looks like everything is in order here." Giving his full attention to L. B., he said, "Even though your position doesn't require a license, L. B., I'll expect no less than your best effort on this ship. You'll answer to Cornelius, but you're under my command." Eyeing her sternly, he said, "Welcome aboard." The flash of a dazzling smile lit the captain's face, and Lannie thought her weak knees might collapse under her.

Her attention was centered on the man, Jake Chamberlain. He belonged here in this element. His voice was full of authority and his face full with confidence; it was obvious who was in charge. He seemed to handle his affairs and cut through difficulties with the grace and ease of a ship through choppy seas.

Momentarily in awe of the captain's presence, Lannie blinked and turned her attention to Cornelius, who was masking a grin. They had not expected to pull off the disguise under the scrutiny of the captain quite so easily. She felt sure the captain would've seen right through her. Pulling her cap down tight and low over her eyes, she held out her hand and gave him the firmest grip she could muster. "Thank you, Captain," she murmured, deep and low.

"The captain's word is law out here, so don't you forget it," Cornelius reminded her sharply. Then they went out the door and down three decks. Cornelius smiled, satisfied that they'd made it past the first hurdle. "Stomp, L. B.! Your feet are as light as Tinkerbell's. Shove, stomp, push, and spit."

His joyful demeanor had a soothing effect on her frayed nerves.

"Oh-eight-hundred, now we can get to work!"

Lannie had no idea what the position of Assistant to the Chief Steward was really all about, but from what Cornelius had described, it sounded a lot like what she had always done: cooked, cleaned, and served. She wasn't to talk much, just follow orders, and that suited her just fine. She really hadn't been in the mood to talk since Cade died, anyway. Now she had an excuse to be unsociable.

Cornelius tossed a white apron to her and waved his hand in the direction of a huge, stainless steel sink piled high with dirty pots and pans from breakfast. "You can start there, but first, I'll give you the tour. He led her through the kitchen and the dining hall, pausing in each to give brief instructions as to what would be expected of her. "This place is hard to keep clean. And the captain, well, he can't abide filth. I'll take you to the officers' hall where they take their meals."

"You mean he doesn't eat with his men?" Lannie's brow creased, trying to understand this seafaring world.

"Good gracious, no. There's an order to things around here. You'll catch on in time. You see, the deck officers and engineers grumble at each other and don't socialize. They point fingers at each other and hold grudges. The chief mate and the second in command mingle with all the men and set the tone for the voyage. Captain, well, you know what they say, 'It's lonely at the top,' but every man on this ship has respect for him and nobody wants to disappoint him."

Following closely on Cornelius' heels, listening to every word of explanation and instruction as they made the circuit, Lannie began to understand a little more. Once they were back in the kitchen, she tackled the dishes and then helped Cornelius prepare lunch.

"When the men come in, if you hear fussing, don't pay no mind, that's just how we pass the day." Cornelius brought the knife down hard on the chopping block, producing thick slices of ham. "They'll call me a belly robber, among other things, but don't let that upset you. That's just us carrying on. The language sometimes gets colorful, and I'm sorry you'll have to hear it. But remember, they think you're a guy, so try not to take offense."

Lunch was served without issue. Lannie was then instructed to first clean the officers' hall, then work her way back down to the galley. Taking a broom, a mop, and a bucket full of supplies, she entered the hall. A few men were still seated around the tables, including the captain, but they mostly ignored her activities as they continued their conversation over coffee. Lannie took the heavy broom and swept every corner, under every table and chair, raking out all the trash and piling it up to be deposited in the trash can. One of the men attempted to exchange a brief word with her, but she pretended not to hear and moved to wash down the vacated tables on the far side of the room. She worked diligently all the way around the room and then paused to survey the well-scrubbed floors and clean tables. Satisfied with her work, she looked up and smiled.

Jake raised his head and studied her. She held her breath and quickly got back to the task. Snatching up the Clorox-soaked dishcloth, she began wiping an imaginary spot on the table. The thing that unnerved her the most was that slow, half grin that came across his face, as if she amused him in some way. Then, his eyes were serious again and seemed to look through her to some faraway place. He frowned and thoughtfully looked down into the liquid in his cup.

Lannie gathered her things and stepped from the room, leaving the captain alone with his thoughts.

It had been many days since they had seen either sun or moon. The clouds were thick overhead as the wind picked up, battering the waves against the ship unmercifully. With her appetite long gone and her hope of sleep lost, Lannie gingerly made her way to the deck, hoping a little cool air might ease her stomach.

Jake was standing along the port rail, puffing his pipe to life as he gazed out over the ocean. The sea was troubled, and crashing waves hit the side of the ship with tremendous force. "L. B.?" the captain asked as he spotted her. "Are you alright?" He had to raise his deep voice to be heard over the crash of the sea.

She leaned over the rail, inhaling the stiff salty air. "I hope to be," she moaned soft and low, but her words were carried away on the wind.

Sizing up the situation, he commanded, "Follow me to sick bay, son."

Looking up quickly proved too much as Lannie's head swam, and she helplessly retched over the rail of the ship. Humiliated to the very core of her being at having Jake witness her misery, Lannie groaned as she clutched the bar of the rail. Pressing her head against the cool metal, she wished for a thousand ways to disappear. Soon, she felt a cool rag on the back of her neck. After a moment, a deep voice close to her ear asked, "Feel better now?"

Lannie nodded her head, unable to find the courage to peer up at the captain.

"Good, take this medicine." He held a pill and a glass of water.

Lannie took the medicine from his hand and popped it in her mouth. Taking the glass, she took a large swig and handed it back to the captain. "Thank you," she mumbled. "Night, Captain."

"Good night." The captain studied her a moment, and then he said, "L. B., keep away from the railings of the ship. One wrong move or slip could prove fatal. If you go left instead of right on board a ship you could be dead or maimed in an instant. Watch your footing."

"Okay, Captain."

The morning broke on a bright sky with white puffy clouds floating along on an ocean of cerulean blue. Cornelius hummed as he chopped onions and bell peppers for the omelets he was preparing. "Lannie, clean the rain locker in the captain's quarters first thing this morning and then change the bedsheets. Go to the quartermaster's quarters next and do the same thing. Tomorrow, you can finish two more officer's quarters and work your way down." Wiping his hands on a kitchen towel, he added, "Just get in there and get out. No one should interrupt you, but if they do, keep working and don't say too much."

Nodding, Lannie seemed to fully understand what was required of her. "Okay…but what's a rain locker?"

"The shower."

"Got it."

Lannie scrubbed the captain's shower, rinsing it out and rubbing it down until it sparkled. A man cleared his throat behind her, causing her to jump. Turning, she saw Jake stripping off his shirt, his face half covered in shaving cream, as he leaned over the sink. The light above the sink glinted off a small, silver medallion that hung on a long, braided silver chain around his neck. It was her medallion! Embossed with the imprint of a silver leaf! The one she'd thought was lost forever. How many times had she returned to the second floor of her house to seek the medallion? Her heart pounded in her chest, and her breathing grew quick and uneven.

Turning a casual eye to observe her, Jake asked, "Did I scare you?"

The gray eyes widened. "Uh…yeah." It was hard for her to pull her attention away from the fascinating play of the muscles that rippled along his arms as he shaved. The medallion winked at her with every movement. Trying very hard not to touch him, she squeezed by, grabbing the dirty linens from the floor beside the bed and left the room. A low, throaty laugh sounded from behind her as the door shut.

Chapter 16

The long summer days aboard ship slipped by as Lannie stayed busy in the galley and about her duties. Coming in and out of port had been, as Cornelius had said, uneventful. She chose to stay on board at each South American port, spending her downtime reading, painting her toenails, and eating chocolate. The ship's store, called a slop-chest, carried toiletries, soda, and candy, and proved to be a lifesaver for Lannie. Chocolate seemed to soothe most ills, and Lannie was grateful for the supply. Although she couldn't say as much for the narrow selection of reading material, she did happen to find a section of C. S. Lewis books tucked away on a dusty shelf.

The ship was quiet. Most of the men went ashore, leaving behind very few to handle the unloading operations. Work continued late into the night after several malfunctions and delays hampered the unloading process. When morning dawned and the cargo was successfully unloaded, the men headed for their cabins to find much-needed rest.

"More coffee, Captain?" Lannie asked, as she stood beside him, watching his expression intently.

Jake grunted and swigged down the last of his coffee. It had been a long night, and he was in no mood for talk. He placed his empty cup down on the table and stared at it as L. B. slowly poured the dark brew. Noticing her hands, he remarked, "Cornelius has been too soft on you, L. B. You have the hands of a woman."

Lannie snatched her hand back as if she'd been scalded. "I get my work done, don't I? And, with no complaints!"

Jake smiled despite himself. Rubbing his hand down his scruffy face, he closed his eyes. They felt scratchy and dry; he needed sleep. "I'm headed to my quarters; come get me at oh-twelve-hundred."

Lannie nodded and without a word, pulled her cap down lower on her head and walked toward the galley, hitching up her pants as they sagged from her waist.

"You need to locate the cookie jar, L. B. That's twice since I've been sitting here that you've almost lost your pants. Spare me the sight of your boney rump, please!"

Turning around, Lannie gave the captain a scathing look, hitched up her pants, and kept walking.

Jake shook his head, too tired to even reprimand the boy.

With mop in hand, Lannie vigorously swept over the floor of the officers' mess hall, careful to keep her gaze down as a few officers entered the room. Brenon, Jake's chief mate, eyed her with interest. She looked at the clock, mindful to wake the captain at noon before lunch was served.

"Well, would you look at this, boys. Don't let that mop fool you, this boy has untapped potential, and he's hoping the captain will see it. Ever wonder why he's always hovering around the captain? He's looking for promotion…to move up in the world." Brenon motioned for L. B. to come near.

"Sir?" Lannie questioned, as she propped her mop against the table and approached him.

"Get that mop and swipe it under here, boy, my feet are sticking to the floor."

Lannie reached back to retrieve the mop. She bent down to shove it under the table. As she did, Brenon pushed her, sending her sprawling backward across the floor. She slid into the mop bucket, spilling the contents and soaking her clothes.

Brenon laughed out loud, pounding the table with his fist as he watched L. B. try to get up off the floor without slipping. Her feet slid out from under her, and she grabbed the end of the table to steady herself, pulling herself up off the floor.

The laughter came to an abrupt halt as the captain walked in. "You men!" Jake barked out. "What's going on here?" Looking down, he saw L. B. trying to get up off the floor holding the mop handle for support with one hand and the lip of the table with the other. Turning an angry eye to the officers, he yelled, "Timmy, explain!"

"Well, Captain," Timmy drawled. "Brenon was just having a little fun, I reckon. He just shoved L. B. down and sent him flyin'." Timmy smiled and shook his head. "That's when the bucket spilled…when L. B. plowed into it."

Brenon turned crimson as the captain's eyes shifted in his direction, nailing him with a penetrating stare.

Jake turned to L. B. and watched as the boy began quietly mopping up the spill. "L. B.!" the Captain commanded.

Lannie refused to meet the captain's eyes, but raised her head in his direction.

"You're dismissed. Leave everything and return to your cabin at once."

Once she was out of the room, she headed for air. The midday sun was hot, but not hot enough to compete with the rising humiliation she felt climb from her neck. Tears welled up in her eyes, but she refused to give in to them. She had to remind herself that she'd chosen to act like a boy, and that's how boys were treated by certain types of men. They'd picked on L. B., not Lannie McPherson. She was just thankful Cornelius hadn't witnessed it. If he had, she knew he wouldn't have taken it lightly, and then he would've been in hot water for assaulting an officer.

Sensing a presence behind her, she turned and saw Jake walking toward her. She wiped her eyes in a quick gesture, catching her nose with her sleeve before turning to face him.

"Sometimes the guys get bored with ship life and do stupid things to entertain themselves. You alright?"

"I'm alright, Captain. No harm done."

"For the next few hours they're gonna be occupied doing your chores. I suggest you make yourself scarce."

Lannie nodded and stepped away.

Something about L. B. tugged at his heart strings. He seemed so pitiful and to know that someone under his command abused the boy was almost too much to take. It angered him. He was not going to have this kind of bullying on his ship. And, especially not from *his* officers! Then the thought hit him: *If my officers treat the boy this way, what must the crew do to him?"*

Later that evening, well after dinner, Lannie leaned on the door to the captain's office with her hand on the handle, waiting for him to acknowledge her. He'd summoned her to his office.

He looked up finally, and his eyes briefly scanned her before he turned his attention to the papers in his hand. "How often do you get...picked on by the crew?"

Lannie shifted uncomfortably and looked down at the floor. "It doesn't matter. I can take care of myself."

With his attention to the task before him, his eyes remained focused on the paper in his hand. "I thought it was understood that I give the orders around here."

"You do, sir." Oh, how she hated to admit that she took orders.

"Then answer my question." He flipped the pages in his hand, and she could've sworn he was masking a grin.

"Nobody picks on me...except for Brenon."

He narrowed his eyes as he looked up at her. "I find that hard to believe. Brenon is a fine Christian man. I'm sure he just had a temporary lapse of judgment. He brings his bible to the table every morning for devotion. He impresses me as the kind of guy who tries to walk a straight line."

"Christian? Pah!" Lannie spat out the words in disgust; she was quickly losing whatever ladylike restraint she'd developed over the years. The boy L. B. was a lot freer to express himself, and Lannie found that she liked it. Self-consciously she adjusted her cap, hoping its cover hid the flush of her face. Jake's close scrutiny unnerved her. "All that means is that he's a pretender. He's like one of those sideshow sailors y'all talk about—all dressed up for the part but just doesn't have it in him to be the real deal. Brenon is all talk. He's spit and polish veneer."

"You speak like an expert in human nature."

Incensed with the captain's mocking glare, Lannie continued, "I bet I know your crew better than you. I've cleaned their cabins, served their meals, and observed them for the past twenty-five days. Brenon is a snake and a liar to the very core. On the other hand, you can trust Jess Ray with your life. He's the real deal and the only worthy officer you have onboard. And by the way, you'll find his bible safely tucked under his pillow, and the ribbon marker in it moves every day! I know because I check! And if Brenon ever puts another hand on me, I'll wrap my mop around his pasty white face and make him eat it!"

Jake watched L. B. with carefully concealed amusement. With stricter standards of training, the colorful types Jake was used to sailing with couldn't make the program as seamen anymore. But this little fellow was proving to be the exception. No bigger than a child, he had twice the fight of any grown man Jake had ever sailed with. He liked the boy and was beginning to understand Cornelius's fondness for him.

"Let's get some air, L. B.," he said, getting up from his chair.

For a moment, Lannie feared being pushed overboard by the captain. *I probably should've left that last part out.*

They walked out onto the deck in companionable silence as a storm moved closer. In the far distance, lightning flashed between the thunderheads as dark clouds gathered.

Jake crossed his arms over his chest as he turned his face toward the sea, deep in thought. After a moment, he said, "Whenever I find myself growing restless and irritable, I know that it's high time for me to go to sea. But lately, I'm beginning to feel a pull toward home." He ran a hand through his dark hair. Turning to L. B., he asked, "Do you have someone waiting for you at home?"

"I do. I've got a sweet little girl waiting for me back home."

"Ah," he nodded, pulling his pipe out of his front pocket. A moment later he puffed it to life, flipping the match over the rail. The sea was calm, except for the foamy whiteness of the bow waves curling along the side of the vessel.

"What about you, Captain, anybody waiting for you?"

"I had a wife, once." The yellow beams from a passing boat cast wavy reflections across the dark water as Jake drew on his pipe. "I love, even need, the sea. I've always thought God speaks His clearest message way out here. That's why I can't leave it…and I've paid a terrible price for it, too."

"In what way," Lannie ventured, quietly.

"I lost my wife. She couldn't cope with my absence."

"She left you?"

Jake shook his head once. "She left the world." After a long moment of reflection, he said, "She would stand on shore and watch as I sailed from sight. It was like I died to her every time I disappeared over the horizon. I found out later that she suffered from a type of depression that skewed her thinking. I guess there was more than water between us; we never truly knew each other. The gulf was just too huge. But I loved her and felt powerless to help her. She needed me, and I failed her. It's as simple as that."

"It's never as simple as that. You can't help someone unless you know what's wrong. It sounds like she covered up and hid it from you. I'm sure in her mind she was protecting you, out of love."

"None of that matters now."

"It all matters, Captain," L. B. countered.

Lannie's feelings of being frustrated began to be replaced with calmness as her breathing fell into a slow and steady pace matching that of the man standing next to her. The aroma of warm vanilla from his pipe smoke encircled her head. He was mourning, but even in his sorrow his presence was oddly comforting, reassuring even. Without a single word, he conveyed a sense of peace. He, too, was deeply grieving, and in some strange way, she felt close to him.

"What about now? Do you have someone to go home to?"

"I have a home, and I'm anxious to get there. I'm finding my thoughts are there more and more these days. I confiscated this before I left." He reached into his shirt and pulled out the silver medallion. "It reminds me of home, and it brings me a small amount of comfort. But it doesn't belong to me." He tucked it back into his shirt. "I'll have to return it to its rightful owner."

"Maybe you could have one made for yourself. I mean, if it brings you so much comfort."

"It wouldn't be the same. I have a memory attached to this one."

They dropped anchor at the last port before heading home. Brilliant sunshine filled the morning air as most of the men on board headed for shore. The day was uneventful, wonderfully uneventful, giving Lannie time to do pretty much what she wanted to do. The sight of the deep-blue sky with wisps of white clouds hanging over the moist air seemed to impart a quiet to the mind, and she wanted to experience it. Taking a book, she set out to a secluded spot she'd found where no one ever ventured. Reclining against a hard steel wall, she stretched out her legs and rolled up her pants legs, intent on catching a little sun.

"Captain?" Cornelius looked concerned as he entered the bridge. He never once remembered being summoned to the bridge by the captain. "Did you need me?"

Jake cast a doubtful glance over his shoulder at his chief steward before turning his attention back to the pair of legs tapping out a rhythm with pink toenails flashing in the sun. "You may not have noticed, Cornelius, but most of the men of this crew don't polish their toenails." Handing the binoculars to Cornelius, he waved in the direction of the tanned and shapely legs. "I think that's L. B."

Swallowing hard, Cornelius complied, looking through the lenses at the unmistakably feminine legs. "I was gonna tell you, Captain, sooner or later, but…"

Just then, Jess Ray entered the room and the conversation stopped.

Jake knew he'd been maneuvered, but he didn't want to make it known to Jess Ray that there was a woman on board. So without argument, he lowered his voice. "Explain." He casually sipped his coffee, leaning over the instrument panel. He considered the nervous man as Cornelius struggled to explain his part of the deception.

"Well, Captain, it's like this. She badly needed this job, and I helped her get it. This one voyage will pay off the debts left by her husband and allow her to start fresh. She has Sadie to think of now, too."

Coffee spewed from Jake's mouth. Slamming down the cup, he turned to Cornelius with an incredulous stare. "What?" He snatched the binoculars and peered once more at the shapely legs. "Well, I'll be a..."

"Captain, is everything okay?" Jess Ray asked, stepping closer to the men.

Regaining his composure, he put down the binoculars and ran a hand through his hair. "Fine, fine. Cornelius and I were just discussing a mutual acquaintance. Cornelius, if you don't mind, send L. B. to my office as soon as possible. I need to have a word with him."

Cornelius reluctantly left the room, mumbling under his breath.

Jake casually moved to the front of his desk as Lannie entered the captain's office. Leaning against the edge, he calmly spoke in a low voice. "It seems we've had a little misunderstanding as to your identity aboard this vessel."

Lannie grimaced, realizing he recognized her. With wide eyes she stared up at him. But a moment later she had to divert her eyes from his stern gaze. The lack of emotion on his face unnerved her no small amount. She took a deep breath, not at all sure of what would come next. Suddenly an image of "walking the plank" above a sea swirling with sharks flashed through her mind, causing her to shudder.

"I suppose it never occurred to you to tell me you were in need of money," he said firmly, then cautiously lowered his voice. A muscle twitched on his shaded jaw. "Are you unaware of the dangers aboard a ship or how an accident or even worse, death, could rob Sadie of a mother in an instant?" His blue eyes narrowed as his jaw muscles flexed.

Lannie's pride rose to the forefront. "I would *never* ask *you* or anybody else for a handout. Obviously, you don't know me. I work for what I have, and I can take care of my own!"

"I was very wrong about you," he observed gruffly, "for ever thinking that you and your cousin were so different. You're both deceivers and will manipulate to get what you want!"

Snapping gray eyes found the hard steel of his stare as he met the challenge there.

"I suggest you keep up the disguise until we reach land. I'm not sure how the men will react to the news." Turning from her, he effectively dismissed her as he held open the door.

"Now that *you* know, it doesn't matter to me what *they* think." *A suggestion is not a command, and I'll do what I want,* she thought, not showing the slightest inclination to obey his suggestion. She was still angry over the comparison to River and the way he was casually dismissing her.

Looking down into her set face, Jake could not help but wonder at the woman before him. He'd never met another quite like her. Whatever the disguise, she seemed capable of disrupting the entire course of his life. Besides that, she caused him to question everything he'd ever believed about women.

Lannie could see a hint of a smile playing across his lips, and she wondered at what could possibly amuse him about the situation. "If that's all, Captain, I have some work to do," she said, making her exit as if she'd been the one dismissing him.

"Try harder to stay out of trouble, Lannie," Jake admonished. "I don't like disruptions on my ship."

On her way back to her cabin, she scanned her clothing. She had the sudden desire to take a shower, scrub her heavily greased hair, and dress in something pretty. She wanted to be treated as a woman, and she wanted to smell like one, too. With that thought, she headed for the shower, grateful now that she'd packed a few personal items, including her favorite scented soap.

Chapter 17

*A*ll eyes were fastened on Lannie as she moved between the tables, sweeping up the last of the dinner fragments that made it to the floor. No one moved. Dinner had been over for a while, but the crew couldn't pull their attention away from the trim figure in blue jeans and a white, short-sleeved seaman's shirt. Her silky, light brown hair fell across her shoulders as she moved gracefully in and out of the chairs. A whiff of fragrance lingered behind her, and you could hear the men exhale as she passed. No one was out of line; in fact, they all seemed completely content and subdued in her presence, watching her hands perform her task.

Cornelius was not happy. It was a torturous moment when he observed every man in the mess hall with their attention fixed solely on Lannie. No one had ever taken more than a casual notice of L. B., but that had certainly changed. He'd had about enough of their ogling. At the end of his patience, he called out, "Lannie, leave that and head to the officers' mess."

Much to the disappointment of the crew, Lannie grabbed her dustpan and left the room.

Jake watched, unnoticed, from his chair in a darkened corner of the officers' mess hall as Lannie went about her duties. He'd learned the channels of most every waterway along the East Coast and the Gulf of Mexico, carefully charting their courses. He had learned the bends and curves along the bays and waterways of Virginia, watching out for the shallows and carefully navigating around them. But this one small woman had proven to be the most difficult thing he'd ever tried to navigate. In fact, more than once he'd felt at the mercy of her unpredictable moods. One thing was certain: Lannie McPherson did exactly what she wanted and didn't ask permission from anyone.

Lannie looked up when voices sounded from the doorway. Several officers entered, and Brenon was among them. Pulling her mop bucket out of the way, she started for the door. As she passed by the men, Brenon reached out and grabbed her arm.

"Don't go on my account. I enjoy watching you mop." He began pulling her backward.

Before his words registered with the others, Lannie snatched her arm away, stepped back, and lifted the mop from the bucket. "Lay another hand on me and you'll eat this mop, not to mention all the questionable things I'll put in your food!"

"You're out of line, Brenon!" Jake's sharp bark exploded across the room as he shot up from his chair and made his way toward him. "One more action like that and you'll be off this ship! Do I make myself clear?" Jake was now scowling inches from Brenon's face.

"Sorry, Captain. It won't happen again. I owe L. B. an apology. I only meant to tease, not to offend."

Warily eyeing the officer, Jake nodded. "In the future, keep your teasing comments to the boys and your hands to yourself. Report to the bridge in ten minutes."

Squaring her shoulders and lifting her head, Lannie moved out of the room, thumping the bucket along behind her as she disappeared from view.

"She's not a lady, Captain. A real lady wouldn't be caught dead on a cargo ship filled with men," Brenon argued, shifting nervously from foot to foot.

Jake never took his eyes off the instrument panel, tracing the screen with a lean and steady finger. He didn't like the man's tone or his narrow opinion of women. A muscle in his jaw tightened. "Your ignorant view of what makes a real lady doesn't concern me, Brenon. What *does* concern me is how you treat this particular lady." He turned his attention to Brenon, fixing him with a penetrating stare. "Understood?"

"Yes, Captain. It won't happen again."

A knock sounded on the door. "Come in," Jake commanded.

Lannie eased the door open. She had once thought Jake Chamberlain was just like all the other men she'd ever known: easy to control. But, she was beginning to have second thoughts about that. He was unlike any man she'd ever known, and that realization scared her to death. No man had ever caused her to tremble, but it seemed lately that this Yankee could do it with only a glance. Clearing her throat, she found her voice. "Captain…"

Jake straightened, his height towering above her as she met him squarely.

"Uh…Captain." She shifted her attention to Brenon, who was standing behind Jake. "I need to speak with you…privately."

Jake glanced over his shoulder. "That'll be all, Brenon."

Once the door closed behind Brenon, Lannie raised her eyes again to meet the captain's. His blue eyes tore at her heart. She hadn't meant to deceive him; she just wanted to provide for her family. But here she was, about to apologize to one of the few decent men she'd ever met. Taking a deep breath, she repeated, "Captain…I'm sorry…"

The door suddenly flew open. "Captain!" Jess Ray called from the doorway. "You're needed by the quartermaster."

Jake nodded and started for the door. "We'll talk later, Lannie."

With that said, the men were gone. Lannie took a deep breath and let it out slowly. "A few more days and I'll be home."

Something was different, very different. Lannie could sense it in the air. The crew members she'd passed seemed preoccupied with their work, busily going about as if they anticipated some disaster. Even Cornelius was quieter than usual as they prepared and set out the night lunches for the watch that night. Cornelius had told her to make plenty of extras; it was going to be a long night.

"What's going on, Cornelius? Why is everyone acting so strangely?" Lannie folded down the top of one lunch sack and moved to the next one.

"Storm's comin'."

Lannie's eyes widened. "A bad one?'

"There ain't no good ones, but we'll be fine, just have to pass through it." He looked at her and smiled. "Don't you worry none. The captain's got this. You just go on to your cabin and hunker down for the night. I'll come and get you if things get rough." With a pat on her back, Cornelius tried to reassure her. "Go on now."

"I'm not leaving," she declared, looking him straight in the eye. "I can help."

The chief steward raised his bushy eyebrows. "Fine then, you can make more coffee and get about your duties." He patted her hand reassuringly and rushed off to the mess hall to make up a few sandwiches.

After making a fresh pot of coffee, she kept busy, serving the crew whenever they rushed in for nourishment or to refill a coffee mug. Determined to keep her resolve, she pulled out the mop bucket and began mopping up the excess water that found its way inside the hall. She began to pray, not just for herself, but for the entire crew and their safety. She gripped the mop handle tightly in her hands as her mind turned to Sadie. A panic set in, one she'd never before experienced. Her heart raced, forcing droplets of cold sweat from her pores. The possibility of what might happen to Sadie frightened her beyond anything else. Her thoughts raced. *Wren will get her*, she reasoned. But in her heart, she knew that the State of Alabama would decide Sadie's future. Fear swelled in her, and she could not hold back the tears that came at the thought of strangers having Sadie until custody could be worked out. She swallowed hard and brushed away the wetness from her eyes. Choking back her panic, she prayed, "Lord, I promise never to risk my life so recklessly again. Please protect Sadie and watch over her, no matter what happens to me. Forgive me for once again taking matters into my own hands without first coming to You."

The hours passed as she listened to and felt the awesome power of the storm. The ship rocked and creaked. Her heart raced and her breathing quickened as desperation shook her frame. What if she never saw Sadie again? What about Wren? The horror of that prospect choked her. A shudder shook her until all she could do was twitch sporadically and stare wild-eyed at the door as each man made his way into the mess hall.

She was beginning to let fear freeze her when she looked up and saw the captain enter the room. Noticing his damp hair and scruffy appearance, she quickly stepped to the galley to fill a large mug of coffee for him. He was far too busy now to bother him with questions, but she desperately wanted to know what she could expect from the storm.

Seeing the fear in Lannie's red and swollen eyes, Jake tried to reassure her. "Storms are very common at sea," he told her in a calm voice. "The worst of this one will be over soon." Taking the cup from her hand he smiled and took a long pull of the coffee as he observed her. Her teeth chattered slightly. Seeing her trembling lips, he leaned back, angling his head for a better view of her face. He could tell she was trying hard to put on a brave front, but she was clearly terrified. "You okay?"

Lifting her chin with determination, she responded, "I'm fine."

He leaned down until he was only an inch or two away from her cheek, so close she could smell the familiar scent of him—the same scent that had haunted her ever since their kiss. "No need to be frightened, Lannie. It's going to be alright," he spoke softly and comfortingly into her ear. "You'd be proud of the crew. They've worked hard at keeping us afloat." His warm, tobacco-scented breath touched her cheek. "Storms at sea can be fierce, violent, and noisy, but they're usually followed by a period of calm."

She released a trembling sigh, easing her shoulders. Jake's presence brought a feeling of security. He was safe and strong. She couldn't deny how good it felt to be under his command.

He pulled back and looked at her. "You okay now?"

She nodded.

"Good, I've got to get back."

"Jake," she called out softly.

He turned at the door, looking back at a vulnerable side of Lannie, one he'd never witnessed before. He concluded in that instant that she was the most intriguing person he'd ever met. It seemed every facet of the woman was captivating, but this particular one was by far the most alluring.

"We'll keep the men fueled and prayers going up."

Jake smiled, reassured now that she'd overcome her fear. He knew the night would be long, longer now as he would once again try and banish her from his thoughts. He wondered at the power the slight girl held over him. More than once he'd marveled at it.

The last two days of the voyage had been relatively uneventful. The ship sailed along over gently rolling seas toward Mobile Bay, lighter and higher in the water on the return trip. The ship cut its way through the frothy whitecaps at a good clip. They were heading home.

Since the night of the storm, Jake had kept his distance from Lannie. They'd pass each other with nothing more than a casual nod. Lannie felt she'd betrayed Jake, but she didn't quite know how to apologize for it. Once they docked, she collected her pay from the captain, like all the other men, and headed straight home, where Wren and Sadie were waiting for her.

Chapter 18

$\mathcal{P}$assing through the old iron gate, the sight of Beauchene in the distance warmed Lannie's heart. Shades of orange and gold like melted sunshine bled across the sky as the sounds of morning cicadas filled the air. Knowing she would soon see Sadie and Wren caused her heart to beat wildly. She was finally home.

The early morning fog rolled out to sea like a silent ghost as Jake walked along the dock. Seagulls cried overhead as the gentle lap of swells reached the shoreline. He paused in front of the Hotcakes and Coffee Café, pulling open the door to allow a couple to exit. As they slipped past him, he entered the restaurant and was met with the familiar smell of coffee and bacon as it permeated the air of the small and quaint café.

Heather smiled from behind the counter as she watched Jake walk in. "The usual?" she asked, already turning to grab the coffee pot.

Nodding, he wandered over to his favorite table near a front window. Sliding into the seat, he reclined against the vinyl-covered bench and stretched out his legs.

Heather followed him to the table armed with a steaming pot of fresh coffee. Turning over his cup, she began to pour as her eyes took him in. "You all right?"

"Yeah...just tired." Rubbing his scruffy chin, he turned his attention to Heather. This is how they'd met: she'd served him breakfast. And, since the first day their eyes met, he'd sought her out. She was pretty, there was no doubt about that. With long, strawberry blonde hair, a warm engaging smile, and an easy disposition, Heather would be a delight for any man. *So what is wrong with me?* "How have you been, Heather?" he asked, casually.

"Oh, I've managed to get along without you these last few weeks," she smiled, taking the bite out of her words. "I've been out a few times, different guys of course, nothing serious. I've kept myself occupied." Heather waited for a jealous reaction and was disappointed when none came.

"That's good, Heather. You're much too young and pretty to sit at home on a Saturday night." He smiled and took a long pull of his coffee.

"Want breakfast?"

He shook his head. "Not today, this is fine."

As Heather stepped away, his thoughts gradually turned to Lannie. Widened gray eyes crept into his thoughts as he pictured her standing before him the night of the storm. An image of L. B. flashed through his mind. After he'd confronted her about the disguise, he'd had to carefully guard his expression to keep the seriousness of her action in the forefront. After all, she *had* deceived him. Yet, another part of him had wanted to stare in amazement at what she had accomplished. She, very convincingly, had portrayed a young boy on board a cargo vessel and did the work of the lowest position without complaint, and very well at that. Rubbing his jawline, he gazed into his cup. In the short time he'd known her, Jake had seen those same gray eyes heavy with sorrow and pain, laughing with joy and mischief, and fearful and in need of comfort. She was unpredictable, yet at the same time faithful and sure. *I wonder what love would look like in her eyes?* He chided himself for his runaway thoughts. Glancing up, he saw Heather smiling at him from across the room. He realized now that he'd made a mistake in coming here. What had once been a welcoming sight to him now seemed all wrong; it was the wrong place and the wrong woman. Standing, he drained his coffee cup and placed it down with a clink. He tossed a twenty on the table and, with a wink to Heather, walked toward the door.

"Jake! Wait!" Heather called to him. She folded her order pad and stuffed it into her apron pocket, taking a few quick steps to reach him. "Are we still on for dinner? You promised to take me to that new little place in town, remember?" Heather's appeal was soft and warm. She flashed a smile as she waited for his answer.

"I do remember, and of course I'll take you. I'll call you later." He forced a smile and turned to leave.

"I'll be expecting you," Heather said.

Then he was gone, leaving Heather staring after him as she watched him disappear into the morning fog.

When Jake first stepped into the entry hall of Beauchene, he inhaled. The familiar smell, the feel of the place, even the coolness of the crystal doorknob in the palm of his hand, all felt like the home's greeting. He felt again the strong sense of place he'd experienced when he'd first passed through the rusty gate. Beauchene was a sanctuary in a world of commotion and chaos. The sense of belonging was both odd and comforting, a feeling he'd never once had in his life except at sea. The sound of tiny footfalls across the wooden floor from the other side of the wall interrupted his thoughts and caused him to smile. "Sadie." Such simple family joys had never been part of his life's experiences; they had always been a normal part of someone else's life, never his own.

The knob of Lannie's door twisted as frustrated little hands tried to open it. Placing his bag down, he waited as he heard Lannie approach. She gently admonished Sadie for trying to open the door. As the door opened, Sadie flew to him, wrapping her tiny arms around his legs. He lifted her into his arms, hugging her tightly. "Did you miss me, Sadie girl?"

"I'd say the body language is a definite yes." Lannie crossed her arms, leaning on the door frame.

Lannie waited in silence as he unlocked his apartment door, tossed his seabag inside, and pulled the door closed. "I want to check out the sea cottage, have a look around, how about you?"

"Lead the way," she said, motioning with her hand.

The morning was unseasonably pleasant as the trio walked down the path. The grass was wet with dew and smelled fresh and sharp on the air. The branches of the silver leaf tree swayed gently in the cool, languid breeze as they passed beneath her rustling leaves.

The first things Lannie noticed as they came to the sea cottage were all the plants and flowers surrounding the small house. The long forgotten and forsaken flower garden had been brought back to vibrant life. It was stunning. She smiled as she looked around in amazement. "Telie," Lannie said, shaking her head. "She knows I don't like 'tight' and formal plants. That's probably why she chose these pink asters." She ran her hand lightly over the mass of color. "I love the way they look when the wind is blowing. Oh! Look!" she said with excitement, pointing to a secluded little alcove next to the cottage. "She's used the old baptismal font in the garden!" Looking up at Sadie, held high in Jake's arms, she explained, "Your daddy salvaged that for me from a church fire in town. He even convinced the old priest to let him have it, promising to put it to good use." Patting Sadie's leg tenderly, she glanced around, continuing to explore. "And just look at all of the Gerbera daisies. Is there anything more cheery than those in a garden?"

Jake looked down at Lannie, thinking that nothing in the garden even came close to the vision he held in his line of sight. She wore a light yellow sundress, loosely fitted and simple, but the way it illuminated her complexion was no less than magical.

Animated in her enthusiasm, Lannie tucked strands of hair behind her ear as the wind danced through it. "A swing and a few chairs arranged on the porch and that's all you'll need down here. This place will be wonderful on a balmy night." She sighed with a soft breath. "And…Moonflowers, my favorite, and right next to the porch! They're so luminous at night you won't even need candles after dark."

Lannie chattered on and on, flitting from one thing to another like some kind of garden fairy caught up in a summer morning dance. Sadie seemed to enjoy the jubilant mood. Reaching over, she pulled the head of a daisy off its stem and handed it to Jake.

Jake put Sadie down and clasped her hand, helping her up the porch steps. "The porch is sturdy." He grasped a post firmly in his hand, testing it for strength.

The smell of fresh lumber filled the air as they opened the door to the cottage and peered in. A sand-toned sea grass rug anchored a seating area in front of the fireplace. Lannie looked around with delight. "I'm going to have so much fun with this place. But," she cautioned, "you have to be careful to navigate the fine line between furnishing and cluttering. Less is definitely more in a place like this. Oh! And I love the louvered shutters on the windows. They add so much character. Real shutters are rare these days." She smoothed her hand over a gray-washed shutter.

Jake stepped up behind her. "I chose them because they're functional. They'll help block out the sun while still allowing a little air to circulate inside. I'm hoping they'll offer some protection during hurricanes and tropical storms." He looked to the roof line extending over the porch. "The metal roof should reflect the heat while the overhang allows the windows to remain open, even in storms. I love hearing rain on a metal roof; I thought Cornelius would enjoy that, so I added it."

Eyeing him uncertainly, Lannie took hold of Sadie's hand. The little girl strained against Lannie's hand in an attempt to get back to Jake. A slow smile crept from the corners of Jake's lips. Lifting Sadie into her arms, Lannie ignored the child's protest. "Was this design your idea?"

Shifting his eyes away from the whimpering child, he said more gently, "It was a joint effort. I had my plans drawn out, and Michael added his thoughts and ideas. He is more experienced with what you need to survive in this African heat than I am. I'm accustomed to a more...hospitable climate." He smiled at the smirk on her face. "Remarkably, Michael and I think a lot alike. I'm headed over now to pay him for the work he's done. I thought I'd better check it out before we settle up." He looked at her as she brushed past him, her all-too-familiar scent following close behind her as she stepped into the cottage. He found it hard to drag his eyes away from her slight form. *How could she have fooled me so completely? There's no mistaking her for a guy now.* She was all soft and feminine, nothing at all like the dirty and scrawny steward they called L. B.

Lannie sensed Jake's eyes on her and wondered about his thoughts. She knew he was still somewhat annoyed with her. *I can't blame him. I made him look foolish in front of his entire crew.* "I…love what you've had done to the cottage," she murmured softly, lowering her gaze from his piercing blue eyes. "I never expected this kind of an investment, though. It'll take me a while to pay you back."

"Our agreement was that I'd get the place livable and you'd furnish it. Nothing has changed has it?"

"Oh no, I'll hold up my end of the bargain…I promise. It's just that my pieces will be…refurbished and not brand new. I hope you won't be disappointed. I'm just not in a position yet to invest in…"

Jake waved away her concern. "Whatever you have will be fine. You have a gift, Lannie, of taking something old and breathing fresh life into it. I know that whatever you do, it'll be comfortable and livable."

She smiled shyly from the compliment and turned away before he could notice the flush creeping into her cheeks. His praise warmed her through and through.

The cottage still smelled of fresh paint and sheetrock. Softly gleaming wooden floors and dove gray walls with bright white trim gave the place a homey feel. The fireplace was left in natural stone with the same tones reflected throughout the room. An old iron fire screen covered the opening to the fireplace; Lannie recognized it immediately as one she'd salvaged and had stored in the barn.

She continued with her observations. "As an avid reader, it's important to me that every chair is comfortable enough to curl up in with a book. I think two overstuffed chairs in front of the fireplace will do nicely. Nothing fancy, though. Nothing you wouldn't want to sit on with a still-damp bathing suit. Of course the most important place is the master bedroom." She stepped across the room. "It has to be a place of escape, rest, and relaxation. Rugs in here should be extremely soft on bare feet. And the bed," she waved her hand in the direction of where the bed should be, "will be piled high with downy comforters and pillows."

"If you don't quit talking, I'm gonna boot Cornelius out and move down here myself."

Lannie looked at him sheepishly. "Sorry, I sometimes get carried away." She turned pensive and lowered Sadie to the floor. The little girl immediately ran to Jake. She broached a subject she would have preferred to avoid. "I owe you an apology, Jake. I'm sorry I deceived you. I was wrong. All I wanted was enough money to settle my debts, and I saw the job as a quick way to do it. Cade's funeral expenses kind of left me in a bind. Cornelius and I knew that if we'd asked you, you would have refused to let me come aboard."

Jake's voice was subdued, but she heard the displeasure in his tone. "I see...better to ask forgiveness than permission."

"I was up against it, Jake. Surely you can forgive me for taking care of my own. But in doing so, I hope I haven't lost your respect along the way. It's not my practice to be deceptive. And, I won't deceive you again."

Jake lifted Sadie off the floor and eyed Lannie. He could hardly mistake the reluctance he saw in her face as she tried to apologize, and it amused him. He got the impression that apologizing was something she wasn't accustomed to. He walked toward the front door and out onto the porch. He settled on the steps, bracing his elbows on his knees with Sadie nestled beside him. Lannie sat down and faced him with her back against the railing. A briny breeze blew in from the bay, rustling the canopy of branches over their heads. Jake casually remarked, "I remember a time in my past when I did the very same thing. I was a stowaway on a ship heading for England. Cornelius discovered me in a grain hold. He helped me out by putting me to work under his supervision, and, I might add, under his constant flow of sermons and lectures." He grew pensive. "I've learned a lot from that old man. I can never repay him."

"Why did you run away?" she asked; her voice soft and feathery.

"Why does any sixteen year old run away? Adventure! To my way of thinking, my dad just wasn't exciting enough. I had to breakout and go experience the world for myself."

Lannie peered at him with a question in her eyes. "Are your parents living?"

Jake shifted, relaxing back with his hands pressed against the boards. "My father is. I never knew my mother. My dad didn't like to talk about her. All I know is that her name is Elizabeth, and at the time I asked, she was still alive." Turning his head, he glanced at her, squinting in the early morning sun. "So, I'm missing a mother and you're missing a father. I don't even want to think what a therapist could do with that kind of information."

Lannie fought against a smile. "And surely, to combine them would make a pretty pathetic pair. Throw Sadie's story into the mix and…well…"

Jake's deep laughter drowned out Lannie's comment. A giggle bubbled up inside of her. She stared at Jake with fascination; he looked every bit the swarthy pirate. This was a side of the man she'd never seen. And, much to her astonishment, one she was finding she definitely liked. She settled against the post to observe him in a new light. Something was familiar about his laugh, but she couldn't quite put a finger on it. Suddenly he glanced at her.

Uneasy beneath his casual grin, she looked down, fidgeting with the hem of her shirt as she asked, "What's your father's name? And what's he like?"

"Saul Chamberlain and he's a man's man. He's quiet, hardworking, and not too concerned about anything that doesn't involve water or fish. Oh, he'd love you," Jake remarked. "You're like lightning: unpredictable, strong, and beautiful. My father likes nothing better than to sit on the dock, whittle, and watch storms as they roll in. He could stay out there for hours, just watching and whittling. He's quite good at carving. Women seem to love his wooden boxes; he sells a lot of them to tourists this time of year."

"So, does he live in…where are you from again?"

"Cape Charles, Virginia, and yes, he lives there. He owns a small marina on Chesapeake Bay called *Captain Jake's*. He changed the name after I became a captain. He rents slips and charters fishing boats, even has this bait and tackle shop right next to the dock. Right now it's the peak season for amberjack and flounder, so he's busy. But, he'll make his way down here once the season ends." When he spoke again, his voice was warm and had a texture to it you could almost feel. "He told me he missed his sister. They spoke every

Saturday night during old Lawrence Welk reruns. He said he'd made a sizable contribution to the Little Sisters of the Poor in honor of Tilda. Apparently, that was her favorite order."

A light sigh escaped from Lannie. "Whatever you do, don't tell that to Brother Ignatius. He'll argue that none of the Sisters had to put up with half as much as he did."

"I gathered that the first time I met the good Brother." Drawing his brows together, Jake seemed to contemplate something. "Back to the whole deception thing…the way I see it, you just can't get off scot-free. I think you owe me."

Lannie raised a brow. "Oh?"

"You owe me dinner… me *and* Cornelius. He was just as much a victim of your scheming as I was. I'm sure you used the full force of your charm and persuasion on him. The poor guy—he never had a chance."

Lannie slapped the wooden porch boards with the flat of her hand. "Fair enough. Dinner will be served at 6:00."

Later that morning, Jake got in his truck and headed for Christenberry's Landscaping Company. Pulling up in front, his eyes scanned the property as he got out, slamming the truck door. A vast array of plants and trees greeted him. On closer inspection, he saw a splashing fountain surrounded by containers of colorful flowers with trailing vines spilling over the sides. The sound alone made the place seem cooler as the wind tousled his longish strands of brown hair.

Telie stepped from the office and smiled. "Well, I'm glad to know that my hard efforts to attract visual interest in this place are paying off."

"I should have known this was *your* doing. You kinda have your own signature style. What you did to our place is beyond words. I've never seen Lannie so excited. You certainly made her day."

"I'm glad she liked it, and I enjoyed doing it." Telie looked over her shoulder and pointed. "You'll find Michael back there."

Maneuvering through a maze of potted trees, Jake made his way to the back side of the property. "Michael," Jake called out.

Michael tossed the last sack of mulch on the pile before turning to the voice. Lifting his sunglasses to his head, he squinted in the glare of the sun, watching as Jake approached. "Well, I see you *finally* made it back to dry land."

"Finally." Jake stuck out his hand. "You did a good job on the cottage...way beyond my expectations."

Tugging off his work gloves, Michael clasped his hand in a firm shake. "What? No confidence in me," he teased, as he reached in his pocket for a cigar. Putting it in his mouth, he rolled it over to his cheek and bit down firmly. "I can't take all the credit; Telie had a lot to do with it," he said between clenched teeth. "The garden is all her. She fussed over those plants for weeks. We had to have certain flowers she knew were Lannie's favorites."

Handing Michael an envelope, Jake said, "Lannie was overjoyed. In all the time I've known her, I don't think I've ever seen her that excited."

Michael eyed him, then spoke as he looked away, running a hand through his hair, "Yeah, well I guess she hasn't had too much to be excited about lately. She used to be so full of life and happy. Put on a little of that Creole music and she'd come to life. It's like nothing you've ever seen. It was impossible for anyone to stay in a bad mood around her." He gave a half laugh. "She hasn't always been like this...sad, I mean."

Curious now, he had to ask, "Did you two date?"

"No, I dated my first wife through high school. She was the only one for me until the day she died...and even a few years after that."

Sorry now that he'd asked, Jake looked down at his feet. "Sorry to hear that."

Michael crossed his arms and leaned against the shed, grinning. "My friend Samuel dated her though and was head over heels if I remember correctly. She nearly drove him crazy. He told me once he didn't know if he wanted to kiss her or arm wrestle her. She kept him guessing, that's for sure. He called her 'Action Figure Barbie.' If she didn't like something, she wouldn't whine or pout about it, but you'd best duck 'cause something would soon be flying in your direction." Michael shook his head grinning. "Of course, Samuel probably deserved most of what he got. He used to be a rounder before he met his wife, Madeline. That little girl straightened him out fast."

Jake smiled, rubbing his whiskered jaw as he pictured Lannie giving that poor guy Samuel the ride of his life. It wasn't hard for him to imagine.

"You don't push Lannie." Michael paused before adding, "I tried to tell Samuel, but he wouldn't listen. She's like something wild in nature that has never been fully tamed. I can't think of anything worse than someone trying to change her. She's kind, has a tremendous heart, and is loyal. If someone can't see the value in that, then they'd best leave her alone."

Jake was beginning to feel as if he'd just been warned. He liked Michael and decided to receive the warning in the spirit in which he felt it was given, out of love for Lannie. "I see the value, Michael, and I understand."

Michael changed the subject. "I sent Joe back down to the cottage to finish up some of the trim. We've had rain for the past few days, and I didn't want him tracking up the place so I pulled him off the job early."

Jake cleared his throat. "Good deal, and thanks again, Michael. I'm very pleased with the work."

As the men shook hands, Michael appraised him. "She's a good woman, Jake. A bit strong willed and independent, but you can always count on her." He grinned. "I understand she went out to sea with you."

"Without my knowledge *or* consent," Jake's eyes darkened as he frowned.

Michael threw his head back and laughed. "Yep, you better get used to it. That's life with Lannie."

Chapter 19

On the drive back to Beauchene, Jake's mind drifted to his wife, Belinda, and her clinging, almost desperate ways. Belinda had loved him, and he'd loved her. He knew that, but she'd needed more than any one person could ever give to another. It was as if she wanted to meld into him and become so much a part of his being that she disappeared entirely. Shaking his head, he tried to clear his thoughts.

Bumping off the smooth pavement, Jake drove down the dirt road through Bell Forest. He'd not gone far until he noticed a car parked on the side of the road in a patch of Queen Anne's lace. He slowed, wondering if he could be of assistance. The couple in the car looked as if they were in a heated discussion. They were waving their hands in the air, but no one was getting hurt. The driver, a male, turned away from the window as Jake passed. *Lovers spat,* he thought, and drove on by. But before he entered the gate at Beauchene, he noticed the car in his rearview mirror was heading slowly toward him. Because their road was the end of the line, he wondered out loud, "Now what do you suppose they want?" Jake thought of every possibility, and then a thought hit him.

Lannie was on the porch swing folding clothes into a basket when Jake pulled up. Sadie was sitting at her feet attempting to fold a washcloth. He quickly hopped out of the truck and hurried up the steps as steam from a passing rain shower rose from the ground.

"You and Sadie get in the house. Stay there until I tell you to come out." He barked out the order.

She stopped the swing with her foot, an incredulous look on her face. "What?"

He didn't blink. "You heard me, go!" Crossing the porch, he jerked the screen door open, motioning them inside.

Lannie was inside the house before she could even find her voice. "The nerve of that man, who does he think he is, ordering me around like I'm still on his ship!" Just then, she heard a car pull up outside. Peering through the window panel of the door, she saw Dawson, Mindy's on-again-off-again boyfriend. He got out of the car and casually approached Jake.

Jake squared off with the man, slowly and thoughtfully assessing the situation.

"My name is Dawson, and I'm here to see Lannie. Is she around?" he asked, wiping rain from his forehead.

"She's not available to you. May I help you?" Jake looked at the man pointedly. He'd never intended to get involved in Lannie's life, but circumstances changed his mind. "I live here."

Dawson nodded, and a wicked grin spread across his face as he understood the meaning behind the words. "Look, all I want is what's fair for Mindy. Sadie is her baby. She's worth something. We heard in town that Lannie paid off some debt today, figured she's come into some money, and we want what's comin' to us."

Jake sized up the man in an instant, knowing exactly where to strike the first blow. "Lannie has been meaning to talk to her sister about that. Seems there's a little matter of back child support to consider. Course, I told her that y'all were probably across the state line by now. You know how hard it is to collect support once you cross the state border."

Dawson furrowed his brow like the thought had never occurred to him that Mindy might actually be the one responsible for her own child. Rubbing his sweaty hands up and down the front of his pants, he smiled and said, "Well, there's no tellin' where we'll end up. All that movin' around is bad for a baby anyway."

"So true." Jake turned and headed toward the house. He'd relayed the message loud and clear. Before his feet hit the porch steps, he heard Dawson's car crank and listened as he whipped it around, slinging gravel behind his spinning tires.

Lannie's teeth worried her lower lip as she watched Jake come into the entry hall. "Well, what did he say?"

"Looks like Dawson and your sister may be moving out of state."

Lannie let out a relieved sigh. "Oh, thank goodness."

Joe Gregory was now legally a man. At twenty-one years of age, he sported a new, shorter haircut, which made him seem older somehow. His slow movements and deliberate steps seemed less lazy and more confident these days. He had a swagger to his walk.

Thunder rolled off in the distance and steam rose from the metal roof of the sea cottage as he plodded through standing water left over from a passing shower. He slowed his pace, coming around the corner of the porch where he'd been tacking up lattice under the floor.

At a glance, the sky showed no sign of the thunderstorm. The sun was out, making the air humid and hard to breathe. A noise behind him caused him to turn. Pushing up the rim of his cap, he squinted until he made out the figure of a girl through the swags of Spanish moss hanging from the tree limbs. She was leaning against the spreading oak with her hands behind her.

Mindy Melson. He turned back to his work, completely snubbing the girl. Sure, Mindy was cute, always had been. But he'd never known a more selfish, spoiled, self-centered girl in his life. She was nothing like her half-sister, Lannie. He shook his head. Whatever she was doing, he couldn't care less. And if the thought ever crossed his mind to ask her, he'd nail his boots to the ground before he could go over and talk to her. She could just stand there and stare for all he cared.

A minute or so later, Mindy walked up to where Joe was kneeling down, driving in a tack. "You look different, Joe. I didn't recognize you at first. You look...older."

Joe didn't respond; he just kept right on ignoring her. He didn't know what she was doing here, and he didn't care.

"Joe, why are you ignoring me?" Mindy crossed her arms and thrust out her bottom lip.

The hammer stilled. Without turning around he drawled, "'Cause I ain't got no use for the likes of you."

"What makes you say that, Joe? You've known me all your life!"

Closing his eyes, he shook his head, exasperated. "Anybody sorry enough to chase after their sister's husband, sleep with him, and use their very own child as some kinda pawn to get what they want is somebody I ain't got no use for. What are you doin' now, plottin' some way to get money outta Lannie? I'm tellin' you just this once. If you don't get away from me, I'm gonna cut me a switch and give you what you've been needin' your whole life long—a good old-fashioned whoopin'!"

Mindy's eyes were huge, wide with shock. She'd gone through twelve years of school with Joe, and in all that time she'd never heard him say more than a few words. Strangely, she'd never really paid too much attention to him before. Now, she felt oddly attracted to him. Her heart began to beat rapidly. Swallowing hard after the harsh spew of words, she ventured, "What are you doing now, Joe? I mean besides hammering up that lattice."

Lifting the hammer, he began pounding in a tack. "I'm gonna join the Merchant Marine. Captain says I'm what they're looking for, not that it's any of *your* concern."

"What about Christenberry's? You mean you'd leave Michael?"

"The sea is callin' me, Mindy. I don't reckon *you'd* understand, but Michael does. I've already talked to him." Joe peered around the cottage toward the house. "Was that Dawson I saw up there a while ago?" He turned around and for the first time nailed her with a look dead in the eye.

"Uh…yeah."

"You with him?"

"Kind of." Mindy glanced away, unable to meet Joe's stern appraisal.

"Figures." He turned back to his work, dismissing her thoroughly.

Not wanting Joe to think ill of her, she offered, "We're just checking on Sadie to see how she's doing."

"Is that so? Then why ain't you up there; you're her momma, no wait...I take that back, Lannie is her momma, you lost that right. You're just the person who had her, and any idiot can have a baby."

With that last statement, something began to crumble inside of Mindy. Her throat tightened and her lips quivered. "You're mean, Joe Gregory!" she said, her eyes brimming with tears.

"Your bawlin' don't bother me none. You *need* to cry and think of somebody else besides yourself for a change, like poor Sadie. How do you think she feels when her own momma don't even want her?"

Mindy was now in a full-blown bawling fit. Tears streamed down her cheeks, and her shoulders jerked with her quick catches of breath. Joe was indifferent to her tears; the sight of Mindy's distress didn't seem to faze him.

Finally, spent from the raw emotion, Mindy sat down on the ground, took a deep and shaky breath, and asked, "What can I do, Joe?" Her tiny, weak voice continued between hiccups "To make it right, I mean?" She picked up a twig and began making circles in the sandy dirt as she waited for an answer.

"The right thing."

"What's the right thing?"

"God holds the answers. Why don't you go someplace and ask some questions?" Joe had heard the captain say that very thing to one of his crew members down at the dock. The way he'd said it made an impression on Joe. He'd been waiting for an opportunity to use the phrase and sound just as authoritative. It seemed to fit the situation.

Sniffling loudly, Mindy got up and brushed herself off. A car horn sounded from the direction of the road. "Thanks, Joe." She walked over and kissed his cheek. "I really needed to hear that." Turning around, Mindy walked toward the road and disappeared from sight.

Joe watched her leave, rubbing his hand over the place still warm from her lips on his cheek.

Chapter 20

The savory scent of roast filled the entry hall as Jake, Cornelius, and an unexpected guest, River, entered Lannie's apartment.

"Have a seat," Lannie called from the kitchen. "Dinner is almost ready."

A table for three was set in the living room. Jake gestured for the others to sit while he stepped into the kitchen to speak to Lannie about another place setting. "Smells wonderful," he said, just above a whisper as he walked up behind Lannie. "We have another guest."

"Oh?" Lannie lifted her brow in surprise. "Well, I have plenty. Just grab a chair and I'll bring an extra plate."

"It's River."

Turning her attention away from the stove, she glanced at him a moment, shrugged, and began stirring the potatoes. "She's welcome at my table."

Looking around, he noticed something missing. "Where's Sadie?"

"Asleep. I think I wore her out today. She's out cold." Removing her apron, she draped it across the back of a chair. "Here, help me get these bowls to the table."

Jake lifted a plate of warm biscuits and a pitcher of iced tea and headed for the table with Lannie right behind him.

After dinner and a lively conversation, which included many stories of sea adventures, Lannie excused herself to check on Sadie. Jake stood and began collecting dishes to clear the table.

River was now certain of Jake's interest in her cousin. After all, what man would ever volunteer to clean a table? She began to plot a full blown attack on Lannie's character. Her conversation turned to vicious comments and insinuations of Lannie's behavior, both past and present.

Having about enough of it, Jake spoke out sharply before Cornelius had a chance. "It's obvious you don't care for Lannie, River. So, let me put you out of your misery by walking you to your car."

Stunned, River quickly tried to make excuses for her comments even as she was being escorted out the door.

Upon returning, Jake flashed a grin toward Cornelius and offered, "More coffee?"

"No, no. I'm completely satisfied, *now*," he emphasized, pushing back from the chair. "That was the finest peach pie I believe I've ever put in my mouth. I'll sleep like a baby after that meal."

Lannie stepped into the room. Looking around, she asked, "Where's River?"

Jake and Cornelius exchanged a quick glance. "She had to go," Jake stated, without explanation.

"That meal was delicious, Lannie darlin'," Cornelius said, rubbing his belly. "If I had known you could cook like that I'd have turned my galley over to you. Bad as I hate to leave," he said, drawing in a deep breath, "I'm going to turn in early. Thank you for that delicious meal." He reached out and took hold of her hand, placing a kiss on her knuckles. "For my part, all is forgiven. I'll be waiting expectantly to be put under another one of your spells," he said, winking. "Jake swears you bewitched me, and I'm inclined to believe it's true."

As Cornelius closed the door behind him, Lannie turned to Jake with fire in her eyes. "It took all I had within me not to come in here and physically remove River from my table. I heard some of what she said. How can *anyone* eat at your table and enjoy your hospitality and the minute your back is turned attack you viciously with their words!" Crossing her arms, she began to tap out a steady beat with her slender foot. "I should have..."

Jake held up his hand, "Easy now." He wagged a finger at her, his teeth gleaming white in his slow grin. "That temper of yours, Lannie, it's getting out of hand. Think of the example." He made a motion with his head toward Sadie's room.

"Ooooh!" Lannie gritted her teeth as she collected a few plates from the table and stepped into the kitchen. Sliding them into the sink, she wrung out the dishrag, twisting it into a tight knot as if she were strangling it.

Jake resumed clearing the table, bringing the dishes to the sink. Suppressing a grin, he reached for a dishcloth, wishing to change the subject. "You know, when a man is at sea for months at a time, it's usually not hard for him to spot a woman, but I must admit, you had me completely fooled."

She plunged the dishrag back down into the sudsy water and began vigorously washing a plate before rinsing it. "In some ways, I guess I've always been kind of tomboyish."

Jake took the clean plate and began rubbing it dry with slow steady movements. The room was silent but for the sounds of their task. Jake spoke quietly, "I never let you out of my sight, you know, once I knew your true identity."

Lannie's eyes skimmed the long, corded veins of his arms as he dried the dish. "I bet you laughed when you saw how scared I was during the storm."

Jake gently stacked the dried dish on the counter. "I admired your hard work and determination. I found you to be a better-than-average steward, so did Cornelius. A ship's galley, pantry, and eating areas are notoriously hard to keep clean and sanitary. Throw the officers' quarters into the mix and you've got a lot of work on your hands. You did your job extremely well." Their hands brushed as he took another dish from her, and she nearly trembled.

He asked, "Why were you looking for me earlier? Cornelius said you asked about my whereabouts." Their eyes met in the reflection of the darkened window over the sink.

Lannie lowered her head, embarrassed as she tried to come up with an excuse for asking about him.

"Was it Sadie?"

Letting out a breath of relieve, she responded, "You shouldn't be surprised; you know how she feels about you." Was that a lie? Her conscience was nipping at her, but there was no way she was going to let him think she was interested in his whereabouts. "I guess if I'd thought about it, I would have known you were with River."

Jake raised an eyebrow. "You'd be wrong. I was alone."

"I'm sure that's just a temporary state for you."

"You're sure? What do you know about me, Lannie?"

Uncomfortable with the warm and thick texture of his voice, she responded, "I guess about as much as you know about me."

Jake studied her as he reached for another plate. "I understand more about you than you realize."

Curiosity widened her eyes. "Do tell," she teased.

Wiping the dish slowly, he began, "You've never had a time in your life when someone else held the reigns. You've always had control. In fact, if you were to move forward at all, you had to be the one to do it. Others in your life selfishly left all decisions to you, and that includes your husband. They just stood back and let you do it all."

His words struck a chord within her. It was true. Even Cade had left the responsibility of the household and the decision making to her. His boyish charm had won out most of the time. She'd easily assumed the role of leader of the home. After all, Cade was seldom there and that was the life she was accustomed to. Was that wrong? "And you control *everything* in your relationships."

Jake laughed shortly. "Not really, not even in my marriage."

"What was your wife's name?" With her hands in the dishwater, she turned to him, waiting for his answer.

"Belinda." He whispered her name like a prayer.

It was like Lannie was seeing the man, Jake Chamberlain, for the first time. She knew him to be an excellent captain, working harder than three men put together. She knew him to be kind and loving to Sadie, and she also knew him to enjoy the company of different women. Now it dawned on her why he had so many women: to take away the awful emptiness he must be feeling. "What was she like?"

Jake inhaled, letting the breath out slowly before he responded. "She wasn't a strong person, but I deeply loved her. Her love for me was not healthy, though. It was a consuming love. She took her life while I was out at sea." A shadow crossed his face as he continued to rub the bowl in his hand.

Her heart went out to him, but she sensed he didn't want or need pity. Understanding that, she asked, "She was very dependent on you, then." It was a statement, not a question.

"In an extreme way. She never adjusted to my way of life, and I didn't see it coming. I knew she would get depressed from time to time, but I thought that was common for new brides. It never occurred to me that she suffered from an imbalance." He shrugged, "I guess I was never around long enough to notice what was going on with my very own wife."

Lannie continued to stare out the kitchen window, lost in thought. In a brief moment of perfect clarity of mind, she spoke. "So, Belinda never told you that she suffered from depression?"

"No. She never acted like anything was wrong; she just told me that she missed me, which at the time I assumed was normal. She clung to me when I was home, but I thought that was typical behavior for a woman whose husband had been gone a long time." He smiled. "In fact, until I met you, I thought all women behaved like that. I haven't had too much experience with women of your sort."

"Then you had no way of knowing. All you knew was that you loved her. And if you had known, you would have done everything in your power to help her...but you were never given that chance. Things like this need to be put in God's hands. He knows not only *what* we do, but *why* we do it, and above all, He's merciful."

The conscience-cooling effect of Lannie's words seemed to release tension in his muscles that had long held tight and firm. Closing his eyes, a brief smile pulled at his lips. "You're right."

"I'm seldom wrong," she teased.

"You've just saved me months of therapy; I owe you."

Billowing clouds in the moist summer air sailed across the bay like racing ships. A hovering gull cried overhead, the sound fading on the wind as the sea rushed to shore.

A car horn honked from the yard of Beauchene. Lannie looked up from her novel in time to see Heather pulling up. She settled back into the metal swing Cornelius had placed near the beach and continued reading. Another blast of the horn sounded. She looked up again and watched as Heather jumped out of the car and began running across the yard and up the porch steps. Jake stood in the doorway as she slid past him, going into the house.

Casually, he began stepping down the wooden steps, walking toward Lannie. She held her breath. He was dressed in khaki pants, loafers without socks, and a white button-down shirt. The sleeves were rolled up, revealing his tanned and corded arms. His dark brown hair was slightly damp and his jawline neat but unshaven. To say he was handsome just didn't do him justice; he was masculinity personified.

Jake plopped down in the swing beside Lannie and let out a deep breath. "She was in a rush to reach the bathroom," he commented dryly. "I guess it is a long trip out here."

"Why is everybody always rushing around?" Lannie replied, trying hard not to let her eyes travel over him. Her heart decided to beat rapidly, and she could feel the heat creep up her neck.

A slow grin spread across his face. "Maybe she is just anxious to see me."

"So, you're saying Heather is so excited to see you that she almost wet herself. I used to have a dog that would do that." *Did that sound snippy?*

Jake furrowed his brow, giving a lopsided grin. "You've never been excited to see someone?"

"On occasion," she said, snapping her book closed. Being around Jake was unnerving. "But it's been a long time."

"You've endured a lot lately, Lannie." He leaned forward in the swing, bracing his elbows on his knees as he turned to look at her. "I'm glad to see that you're taking it easy. I know it can get lonely at times, but you're doing the right thing by taking it slow."

"I'm not lonely. I have the Lord, and I have Sadie. And, I have a few friends. As a matter of fact, June stopped by to see Sadie. She and Cornelius are inside the sea cottage right now sharing homemade ice cream with her."

"Yes, you have good friends," Jake agreed. "But, sometimes you need a person to sit across from you to share your feelings with. You need a man."

"I agree. That's why I'm going out with Jess Ray tonight. I feel a need to…live a little. I'm tired of being sad and just existing."

Sitting back in the swing, Jake eyed her intently. "Jess Ray? What about Sadie?"

"What about Sadie?"

"Does he know you have a child?"

"Of course he does," she said, her voice sounding incredulous. "That's why he suggested we go to the amusement park after dinner. He said Sadie will enjoy the new glass-bottom boat they've recently added."

A wave of inexplicable jealously swept over Jake. Before he could make a comment, Heather crossed the yard to join them.

"Let's go, I'm starving," Heather said, wrapping her arms around Jake's neck from behind. "You promised me dinner on the bay, remember?" She bent over to nuzzle his neck.

Jake was surprised by his strong emotions. He'd never been prone to jealous fits, but he felt one coming on. He cleared his throat and spoke as if reluctant to do so. "I hope you have fun tonight, Lannie. I'm sure Sadie will love the boat ride." He got up and waited for Heather to go before him. Turning back to Lannie, he smiled. "I almost forgot." He reached under his collar and pulled out the medallion, lifting it over his head. "I think this belongs to you."

Lannie took the medallion, still warm from his skin, and whispered, "Thank you." She felt like crying. "Be safe."

Chapter 21

$\mathcal{R}$ ain quickened from a light drizzle to a heavy downpour in less than five minutes as Jess Ray stared nervously out the windshield of his car between rapid slaps of the wipers. "We'd better take a rain check on our plans for tonight, Lannie. It looks like this rain is settling in. I wouldn't want you or Sadie to get wet."

A dense fog crept out of the bayou as they drove silently through Bell Forest. Lannie sat staring straight ahead without a word, but her thoughts were running wild. Was he kidding? Rain was part of life, especially here. The thought that a little rain would deter this man from going out with her made Lannie suddenly want to be anywhere but with him. She knew Jess Ray was a good man, but obviously not the man for her. He was kind but overly cautious.

"I agree," she blurted out. "Good thing we haven't gone far. You can turn around at the gate of the monastery. Better yet, just drop us off there, at the front door. I've been meaning to stop in for a visit. One of the Brothers will drive us home." As the rain continued, Lannie suddenly felt elated to not be going out with him.

Jess Ray took his eyes off the road and looked at her hesitantly. "Are you sure? This place looks creepy...like something from an old horror movie."

Lannie smiled, thinking how much she'd prefer the company of monks, or even Dracula, to his company right now. "I'm sure. They're friends." She stopped short of telling him exactly what she thought, no sense in upsetting him. He couldn't help it, he was just too naïve for her. She knew it would take a much stronger man than Jess Ray to handle her. One outspoken word from her and he'd likely shake in his shoes.

Standing on the stoop outside of the monastery, Lannie watched as Jess Ray pulled away. *He didn't even give me his umbrella!* It was then that she realized there were worse things in life than being lonely, and being with the wrong person was one of them.

Moisture from the rain fell on her cheeks as she watched the glowing red taillights disappear into the fog. Her mind turned to Cade, remembering the countless times he'd risked life and limb just to check on her whenever he worked a hurricane as a first responder. She had always been his first concern during bad weather, and nothing ever deterred him from being with her.

She looked down into Sadie's innocent and confused face as they stood there on the stoop. "Your daddy was a good man, Sadie." Surprised at her own admission, Lannie smiled, feeling lighter than she had in months. She lifted Sadie into her arms and nuzzled her neck. "Come on, I want you to meet some friends of mine."

Tapping on the thick and imposing wooden door, Lannie was certain the knock wouldn't be heard over the rain. Trying the knob, she found it unlocked. She poked her head into the deserted entry hall. Silence enveloped them. Nothing could be heard in the cavernous room except the ticking of a grandfather clock on the far wall. Placing Sadie's feet on the floor, she lifted a corner of the hem of her skirt and patted the little girl's cheeks dry.

A table just inside the entry hall held a small, brass bell, placed there to announce a guest. Lannie picked it up and rang it. The sound reverberated throughout the monastery. Clasping Sadie's hand, she tiptoed into the great room, feeling as if she'd disturbed a great sleeping dragon as pops and creaks echoed through the halls.

The smell of leather, old books, and wood polish permeated the quiet surroundings. From somewhere down the long, dark hall, a shadow began to come toward them, taking shape as it neared. She held her breath, holding Sadie's hand firmly in hers as the form of Brother Raphael seemed to materialize before their very eyes.

"Lannie, it's so good to see you!" Brother Raphael opened his hands as if to pronounce a blessing on them. "And who is this little one?"

Lannie lovingly brushed the hair out of Sadie's eyes. "This is my Sadie."

"Well, I'm certainly glad to meet you, Sadie. Why don't we sit down and make ourselves comfortable." He motioned toward a dark leather couch in the center of the room. It was flanked on either side by large mahogany end tables and anchored with two heavy brass lamps that glowed dimly. High ceilings and an enormous stone fireplace seemed to call for large pieces just to keep the room from swallowing up the furnishings.

As Lannie and Sadie sat down, a low moan howled around the corners of the stone structure. The wind picked up. Pelting rain began hitting the windows with force.

Brother Raphael stepped over to the tall mullion windows and flipped a switch. The outside lights came on, illuminating the swirling trees through the framed windows as they bowed and tossed their branches in a wild dance. "Look, Sadie, every tree is excited, waving gloriously to the Creator!"

Sadie began sucking her thumb rapidly and held on tightly to Lannie. With eyes wide, she watched Brother Raphael from across the room.

Brother Raphael was young—not quite forty. He spoke with a slight Middle Eastern accent. Dark, almost black hair and warm sparkling eyes added to the mystique surrounding the monk. He was kind and approachable and known to be wise in his counsel. Lannie was glad he had been the one who answered the door that night.

A slight shuffling from the hallway drew their attention as Brother Simeon came into view. The old, white-headed, Irish monk held a plate of cookies in his hand as he motioned for Sadie to follow him into the kitchen. Sadie slid off the couch timidly, and her feet hit the floor with a thump. Without a backward glance, she followed the old monk down the darkened corridor.

"I can't believe she just did that," Lannie whispered, staring with her mouth open as Sadie followed the monk.

"Brother Simeon has a way with children." He gave a soft laugh. "In many ways, he relates to them better than to the adult versions. He always enjoys milk and cookies before bedtime."

"Who doesn't?" She smiled at Brother Raphael.

"You sound like Telie," he said, smiling. "I've never seen anyone over the age of twelve get as excited as Telie does when we send over cookies, especially chocolate cookies. And, now that she's expecting, we've all determined to spoil her rotten. We feel as if we're all about to become uncles."

"And you'll all make excellent uncles, too."

Brother Raphael came to sit across from Lannie in a comfortable looking captain's chair. The soft leather gave under his weight as he settled in, adjusting his elbows on the armrests. He caught a quick breath and held it, hesitating as he settled back into the chair and looked at Lannie. "You're exhausted."

"I sleep well. In fact, I'm even finding time for naps these days." Lannie shrugged. "Lately though, I do seem to be tired a lot."

"You sound like most mothers of small children." He tapped his fingers together lightly and then stopped and held them in a steeple position. "Isn't it amazing how God provided a door to motherhood for you through a completely different means?"

Lannie raised an eyebrow. "A different means? Well, I guess that's one way of looking at it, Brother." She laughed softly, then furrowed her brow.

His gaze settled on the tight worry lines across her brow. Whereas he'd known her earlier to be a happy and fully alive girl, he now perceived a heartbroken seriousness about her. Still, she moved with the fluid grace and intent directness he'd always admired, although he sensed a change that troubled him. "What is at the heart of what's bothering you, Lannie?"

She looked deep into Brother Raphael's warm, dark eyes. She'd forgotten how potent they could be. They seemed capable of stripping away the pretense from whatever passed before them. With a heavy sigh, she ran a hand through her hair and fell back against the couch. "I don't know where my husband is."

"Tell me what you *do* know," Brother Raphael pressed, sensing that Lannie needed to get something off her chest.

It was all she could do to answer his question and not retreat into the safety of silence. Bringing up what troubled her opened and exposed a painful wound. Nevertheless, she knew she needed to treat the wound, and she trusted Brother Raphael to tend it. Everyone in Moss Bay, including the monks, knew what had happened. Small towns held few secrets. "I know that Cade wanted to make things right. I know he was a believer in Christ. He told Shane, his best friend, that he was going to our pastor to get council on what he needed to do. He was tired of living with the guilt, and he wanted forgiveness, not just from me, but from God. But he never got the chance to ask for it."

Brother Raphael sat forward in his chair. "That's good to hear. The scriptures tell us in 1 John that if our hearts condemn us, He is greater than our hearts. And He knows everything. God forgives, and He alone knows the intent of a man's heart. But in the end, we must place all these things under the care of God, who truly loves us, and rely on His grace to cover our sin. I do know this, Lannie: God is merciful, and it is not His wish that any perish. He has provided what we all need in his Son."

There are moments when something that should have been known all along suddenly becomes crystal clear; sometimes it takes a person on the outside to bring the truth home in a simple way. Lannie now realized the truth: that God loves His children, and that none are without sin. He loves His children so much, in fact, that He sent His Son as a sacrifice to pay for their sin...all of it! As those words sank in deep, Lannie felt a weight lift from her shoulders. The weariness she'd felt for the past months seemed to seep out of her spirit and float toward the high ceiling. Lightness replaced the heaviness, and for the first time in a long while, Lannie felt joy in her soul.

Later that night, Jake returned home as the rain dwindled into a swirling gray mist that hovered close to the ground. As he approached the house, lights from Lannie's apartment shone out into the damp night. The sound of music hit Jake as he opened his truck door. He turned his head, looking for Jess Ray's car. He stood there in the damp mist, as indecisive as the raindrops on the tips of the silver leaves above his head. He wasn't sure he could stand the thought of Lannie enjoying the company of another man. He ran a frustrated hand through his damp hair as he reluctantly walked toward the house.

A shriek of laughter pierced the night, and in the next instant, the sound of *Born on the Bayou,* by Creedence Clearwater Revival, filled the air. Stepping up on the porch, he couldn't resist a glance through the French door of Lannie's apartment. Relief flooded him as soon as he saw Lannie with Sadie in her arms, dancing in carefree abandon around the living room. The sight captivated him. Unable and unwilling to move, he watched as she sashayed around with an easy rhythm and a graceful form. She was laughing...she was actually laughing!

Lannie laughed as if she were about to plunge into some thrilling adventure, swinging Sadie around in her arms. Jake watched the entrancing play of her features as she lifted Sadie high in the air. The little girl let out a squeal of pure delight. Jake hooked his leg around the rocking chair and slid it across the porch planks. He sat down, regarding the scene with a smile twitching at the corners of his lips. *This must be the girl Michael was talking about,* he mused, leaning back in the chair as he considered this new woman. Decidedly, he liked her...he liked her a lot.

As the music ended, Lannie slowed the dance and hugged Sadie tightly. With a graceful hand, she leaned over and turned off the lamp, and they disappeared toward the back of the house. With a shake of his head, Jake pushed up from his seat, smiling at the image he knew would forever be etched in his memory. Then the thought hit him. *Why is she so happy? That must've been some date.* Unable to settle his thoughts, he turned his attention west toward the sea cottage. The sight of a glowing window from the rear of the cottage proved that Cornelius had settled in but was still awake.

"What's wrong with me? I need to get back to sea...and soon!" Jake said out loud. His mind traveled down a different path. For a moment, he let himself think about how soft Lannie felt in his arms and that haunting fragrance she wore. The very one he smelled each time he entered the house. The thought of her silky hair brushing against his bare arm caused him to shudder. "Enough of this!" he said irritably, as he stepped up to the sea cottage door and pounded on it.

The door flew open as Cornelius stared wide-eyed into the angry face of the captain. "Captain, is everything all right?"

Jake gave a half smile, aware that he'd been scowling. "Just thought I'd check on you, see how you're doing down here."

"Oh, I've never been more content with a place. Keep me here much longer and I'm liable to go soft on you. Maybe even join a book club." Cornelius twisted his lips in a prissy fashion.

"Let's not go too far, Cornelius, or I'll be forced to remove you from my ship," Jake joked.

"I've been meaning to ask you something, Captain." He motioned to the chairs positioned in front of the fireplace. "Take a seat."

Jake plopped down in the chair and looked up at his friend. "Go ahead."

Sheepishly, Cornelius cut his eyes at the captain as he sat down. "You know me well enough to know that I'm not one to see things. But, I see things and hear things I can't explain around this place."

"Such as…"

Rubbing his jaw, he continued in a cautious manner, "I heard a rustling of the wind in the trees earlier this evening while I was sitting on the porch." He pointed in the direction of the forest. "Then I turned and saw a shadow move between the trees."

Jake's grin brazenly declared his amusement. "I've seen things myself, Cornelius, but whether they're alive or long since dead, I have no way of knowing. I blame most of what I see around here on this infernal heat. Tell me, was the shadow small and about yea high?" He raised his hand to indicate the height.

Nodding, Cornelius replied, "Yes, and it seemed to float along the path toward the sea without a sound." He shivered. "Creepy."

"Lannie is bad to wander around the property at night. I can almost guarantee it was her. She and Sadie are still up. They could've wandered down to the bay. That woman wanders all over creation at night." His knowledge and understanding of Lannie was increasing with each passing day. Considering all the aspects of her personality, he seriously doubted that he would ever fully understand her. She was quite an intriguing woman.

With a relieved sigh, Cornelius said, "Come to think of it, the 'spirit' was about the size of Lannie, and she was holding something." He laughed, feeling much relieved. "She sure is a spirited woman. If I was younger, I'd want to tame nothing more than her heart."

"You need a wife, Cornelius. Why don't you come to church with me tomorrow and pick one out of the congregation. I'm finding out Moss Bay has some pretty interesting women."

A bit of rebellion shone in his eyes. "I've yet to meet the woman who could hold your attention for more than a few hours. Lannie may be the exception, though." He threw his head back and laughed. "That little girl has me sleeping with a night-light while she's outside roaming the countryside!" He shook his head. "Honk twice in the morning; I'll be ready for church. I'd planned to go anyway. In fact, I was invited by Lannie's friend, June Meyers. When a beautiful woman asks you to church, you go."

Chapter 22

It was a glorious Sunday morning. The sun, hiding behind a passing cloud, pierced the obstruction with her rays in a spectacular display across the morning sky. Pulling up to the cottage, Jake honked twice. A second later, Cornelius stepped out, dressed in khaki pants and a crisply starched dark blue shirt.

"You clean up well, Cornelius. What's that I smell?" Jake sniffed the air.

"Aftershave…is it too much?"

Jake twisted his lips to keep from grinning. "No, not at all. I just haven't known you to wear the stuff. What's that you call it…foo foo juice?"

Clearing his throat, he replied, "You don't know everything about me, my boy. There may be snow on the roof, but there's fire in the hearth."

"I gotta meet this woman." Jake put the truck in gear and eased down the rutted road toward town.

"I thought Lannie and Sadie would be with us." Cornelius glanced over his shoulder toward the house, noticing Lannie's car was gone.

Jake shrugged, "I guess they left earlier this morning. I didn't get a chance to speak to her about church yesterday."

"Maybe she's already there. Hope so. June just adores Sadie, and I think Sadie feels the same way about her. We made homemade ice cream yesterday. I can't remember when I've had a more enjoyable time." The truck bounced as it fell into a rut and the men shifted. "I guess I'm getting soft in my old age, but I really like talking to that woman. She's had an interesting life."

Jake took his eyes off the road and looked at his friend. "It's nice here. A man could get used to it...nothing wrong with that."

Pulling into the parking lot of the church, the men got out and made their way toward the door. A man greeted them inside the doorway. "Good morning, come on in." Extending his hand, he said, "I'm Nathan, and this is my wife, Sonny."

Jake gave Nathan a firm shake. "Jake Chamberlain, and this is Cornelius Longcrier." Each man nodded to Sonny, "Ma'am."

"We're glad to have you with us," Nathan said, patting Jake on the back as he passed.

"They seem like nice folks," Cornelius observed. "I'll bet that guy knows how to pick a good fishing hole. He has the look of a fisherman about him."

"He certainly knows how to pick a wife, that's for sure," Jake noted.

As they walked down the aisle, June waved from across the church. "There's my date. Wanna sit with us?" Cornelius rifled in his pocket in search of a mint.

"You go on. I'll sit over here." Watching his friend navigate the pews, Jake felt suddenly lighter. Looking up, he saw Lannie sitting near the front talking to a man, and the man was smiling at her, intensely watching her face. A dark scowl began forming on Jake's brow. Suddenly, he felt a presence beside him.

"Sit with us, Jake," River offered, indicating a pew behind her.

Jake moved into the pew, trying his best to keep his attention off Lannie. He picked up a hymnal and started fumbling through the pages. River clamped down on his arm and whispered in his ear, "What did I tell you about Lannie? That man she's talking to is *married*."

"Married!" He jerked his head up in time to see the broad-shouldered man lean over and hug Lannie. An attractive girl with honey amber hair walked down the aisle to join them. The man, still smiling, seized the woman around the waist and pulled her to him in a tight embrace. The girl reached down, lifted Sadie from Lannie's lap, and turned, walking with the man back down the aisle toward the back of the church. As they neared, Sadie spotted Jake and lunged forward, almost jumping out of the woman's arms.

"Whoa now," the man said, assisting the woman with Sadie. He looked down at Jake and smiled. "It seems you have quite an effect on women. This one is just throwing herself at you."

"I've won the heart of this particular one, it seems." Jake stuck out his hand. "I'm Jake Chamberlain."

"Samuel Warren, and this is my wife, Madeline." Samuel eyed the man. "I feel as if I know you already; Michael has told me so much about you." He glanced at his wife as she struggled to contain Sadie. "You better head on to the nursery, honey, before you have a mutiny on your hands," he told his wife, looking back at Jake. "Michael, Lannie, and I go way back. I was relieved to know she wasn't living out at Beauchene all by herself. I'm old fashioned, I know, but I believe a woman needs a man around for protection." He put his finger to his lips. "Just don't tell Lannie I said that, okay?"

Jake threw his head back and laughed. "Don't worry, your secret is safe with me."

Samuel grinned. "You're a smart man. By the way, my father-in-law says he knows you."

"Oh? Who is he?"

"Alexander Gailen."

Jake's lips curled into a wide smile. Before he could respond, a huge hand gripped his shoulder from behind, and he glanced up to see Alexander grinning down at him.

Alexander's eyes sparkled with joy. "Wren told me all about this pirate of a man and his devilish ways, and I knew it could only be one person. How have you been, Captain? It's been way too long, friend."

Jake stood and tightly embraced the man. "Don't tell me you're the handsome man Wren has been talking about. I would have *never* thought of you!" Jake pushed back for a closer inspection of the man. "You look good, Alexander. Life here seems to suit you."

"I'm a blessed man, let me tell you. Let's meet later and catch up. A lot has happened to this old man, and I want to tell you about it." With a slap on Jake's shoulder, he stepped back, motioning to Wren across the aisle. "Better get back before service starts. I don't want to do *anything* to upset that beautiful woman."

As Samuel and Alexander walked off, Jake sat down and looked up, noticing Lannie. She sat by herself now with her head raised toward the cross behind the pulpit. A shaft of light from a window cast a pewter beam across the wooden cross, illuminating it. He wondered at her thoughts as she gazed at it. Her hair, gathered loosely on the back of her head, exposed the slender column of her neck. A silver flash caught his eye from the chain around her neck—the medallion. His thoughts turned to the silver leaf tree. He'd seen that tree withstand high winds and many storms since he'd been at Beauchene, but it held its ground. Its roots were planted deep, drawing up a fresh source of life-giving water that strengthened it for the storms of life.

At the opening song, everyone got to their feet. Jake paused as he listened to the words: *I'll stand and trust, I'll stand in faith, I will not be shaken!* "Wow," he said softly, thinking of the silver leaf tree again.

Pastor Thad stepped up to the pulpit and opened his bible. "Who is Lord of your life?" He paused and looked around. "Careful how you answer that," he warned. "Who do you *want* to be the Lord of all? I know many of you will say Jesus, but be careful when you say things like that. You'd better be sure and know what you're asking. Because if you're serious about it, you'll be changed just like a strong wind changes the course of a sailboat. I don't mean to frighten you, just warn you. It will mean that you no longer have control—He'll determine your course. Ask any sailor and he'll tell you that true north is marked in the skies by Polaris. Finding our true north means to get on the right course, proceed in the right direction; however, the direction of our true north is not revealed in the sky but in scripture. A ship's captain has an unlimited master's license and can sail anywhere he chooses, but, as followers of Christ, we're not the captains of our souls. God alone holds that title, and He alone is the master of our fate. Are you ready to turn over the controls to Him? Are you ready for that kind of change? If you are, then turn with me to God's Word."

After service was over, Jake sat dazed. It was as if the entire sermon had been selected *for* and directed *toward* him. He glanced up as Lannie brushed by, and he wondered briefly if the message had gotten to her, too.

Lannie glanced at Jake as she walked by, noticing River tucked under his arm. River had a smug look about her, as if she'd outsmarted the rest of the women in Moss Bay. Anxious to pick up Sadie from the nursery, Lannie was not in a mood to put up with the likes of River Adams. A bible sitting on the arm of the pew next to Jake slipped to the floor in front of her. She reached down and collected it off the floor, smoothing the black leather surface with her hand. She paused over the name, Daniel Jake Chamberlain, engraved in silver lettering. "Oh, I think I've lost your place. Let's see…" she began thumbing through the pages, "I think this is where you were, right here in Romans 7:2." Risking a glance at him, she saw half of his mouth begin to pull up at the corners. She marveled at his coolness. River, on the other hand, was fuming.

"Are you just going to sit there and let her taunt you?" River asked, as she glared at Lannie.

He had no idea what the passage of scripture said, but, knowing Lannie, it had to be a good one. There was something about Lannie's voice that pulled at him, something whimsical, yet alluring. Disturbed by the effect her voice was having on him, Jake decided to take matters into his own hands. "Uh, Lannie, can I trouble you for a ride home? Cornelius is taking June to lunch, and I'm loaning him the truck."

Turning surprised gray eyes toward him she said, "What? You mean you trust Cornelius with your precious truck?"

He looked at her and smirked. "He's a guy."

"Then are you sure you'll be able to handle a woman at the wheel?"

"Well, actually, I was hoping you'd let me drive," he confessed, trying to keep the grin off his face. He knew he was getting to her, and he loved every minute of it.

River stood and grabbed his arm, giving it a yank. "Forget her, I'll take you home."

Jake sat motionless, unaffected by River's words as he smiled into Lannie's challenging eyes. "First comes the lesson, then comes the test."

"I'll get Sadie. Meet us out front." Her eyes shifted to River, who was seething with anger and barely able to keep her temper in check.

Once outside, Lannie saw Jake near the SUV, leaning against the passenger side door. The wind was blowing a gentle breeze across the parking lot, stirring his hair as he patiently waited for them. His feet were crossed at the ankles, and his arms were folded across his chest. He had the look of being out of place, but trying hard to accept it. Deciding to let him off the hook, she stepped near him as Sadie lunged forward. With one swift movement, Jake reached out and snatched Sadie out of Lannie's arms. "The keys," Lannie said, dangling them in front of his face.

With a look of surprise, he grabbed them and opened the passenger door for Lannie. She stepped up on the running board and climbed in. Closing the door gently, he walked around and opened the rear door for Sadie and buckled her into the car seat. With his sense of manhood restored, he looked around, jerked the door open, and climbed into the driver's seat. "Change of heart?" he asked, as he cranked the truck and looked back over his shoulder.

"Don't push it," Lannie replied, pulling down the visor for the mirror as she applied a light coat of lip gloss.

"Where to?"

"You're driving, you decide."

A slow smile spread across his handsome features. "Music to my ears."

Chapter 23

The SUV pulled up to a tiny little restaurant on the outskirts of town as the noonday sun bore down on the southern fields. The place seemed to sprout right out of the dirt like a stray stalk of corn in a field of cotton. The name was written in faded letters on a rusty sign hanging from an old post, The Cotton King Café.

"I found this place by accident while I was out scouting around one day. That's the Warren and Beckett development across the street in that old cotton field. I eat lunch here sometimes, and I've gotten to know a few of the men from the construction site," Jake explained.

Lannie surveyed the area then turned to Jake. "I saw you talking to Samuel Warren this morning. He owns half of that development."

"Well, so your old boyfriend has made a name for himself."

"What? Did Samuel tell you that?" Lannie blushed with embarrassment.

"I never reveal my sources." White teeth gleamed in a reckless smile. "Don't let the look of the place fool you. It may be old, but they've got the best fried chicken I've ever put in my mouth."

"*I* know that just because something is old, it doesn't mean it's worthless. It has more value, not less. And, that sugar kettle over there," she pointed to a kettle propped up next to the wooden planks of the restaurant, "wants to go home with me."

As Lannie stepped in front of the truck, Jake unfastened Sadie, and they followed her up the creaking steps. She got a good whiff of the Confederate roses clinging to the posts holding up the sagging roof. Pulling the screen door wide, they entered the small café.

"Y'all come on in. I see you're back for more, Captain," a voice as smooth as molasses called from the kitchen. "What is it this time, fried chicken, mashed tatas, and field peas?"

Jake smiled, "Give us some of everything you've got, Momma...and top it off with your blueberry pie."

A low laugh sounded from the direction of the kitchen. Metal pots clanged together as a deep humming drifted through the air from the cutout in the kitchen wall.

Dragging a highchair from the corner, Lannie lifted Sadie from Jake's arms and deposited her securely in the chair. Sliding her up to the table, she handed her a sippy cup full of juice. "I can't believe I've never been here before." She looked around, spying an old rattling box fan mounted in the window. "This is my kinda place."

"I thought you might like it," he said, sitting back as a young girl of no more than fifteen brought out their water.

The table was covered in a plastic red-and-white-checked tablecloth. A bottle of hot sauce and cardboard salt and pepper shakers were the only condiments on the table.

"So, you come here often?" Lannie asked, yanking several napkins from the dispenser.

"Sure do, but…" he paused, tilting his glass to her, "you're the only woman I've ever brought with me." Jake smiled into his glass as he noticed her reaction.

"I can't imagine why. All of your women must have peculiar taste if they wouldn't love the atmosphere here."

Just then the bell over the door clanged as four men walked in, talking loudly and shoving each other. Jake sized up the foursome with a quick glance then pushed back from the table as the cook, who allowed her friends to call her momma, brought over their plates. Momma was close to seventy, kind and easy mannered, with skin the color of coffee with a good dollop of cream mixed in.

"Here you go now, and I made a special plate for the young'un." Momma smiled and touched Sadie's head. "You sure are a pretty little thing…so precious."

As Momma stepped away, one of the boys from the next table, whose cheeks were still covered with the light down of youth, said, "Hurry up, old woman, we're starving over here."

Momma shuffled past them on her way back to the kitchen, waving her hand in the air to give the indication that she heard them.

The sound of Jake's chair scraping across the linoleum floor caused Lannie to look up from her meal. She watched with mild interest as Jake calmly stood and walked over to where a pitcher of tea sat on a side table. He picked it up and moved toward the table where the four men sat.

"Fill your glasses for you?" Jake asked, raising the pitcher in his hand.

The older man of the bunch stalled, not sure whether to take the man seriously.

Without waiting for a reply, Jake began filling the glass of each man. "You boys must be from the Warren and Beckett site. Nice of y'all to support the local economy; I know Momma sure appreciates it."

The older man responded, "Yeah, well...we do what we can. We eat here nearly every meal."

"Is that a fact? Well, if I'd known that, I'd have thanked Samuel Warren personally this morning. I'll be sure to tell him how you boys treat Momma. He'll be real happy to know that you *treat her with respect.*" He emphasized the last four words. He leaned an elbow on the table and looked the older man dead in the eyes. "Where's Josiah?"

"Honeymoon," the man answered. "I'm filling in as foreman while he's gone. The name's Vinson South." He stuck his hand across the table.

Taking the man's hand, Jake replied, "Well, it's good to know, Vinson, that you're the man responsible for these guys."

"Reckon so," he said, looking over the ragtag bunch of boys.

Jake stared at him a moment longer than necessary, and Vinson got the feeling Jake knew exactly what he was doing. The message was loud and clear to all present.

Jake pushed off the table and called over his shoulder, "Let me know if y'all need anything else boys. Momma will be out with your dinner in a minute." He didn't wait for a response before returning to his table. He hooked the chair with his foot and slid it out.

Lannie stared in mute surprise.

"Nice enough guys," Jake said, as he settled into his seat. "Just in need of a little tightening up."

Momma stared in wide-eyed wonder, shifting her attention from one table to the next. She'd watched the whole thing play out from her little cut-out window. Shaking her head, she lifted two plates and made her way over to the table of men.

As Momma put down the plates on the table, two of the three boys yanked the hats off their heads and said, "Thank you, ma'am."

Staring in curiosity at the foursome, Lannie turned her confused expression to Jake. "How did you do that?" she asked, her voice barely more than a whisper.

"I know men," he stated confidently. "They're a little rowdy, but harmless. They don't get out of hand with Josiah. They're just testing Vinson. Now, if he'll step up and take charge, there won't be any more disruptions."

As Jake predicted, Lannie glanced over in time to see Vinson jerk the cap off one boy's head.

After dinner, they drove along the bay and out toward the docks. Jake had to make a stop at the business office to pick up some papers. After that, they stopped for ice cream and slowly meandered along the streets of Moss Bay, with Sadie walking and licking her cone between them.

Stopping in front of a store window, Lannie licked her ice cream and pointed with a graceful finger. "This is where I work."

Narrowing his eyes, Jake looked up at the lettering across the glass: "Keepers of the Past." He leaned forward for a better view. "Yep...this looks like the kind of a place where you'd work."

Lannie pulled her head back sharply. "And, just what is *that* supposed to mean?"

"It means the place looks haunted. I guarantee some of that stuff in there has a spirit attached to it."

Her slow smile shone with mischief. "No, I invited all of them to come home with me. Most came back though, said they couldn't stand your girlfriends."

"Oh, is that right? Well, I'll just have to try to make better selections in the future."

"I'm sure they would appreciate it."

As the long afternoon stretched into evening, they drove through the gate of Beauchene with golden light warming the fields on either side of the lane. Insects floated and swirled in the heavy air. The day was softly fading.

As they approached the house, a fluttering of white paper caught Lannie's eye. A letter was stuck inside the frame of the screen door. The SUV rolled to a stop in front of the house, and Lannie got out and looked over her shoulder to make sure Jake was unfastening Sadie. She made her way to the door and froze, her hand in midair. Looking down at the paper, her hand began to tremble. There, on the paper, was the familiar scrawl of her mother. It simply read: Landis.

Gently, almost reverently, she pulled the letter free. Could her mother be concerned about her? With trembling hands, she turned the letter over and slid the tip of her finger under the sealed flap. Unfolding the note, she read:

Landis,

I didn't want to tell you this way, but you've left me no other choice since you've gone into hiding and turned off your cell phone. Your sister has had some sort of "awakening" experience and wants Sadie back. As it turns out, she has left her boyfriend and has started seeing Joe Gregory, you know, the boy who works for Michael Christenberry. Anyway, she wants to take responsibility for her daughter now and have a family of her own. Of course, I'll be moving to New Orleans with Sheldon, and I won't be in a position to help her. She has already made plans to get Sadie, and it's my understanding that she will contact you soon, maybe even tonight.

She's working at a bank in town and has already moved into a small house behind the library. I know you will fight for Sadie; Mindy knows this, too. But, I ask that you stand aside and let your sister have her daughter. She's asking for another chance to get it right. ~ Love, Mother

A low groan began somewhere deep inside of Lannie's being. She moved to the swing and lowered herself into the seat, staring straight ahead.

Seeing the change in Lannie's countenance, Jake cautiously approached. "Everything alright?"

She held her arm out stiffly, handing the letter over to him. Taking the paper, he began to read. The blue eyes scanned the words as horror dawned on his face. "Not this," he whispered.

Chapter 24

Candis McPherson stood in the pitch black darkness beneath the trees on the edge of the shoreline. The well-masked grove beside the bay and near the cottage provided solitude and the space she sought to sort out her feelings. She wanted to grieve in peace. Reaching down, she began picking up fallen limbs and pieces of driftwood, laying them in a pile on the beach. Striking a match, she set to flame a small pile of dried pine needles and twigs under the twisted wood and then settled against a large rock that was still warm from the day's sun.

A whippoorwill called out from somewhere deep in Bell Forest, haunting her dark hour with its lonesome tune. She had no desire to go back to the cold house, a house now devoid of the company of little Sadie and her silent presence.

Making the transition easy for Sadie had been Lannie's first priority. She'd packed up the satin-trimmed blanket and Sadie's favorite books, a tea set, and the patchwork ragdoll Lannie had found at an antique store. Swallowing down the massive lump in her throat, Lannie summoned her courage and did what needed to be done.

Mindy had come and gone and taken Sadie just as her mother had said she would. Leaning against the rock, she inhaled a jagged breath. Mindy had changed, or so it seemed. There was an air of maturity about her that Lannie had never witnessed before. Sadie did seem happy to see her mother. In fact, the little girl ran into her mother's arms and hugged her tightly. Lannie closed her eyes, listening to the sounds of the sea. Her mind traveled back over the weeks Sadie had been with her. She had been too quiet and relied on that thumb of hers way too much. Could it be that she'd missed her mother? Then the thought struck her. Mindy is *still* her mother, even if she had behaved selfishly. *I would give anything for my mother to come for me. Maybe Sadie feels the same way.* She shook her head to clear her runaway thoughts.

Pulling up her knees, she rested her chin on them and in the privacy of the secluded spot, gave in to the sorrow within her. Tears trickled down her cheeks as she thought of all she'd lost. Sadie had been the only ray of sunshine in the darkest days of her life, and now she was gone. Her throat tightened, and she swallowed painfully. *How do I ever go on?*

Jake crossed the yard, inhaling deeply to push down his own sadness as he made his way toward the fire on the beach. He smiled weakly as he caught sight of the small boots facing the fire, dug halfway into the sand. A lace-trimmed cotton skirt came just above Lannie's knees, an odd combination but it suited her nonetheless. "Mind a little company?" He looked down at her moist face, glistening in the firelight. She stared unblinkingly into the crackling fire that blazed in front of them like a lost child facing the uncertainty of a future that held no promise of joy.

She nodded, suddenly not trusting her voice.

He plopped down, straightening his legs in front of him with a grimace as he leaned against the rock. Gazing into the fire, he was quiet. Everything in him wanted to comfort her. But how do you comfort someone who has lost so much? Besides that, it worried him that he was scheduled to leave first thing in the morning. He'd volunteered to fill in for another captain who was having surgery. The old guilt resurfaced with a stabbing pain; what kind of a man could leave a woman in such a hard place?

After a long time, Lannie turned red-rimmed eyes to Jake and said, "I don't want to go inside. I live in a house full of ghosts and emptiness."

"I'm not a ghost," he informed her, flatly. He'd decided while sitting there that the best way to help Lannie was to challenge her to fight against the darkness that threatened to overtake her and their home. "This is my home, too. Now, the way I look at it we have two choices. We can fold, or we can fight. I, for one, choose to fight. Sadie may not belong to us, but by God's good grace, He will see to it that all is not lost."

She looked at Jake like she'd never seen him before, but before she could respond, Cornelius came out of the cottage some thirty feet away. He filled up the doorway so no light could get out, inhaling in a dramatic fashion as he made a pronouncement.

"Sometimes we need to hold onto our faith while letting go of the outcome. Put this matter in God's hands—and go to sleep." Cornelius turned quietly and shut the door.

They stared at the closed door for a minute before Jake said, "He's absolutely right."

Like a child, Lannie nodded in agreement, realizing for the first time that she wasn't the only one suffering over the loss of Sadie; Jake and Cornelius were mourning as well.

A slow smile broke across her face. "Was Cornelius wearing a baby blue bathrobe?"

Jake nodded slowly as he rubbed his jaw. "Yes, and if you ever want to know what a woolly mammoth looks like in a bathrobe, there's your picture." Lannie laughed lightly, and the sound ran straight through him. "Would you like to go get something to eat?"

The smile faded, and she brushed a hand down her skirt. "I don't think so."

"Don't let yourself fly all to pieces, Lannie. I just think you need to get out for a while," he assured her.

The smell of butter rum Life Savers wafted in front of her as Jake leaned toward her, waiting for an answer.

"I don't think that's such a good idea."

His smile deepened, plainly revealing his amusement at her reluctance. "I was warned about hostile Yankee haters. I just didn't believe such people still existed in the South. I stand corrected." His chiding laughter irritated her to no end.

Lannie faced him squarely. There was silence for a long moment as they sized each other up. "I'm not interested in going out with you, Jake. If I ever change my mind, I'll let you know." She knew she sounded snippy, but she didn't care; she'd just had it. The last thing she needed was for him to come on to her and especially at one of the lowest points of her life. She was not one of his little girlfriends.

Narrowing his eyes, he replied, "Don't confuse me with one of your soft and pliable boyfriends, Lannie."

"Well, if I ever want to know about you, Captain, I'll be sure to ask my cousin, River, or Heather, or any of your other lovers." Her gray eyes began to flash, reflecting the fire's glow.

"Lovers...lovers? What do you take me for?"

She looked at him, perplexed. "You mean...you've never..."

"Don't be ridiculous. I mean, I've learned...the hard way. I wrestle with my flesh just like every other red-blooded man. But, you don't know me, Lannie, or what I have or have not done. Only God knows, and I answer to Him alone. My relationships are casual, and by that I mean that they only go so far. Marriage is a thing of value, but it's cheapened if it's not valued. I may not ever be ready for that kind of a commitment again, but that doesn't mean I don't realize how sacred it is."

Lannie's eyes widened.

A grin lifted the corner of his mouth as he stood up, dusting the sand off his jeans. "Not what you expected to hear?" In a casual tone, he commented, "Never assume you know all there is to know about me."

"I won't. So...where are you taking me?" she asked as she got up, kicking sand on the fire with her boots.

Chapter 25

*P*ap's Cove was a different place at night. By day, it was a great place for the family to dine, with tables placed near large glass windows overlooking the marina. The outdoor seating area, complete with umbrella-covered wrought iron tables, was a perfect way to dine, watch boats come and go from the slips, and enjoy a sunset. White tablecloths and flickering candles graced each table, giving the atmosphere a decidedly charming aura. But at night, the mood shifted to a more relaxed and loose environment. The outdoor tables were pushed to the side to make room for a band and dance floor.

Jake placed his hand on the small of Lannie's back and led her down the garden path. She stopped under a vine-covered arbor at the entrance of Pap's Cove.

"You're not going to believe this, but this place resembled the surface of the moon before Telie got a hold of it." Lannie ran her hand over the lush, green Jackson vine.

"I believe it. I think the girl is some kind of garden pixie. I've never seen anything like it." He yanked on the door, and they stepped inside.

"The earth loves Telie. All she has to do is tickle it with her fingers and out sprouts something green," Lannie said, grinning up into Jake's face.

An attractive woman approached, smiling broadly at Jake as they came through the door. Sliding two menus off the hostess stand, she directed them toward a table in the center of the room.

Jake looked into the hostess's eyes and said, "Caroline, I would prefer a table outside. The one in the corner will do just fine."

Caroline seemed to melt at the mention of her name. Peering shyly over her shoulder, she said, "Certainly, Jake, whatever *you* want."

Lannie had an unexpected urge to push the woman. Instead, she slipped her hand around Jake's forearm possessively and allowed him to escort her outside to the table.

The moment Lannie's soft hand touched his arm Jake felt a river of warmth wash over his entire body. He took a deep breath, becoming more aware of her delicate scent than ever before. *I wonder what she would feel like in my arms again.* Just then, she stumbled as her shoe caught on a board. He grabbed her shoulders to steady her and felt the surge all the way to his toes.

"I should have left my boots on. These slippers seem to hang on everything. I think I'm stuck."

How did she manage to look so soft and feminine in the brief time it took her to change clothes? Grace and poise, he supposed, but there was always that…that underlying self-confidence he found so appealing. "Here, let me help you with that." Jake bent to loosen the fabric of her shoe from the splintered wood. He heard and felt her sharp intake of breath as he wrapped his hand around her ankle. "Don't get all shy on me now, I've almost got it."

After her foot was free, Lannie twirled her toes. "Thank you. That's much better." At the touch of Jake's hand on her back, all her embarrassment quickly fled. He moved behind her, pulling out her chair while the hostess looked on with a mixture of envy and aggravation in her eyes.

"Your waitress will be right out to take your order," Caroline said, crisply.

Looking up at Jake, Lannie said, "I'm usually not this clumsy." Her silken syllables were weaving a spell over him. "I'm pretty light on my feet most of the time."

"Well, you don't have to convince me. The fact that you never went overboard proves it. But we'll find out for sure once this band plays something slow."

The thought of dancing with him thrilled her. It had been too long since she'd danced, and oh how she loved it. "You're on."

Toward the west, a storm was wreaking havoc miles away, giving them an amazing show of lightning flashes between the clouds. The wind picked up, stirring the tablecloth slightly.

"Nothing like the fresh evening air stirring your hair, is there?" Jake remarked, his face alive and charged with the approaching storm.

"I'm just glad I'm on solid ground. Storms at sea are pretty terrifying." Sensing an opportunity, she asked, "Tell me about your work." She settled back into her chair and folded her hands in her lap as she waited for an explanation.

The waitress arrived, filled their glasses, and took their order.

"Hot tea for me, please," Lannie said to the waitress. Looking up at Jake, she explained. "I like to drink my tea slowly and reverently whenever I can, especially on easy nights like this."

"Iced tea may not be as sophisticated as hot tea, but in this Alabama heat, I'd rather be cool and refreshed than boiled alive like a crawfish." Jake turned his attention to Lannie and watched as her hair played around her face. "What would you like to know?"

"What do you do, exactly?" Her eyes never left his face.

"I read charts, plan courses, keep track of freight, and keep order…that's most of it."

"And of all of that, what would you say is the most important?"

"Order and then trust, and *in* that order. When men lose confidence in those who lead them, and when there is no trust, order falls into chaos. And danger for the crew is always the result."

A fresh wind blew off the bay waters, and Jake lifted his head to savor the salt-tinged breeze. The smell of rain was heavy on the air. He noticed Lannie and how she seemed to relax into the slow tune the band was playing.

Lannie felt the intensity of Jake's blue gaze on her as if it were something tangible. A slight shiver ran through her.

"Are you cold, or is that music doing something to you?"

"The music, I suppose. I love that song."

"'Unchained Melody'?"

She nodded, as the waitress brought their drinks. She took a sip of her tea, studying him. Oh, he was impressive. The muscles of his forearms strained against his light blue sleeves as he leaned forward on the table. But it was that air of confidence he possessed that impressed her the most. "It's always been one of my favorites."

"Let's not waste it then." He stood and pulled out her chair.

Lannie walked in front of Jake to the center of the floor, turned, and lifted her arms, draping them lightly around his neck. With her eyes half closed, she swayed side to side with him in rhythm to the music.

Lowering his head, Jake inhaled the haunting scent of the woman in his arms. His face brushed her hair as he pressed closer. They danced in complete harmony, each responding instinctively to the other. Both seemed surprised by the way they moved together, as if some inner sense of balance had been created between them that could not be achieved apart.

The rough, knotted cord Lannie had felt around her throat for months seemed to slip from her neck. The weight of her circumstances fell at her feet as Jake held her in his arms. She inhaled deeply and breathed out a sigh, smelling the fresh scent of him and feeling safe enclosed in his strong arms. Sliding a hand to her chest, she toyed with the medallion around her neck.

He watched her hand and with a small smile, lifted the medallion from her chest. "I really miss this," he said, rubbing it with his thumb before releasing it.

In one smooth movement, she lifted it from around her neck and gave it to him. "It's yours to wear...for your next journey, whenever that will be."

A shadow of sadness fell over his face. "Tomorrow," he whispered and glanced up at the sea. All shades of light on the water seemed to vanish, replaced by dismal gray. "I can't take your silver leaf. Besides, it's missing the most important part."

"And what's that?"

"The memory that was attached to it; it's just gone, faded. Memories do that, you know. You have to constantly refresh a memory," he stated matter-of-factly.

Lannie cocked her head slightly and looked up at him with a question in her eyes. "So, how do you refresh a memory?"

"I'm glad you asked." He slowly lifted his rough hand to her face, tilting it up even higher as his eyes locked onto hers. His arm pulled her close against his chest as he lowered his head to meet her lips.

A sound escaped her lips as she responded to Jake's deepening kiss. The stubble on his darkened jaw felt good pressing into her skin. Reaching around his neck, she ran her fingers through his hair, lifting it away from his collar. Rain began pelting them, and the music stopped. People scrambled around trying to take cover from the sudden onslaught of rain. But Jake and Lannie never moved. Soaked to the skin, the couple remained entwined in their kiss until the waitress tapped on Jake's shoulder, breaking the spell. He reluctantly pulled away and looked over his shoulder. The waitress stood with a dripping umbrella, staring at the couple. "I've moved you to a table inside," she said loudly, over the noise of the rain. Turning, she pointed to the window.

"We'll have our dinner to go if that's alright. I'm afraid we might catch pneumonia if we go inside in these wet clothes. Not to mention the mess we'll make on your floors."

The waitress smiled. "I'll pack it up for you and bring it out to your car."

Looking down at Lannie, he saw the same look of surprise on her face that was mirrored on his own. They just stood there in the pelting rain, staring at each other and blinking away the water from their eyes.

Dragging her eyes away from the attractive crease near Jake's mouth was proving to be difficult. Reluctantly, she looked away and saw that they were drawing a crowd.

Jake glanced at the window where amused onlookers watched the drenched couple. Twisting his lips to hide his smile, he said, "I guess now that we've made a name for ourselves here at Pap's Cove, we can leave." Wrapping her hand in his, he led her to the truck and helped her inside. The truck moved under his weight as he hopped in and cranked it up, flipping on the heat to stave off the chill. "Here," he reached behind the seat and pulled out a blanket.

She faced him squarely. Her lower lip began to tremble as she wondered briefly if this was what it was like to let someone else take the lead.

Jake dropped the blanket over her shoulders and pulled it around on each side, tucking it in. But as his hands closed over the soft flesh of her shoulders, all resolve went flying out the window. Reluctantly, he dropped his hands. *What is wrong with me? I'm acting like a teenage boy around this girl.* Clearing his throat, he stared out the windshield and then said, "I'm...sorry that I'm not going to be here for you. I know it's a bad time for me to leave. I volunteered several days ago to help out a captain friend who's having surgery. I jumped at the chance to captain his ship."

"You're not responsible for me, Jake. It's good that you're helping out a friend. And, *never* apologize for loving what you do, especially to me. I feel the same way about what I do for a living and I don't care if other people understand it or not. It's just who I am, and it's who you are," Lannie replied. She sensed an uneasiness in him and wasn't sure what had caused it. "Speaking of being passionate about what you do, I'm also leaving in the morning."

His head whipped around. She certainly had his full attention now. A strange expression came over Jake's face as he intensely regarded her. He captured her attention and held it. His initial surprise had given way to something else; something that caused Lannie more than a little curiosity.

"Leaving? Where are you going?" he asked, trying to keep a casual tone while his heart began picking up speed.

"Charleston, South Carolina. It's actually on the outskirts of town, near the marshes."

Swallowing hard, Jake nodded. "Charleston...beautiful city. Any particular reason you're going there?"

"Well, Samuel called while I was getting ready to go out and asked if I'd be interested in going on a little road trip for a few weeks. He and Madeline are going up to visit Samuel's brother, Jude. He said that a friend of his called weeks ago and told him about some property that's for sale. It joins his land and has an old, abandoned house on it. Samuel's buying the property and said I could have everything in the house—all that we can haul back in his trailer, that is. Inventory is running a little low at the shop. I've been a little preoccupied lately with other things."

That same streak of jealously began to surface as Jake tried, but failed, to tap it down.

"So…are you friends with Jude?"

"I wouldn't say we're friends, but he's a nice guy and we've always gotten along. He's never had much to do with anyone other than Samuel's wife, Madeline. He had only scraps of time left for everybody else. Jude and Madeline are best friends, have been all their lives. In fact, they're so close that sometimes Samuel has a hard time with it. I think he gets a little jealous of their relationship. He told me once that they communicate on a different level than most mortals."

"That must be a terrible feeling…jealousy. Poor guy, I feel for him."

"Yeah, well, Samuel also knows that he and Madeline share a love that goes way beyond friendship. He's told me that much."

After a long pause, Jake said, "I understand your need to get away. I've felt that way before, too." An image of Belinda flashed through his mind.

"Mostly, I need a change of scenery, and something tells me this trip may be just the right medicine for me. Everything in me wants to run away, but deep down I know this is home. Beauchene is where I belong. It's just sad for me right now."

A tap sounded on the window, breaking the silence. Jake lowered the window, reached in his back pocket, and pulled out a few bills. "Keep the change, and thank you." Placing the bag between them, he reached up, put the truck in gear, and slowly eased away, his mind too disturbed for him to speak.

Chapter 26

Samuel Warren slowly bumped over the sand and crushed shell road, which ran through a lane of oaks and twisted gray cedars, until the abandoned house came into view. They had arrived at Samuel's South Carolina home late yesterday evening. The trip up had been enjoyable as Lannie got to witness firsthand the dynamic between Samuel and his new bride, Madeline. It was plain to see they were perfect for each other and deeply in love, but seeing them together made her think of Jake all the more, something she'd promised herself she wouldn't do. The night before, it had taken four hours and two cups of Sleepy Time tea to settle her mind down enough to fall asleep. Her thoughts had been on Jake, then Sadie, then Jake again over and over until she'd finally collapsed in exhaustion.

The faded white outhouse with its blank stare seemed to call to her. A rush of emotions flooded her as memories from the past seemed to press in on her. But, they were not *her* memories. A melancholy feeling invaded her as she looked around the abandoned homeplace. Goose bumps covered her flesh, whether from fear or nostalgia, she didn't quite know.

"I see this place is getting to you already," Samuel commented. "I told Madeline you would pick up on the place as soon as you saw it...and I was right."

"I know there's a story here...so what is it?" Lannie looked him in the eye as she waited for an answer.

Samuel pulled up next to the house and parked the truck. "Now Lannie, if I told *you* there would be no way you'd ever let me bulldoze this old house down. I'd have a protest on my hands. I can see it now: you chained to the front door and the media swarming." He got out of the truck and slammed the door. Reaching into the truck bed, he lifted out a cooler. "Maddie packed a lunch for y'all," he said through the open truck window.

"Y'all?" Lannie stepped out of the truck, never taking her eyes off Samuel. With his head turned like that, he reminded her of Jake. Shaking her head, she rolled her eyes, disgusted with herself for thinking of the man every two minutes.

"My old friend, Mathias Williams, is coming out to help you. This kinda stuff is right up his alley. He's involved with historic preservation ordinances in Charleston, but he's an architect by trade." Samuel set the cooler on the porch. "Don't let his easy manner fool you; the man's loaded with wisdom. Here he comes now."

Samuel stepped to the lane and waited as the silver Tahoe rolled to a stop and Mathias got out. Gray hair encircled Mathias's dark head like a halo. Lannie watched as he paused, looking up at the house. His face clouded with a play of emotions.

Samuel shook his head slowly. "Oh no, this is definitely not good. I just saw that same look on Lannie's face not two minutes ago." Samuel stepped up to his friend and clasped his shoulder. "Good to see you, my friend. Let me introduce you to a young lady that will most likely become your female counterpart. Lannie, step over here a minute."

Mathias's face softened at the sight of the girl as she approached. He rubbed his jaw and his brow creased. He spoke to Samuel, "She'll do."

Lannie didn't quite know what to think of the exchange, and she looked to Samuel for some clarification.

Flashing white teeth, Samuel broke into a wide grin as he said, "I thought you'd approve."

As if she'd passed some kind of initiation, Lannie watched as Samuel walked to his truck, unhitched the trailer, and, with a wave over his shoulder in their general direction, got in the truck and pulled away.

Turning her attention back to Mathias, she watched as he headed toward the front door, and then she fell into step behind him. Suddenly, she realized she'd not said the first word to the man. *He certainly knows how to communicate,* she thought. *He already has me following his lead.*

She followed him into the house and almost ran into his back as he stopped suddenly in the entry hall. Simultaneously, they looked up the staircase as a cold breeze passed through them. He looked back over his shoulder at Lannie as if to see if she caught that.

"Yes, I caught that, whatever it was," she said in a whisper.

Without a word, he stepped forward in a calm and watchful manner, looking over everything. They treaded lightly and respectfully throughout the house, careful not to disturb the surroundings. They gave only short responses to each other's comments as they came upon something of interest. It was obvious that they were both used to working alone and that they were comfortable with long lapses of silence.

Once outside, they looked at each other with understanding.

"Are you gonna tell him or should I?" Mathias asked, slapping his hands together to rid them of dust.

"I'll tell him. I think he's still a little bit afraid of me," Lannie said with a smirk. "But, I've got to tell you, I like having an expert by my side when it comes to telling someone they shouldn't tear down a place. Some folks get kind of testy."

His lips twisted into a wry grin. "Seems I remember a few times like that. Well, we might as well look in the barn or that old outbuilding for something to salvage."

Cobwebs hung across the corner of the door to the shed. It creaked loudly on its hinges as they pushed it open. The pungent odor of rusted metal and old dirt hit them as soon as they stepped inside. Weak sunlight filtered in through the small window panes as dust motes swirled in the stirred air. Looking around, they discovered a plethora of metal chairs and galvanized buckets, an old iron bed, and dozens of planters. A stack of folded patchwork quilts in a plastic zipper bag sat high on a self. "Jackpot!" Lannie announced with a smile.

Mathias reached down and lifted a heavy binder from the floor. "So, how long have you been a keeper of the past?" Gently, he turned the dusty pages, scanning their content.

Lannie shrugged, wondering how the man knew the name of the antique shop where she worked. Then she remembered Samuel and his meddling ways and dismissed the thought. "From the time I could pull a red wagon over to a trash pile, I guess."

He never looked up from the book in his hands. "Tell me, have you ever reached into one of those trash piles and pulled out something of value? Maybe something of great worth that, at the time, the owner hadn't realized was valuable?"

Lannie pulled a chair over to the shelves and stood on it to reach the bag of quilts. "All the time."

"And, after you restored it, has the owner ever come to you wanting it back?"

Pinching the corner of the plastic, Lannie pulled the bag of quilts down, catching it in her arms. "One time I found an old wooden rocker in an abandoned house. I cleaned it up and restored it, even upholstered a seat for it. It was one of my finest pieces. A woman came into our shop one day and wandered around for a while. I saw her come in, but I didn't see her go out. So, I began looking around for her. And then I saw her, crying and running her hand over the arm of the chair. I asked her if she was all right. She turned from the chair and looked up at me. Right then, I knew she had a history with the chair. She removed her hand and showed me a tiny carving in the rocker's arm. There, scrawled in the wood, was the word 'Mama.' I'd never noticed it before, but sure enough, it was there. The woman turned to me and said that she'd pay whatever I asked for the chair. It had once belonged to her mother, and she'd scrawled the word when she was a small child. It was priceless to her. Of course, after hearing that story, I gave it to her."

Mathias stood still, his hand frozen on the page as he stared across the room. "And how did you feel after the woman left?"

"Sad at first, and then, the more I thought about it, I felt a kind of joy in knowing that I'd helped her get her treasure back. And it belonged...to...her." Realization hit Lannie in the face like a blast of frigid air. She stepped down from the chair and slowly walked across the creaking boards and out the door.

Cedar trees clustered together a short distance from the shed, and Lannie made her way to them. They seemed detached from the flow of things and stood as if observing life from a distance. She plopped down on the ground and picked up a stick, tapping the ground as her thoughts swirled.

After a little while, Mathias walked over and placed the cooler down beside her in the shade. "Lunch?" he asked, plopping down across from her. The sounds of insects and frogs grew louder as he unpacked their lunch. "It's hard to believe that we're hearing only a part of the show. Many songs of insects are outside the range of human hearing. But I love them all, cicadas, katydids, grasshoppers. They always remind me of when I was a young man. They taught me a valuable lesson."

Curious, Lannie took the sandwich he offered and asked, "What lesson?"

"I always wanted to be George Washington Carver," he said, and laughed. "He was my idol. I studied that man and read all he'd ever written. Truth was, I wanted to be the rooster who stood on the fence post crowing for all the world to hear. I didn't want to be the insect nobody heard." He settled back against the cedar tree and took a bite of his sandwich. Swallowing, he added, "But, the Lord showed me grace, that wonderful provision we all need to be able to mature in Him. I began to see the humble nature of God in George Washington Carver, and it changed my life forever. Now, I sing my song for God alone, and I don't care who else, or even *if* anybody else, hears me."

A long moment passed as they ate their lunch. Lannie dug around in the cooler until she located a container of brownies. Popping the lid, she offered one to Mathias. "You remind me of an old friend of mine, Tilda Wheeler."

"That right?"

"Yeah. She noticed things around her, too. Sometimes I'd look around and she'd be staring off in the distance. Then she'd surprise me with some profound statement, as if the message just dropped on her from heaven above."

"I'd like to hear some of your friend's wisdom."

"Okay." Lannie threw her head back and looked up into the tree. "Who needs the shade? Not the tree. A tree is a covering for anyone seeking shelter from the heat of the day. We are supposed to be like Jesus, aren't we? Then you and I should be sure that we have grown outward far enough that we have become shade so that others might sit down under our cool shadows and be refreshed. God made you a shelter. Tribulations will come. The wind is going to blow, and if you don't grow deep and stretch down to the water, you will not be able to stand. Put your roots down so deep that only the voice of God can uproot you. Tap into the life-giving water of God's Word and refresh all that come to you seeking shade." Dropping her head, she looked directly at Mathias.

"Thank you, from the bottom of my heart, thank you. I can't tell you how much I needed to hear that."

"Consider us even." Lannie smiled knowingly at him. "Samuel is at his tricks again. I guess he's told you all about me."

"No, not even the half," Mathias replied, returning her smile.

Chapter 27

Lannie returned to Beauchene a little bit wiser and a lot more at peace with her circumstances. She stayed on the porch a lot in those days, just rocking and reading or watching the afternoon thunderstorms roll across the bay. She never grew tired of the smell of rain on the grass and the way the silver leaf tree shivered with pure delight in the shower.

It was late afternoon and the slanted sunlight cut through the trees, creating long shadows across the yard. Cicadas filled the thick, warm air as Lannie walked toward the shore. Weary from a busy day at work, she'd planned on a little walk to relax her muscles and clear her head.

"Fancy meeting you here," Brother Ignatius rasped, leaning heavily on his cane as he came upon Lannie. He walked the shore each evening for exercise and fresh air. "Sit, sit. You look tired, my dear," he said, gesturing with his cane toward a piece of drift wood.

The truth was Brother Ignatius looked like he could collapse any minute. "I don't mind if I do," Lannie said, taking a seat after wiping off the sand.

"I've been meaning to talk to you, Lannie, about something of importance." He eased his weight down on the log next to her. "Tilda Wheeler, her history is in that house...somewhere up under the eaves just waiting to be discovered. History doesn't care who finds it, but it's always unsettled until it finds the right hands, hands that will take the story and squeeze the good out of it."

Lannie was slow to respond, not sure what to say. "Do you know something I should know, Brother Ignatius?"

"Indeed. But I'm not at liberty to say. You'll have to discover the secret yourself and, hopefully, share it once you do."

More confused than ever, Lannie propped her elbow on her knee and placed her fist on her cheek. "I see...under the eaves, you say?"

He stabbed the sand with the rubber end of his cane. "If my memory serves me correctly."

Jake always felt the excitement of casting off at the beginning of every voyage. But today, he felt an excited restlessness as he stood on deck and watched as the ship headed toward home. The massive vessel moved into Mobile Bay as the white chop of the waves broke across the bow. She sliced through the water effortlessly, as if eager for the journey to end. Staring down at the water, Jake thought about how his life had changed since coming to Moss Bay. He sure never planned on feeling the way he did. Never had he looked forward to going home with such anticipation. The truth was he'd fallen in love with Lannie McPherson, and he wanted to be wherever she was.

As the weeks passed, then a full month, he knew without a doubt what he was dealing with. His thoughts revolved around Lannie nearly every minute of the day. He would smile when he thought about her spitfire grit and determination. He loved the way she gave herself so completely to whatever she did. She stood up to him, outsmarted him, and nearly drove him crazy with her graceful movements and her haunting scent. But there was a vulnerable side to Lannie as well, and it was that side that nearly drove him crazy, keeping him up at night. She was his *bon secure,* the safe harbor he'd been searching for all his life. Lannie had been handed betrayal, unexpected motherhood, and grief, but she never lost her faith in God or in love. Jake admired those qualities, but it was much more than that. He loved her, and it was just that simple.

On his way home from his long sea voyage, Jake was driving through the streets of Moss Bay when he noticed Lannie's SUV parked next to the curb of a vacant lot. He eased his truck behind her vehicle and got out. Following the sound of feminine voices, he peered through a brick archway and spotted Lannie and Telie. Casually he crossed his arms and leaned against the wall to enjoy the view.

Covered in slick mud, Lannie held tightly to the stone cherub, pushing with all her might as Telie dug at the base with a trowel, attempting to free the creature from its surroundings. The lichen speckled cherub sat pensively in its shady spot, as if unconcerned about the attempts being made to free it.

"It's a sight, isn't it?" Michael said, as he came up behind Jake.

"Wander around the streets of Moss Bay and you never know what you'll find just behind the high walls." He motioned with his head toward the mud-covered girls. "I'm not sure which one of them is more determined to unearth that poor creature, but, from the look of it, the cherub is winning the battle." Jake smiled back at Michael, thoroughly enjoying himself.

"You better watch it, Captain. Don't let them see you over here grinning. That smallest one isn't too sociable when she's working. And the other one, digging away with the trowel, won't mind hitting you with something, either. I've seen that determined look before...trust me."

Without even turning around, Jake knew Joe was walking up behind them as soon as the boy opened his mouth. He had an accent that would have placed him in rural Louisiana among the swamps and marshes.

"Well." Joe paused just long enough that you wanted to slap him into spitting out the rest of his sentence. "What's goin' on over here? Thought Telie needed us."

Jake spoke over his shoulder, "We're watching a battle of wills between a reluctant cherub and two determined mud angels."

Joe mumbled under his breath, "Guess that's what some folks call entertainment." He looked at the girls, shook his head, and then looked back at Jake. "Captain, I was needin' to talk to you 'bout something when you get a second."

Dragging his eyes away from the scene, Jake looked at Joe and cleared his throat. "Sure, Joe, what's on your mind?"

Joe adjusted his cap, pushing it off his forehead so he could look Jake in the eyes. He grew serious. "Me and Mindy, well, we're getting married."

"Congratulations! That's good news." Jake stuck out his hand and shook the boy's hand firmly, patting him on the back. "Does Lannie know?"

"Well, you see, that's my problem. Mindy don't want no one taking care of Sadie except Lannie. Not just while we're gone on this honeymoon, but even during the day while she works. But she's scared to death to ask her. You know Lannie. She's liable to haul off and smack Mindy if she has a mind to. Not sayin' I'd blame her none. I mean, after all Mindy put her through, but Mindy's changed." His hat inched forward as he scratched the back of his head. "You see, I'm in a hard spot. We want to leave this weekend for Gatlinburg, Tennessee, and get married in a chapel up there. Michael and Telie paid for us to have a nice honeymoon up there in the mountains, but Mindy won't go unless Lannie takes Sadie."

"You won't have a problem there, Joe. Lannie loves the little girl, and I can promise you she'll be thrilled to have her again." Looking back at Lannie, all slick with mud, he motioned with his head. "Go ask her now; you'll see what I mean. Trust me."

Joe took a deep breath and steeled himself, stepping past Jake. He walked toward Lannie and Telie with that slow, deliberate saunter that was signature Joe. Jake and Michael watched with keen interest as the girls stopped what they were doing and looked up, listening to Joe. Lannie grasped her chest as if trying to still the pounding of her heart, and then, without warning, she flung her arms around Joe and squeezed. He stood there like a limp ragdoll getting tossed about. After Lannie let go, she turned to Telie, and they held each other in a tight embrace. Joe made a break for it and got away before Lannie could catch him again.

"What did I tell you," Jake said smiling, never taking his eyes off Lannie.

Joe shook his head as he wiped the mud from his face and clothes. "Women...do you ever understand them?"

"No!" Jake and Michael answered simultaneously.

Lannie looked back over her shoulder and froze. There, leaning against the brick wall with his arms crossed over his chest watching her, was Jake. His eyes locked on hers, conveying something she understood without a single word passing between them. A slow smile spread across his face, as refreshing as a cool rain. Her heart began to beat wildly within her chest, and for the second time in less than ten minutes, she held her hand to her heart.

"Looks like you girls could use a little help," Jake said as he walked up to them.

"Jake," Lannie half whispered his name.

He loved the way she said his name with that breathy drawl that caused him to shiver. *You're in love with her, there's no denying it. If given the choice, you'd choose her over anything.* It was true, and he knew it. He would gladly give up his life for her, even the sea life. He'd do it...for her. His old guilt resurfaced. *Why didn't I feel that way when I was married to Belinda? I was a different man then; I have grown in the area of love. By the grace of God, I've changed,* came the answer in his heart.

Telie spoke up, "Lannie, can you and Jake take it from here? We're working next door, and I got a little sidetracked when I saw this cherub. I knew you would love the little guy." She wiped her hands down her jeans to remove some of the mud.

"Not a problem," Jake replied. "I've been hauling things in and out of that SUV all summer long. This is just one more treasure to add to the pile."

After loading the cherub into Lannie's SUV, Jake walked to his truck and with a wave, hopped in and headed for Beauchene. Hours later, Lannie had not made it back home. Now, with darkness approaching and still no sign of Lannie, he tried her cell phone only to hear it ring in her apartment next door. "That woman is going to cause me to gray before my time!" A quick call to Wren and he knew exactly where to go: the Parker Place.

Jake watched as Lannie bit her bottom lip in concentration. She twisted and turned the screwdriver in her hand. He was having a hard time remembering why he'd been mad at her. The sight of a tool in her delicate hands was just plain comical to him.

Lannie looked up, halting her pursuit of the crystal doorknob now hanging loosely by one screw. She saw the same maddening laughter in his eyes that drove her crazy. She went back to work, trying her best to ignore him but feeling the tension begin to build.

"Are you almost finished here?" Jake asked, as he pressed against the doorframe.

"Why, you need something?"

"No, it's just getting dark, and I think you need to finish up so you can get on home."

Lannie stopped what she was doing and stared at him. "Are you kidding me? Look, I don't have Sadie anymore, so you can quit worrying."

"I'm not worried about Sadie; I'm worried about you."

Had she heard correctly?

"I noticed some guys camping down the road, and it looked like they were drinking. You need to finish what you're doing and head back. It's not safe," he decided.

As she stood, she studied his face, noticing the hard line of his set jaw and decided to challenge him. "You," she jabbed her finger straight into his chest, "are not going to speak to me like I'm a child. I can handle myself."

For all his easy ways, Jake had steel at his core. Nothing moved the man once his mind settled on an action. "You *will* come with me."

Her mind grappled with his firm decision. She felt the warmth and strength of his hand on her shoulder and looked up into his eyes.

"Behave yourself, or I'll be forced to meet that challenge in your eyes," he said sternly.

"You sound real impressive saying that in that deep voice and all. It just so happens, I'll be finished here if you don't mind helping me with one more crystal doorknob."

"Glad to help." Jake adjusted his cap. "Tell me, what's so all-fired important about doorknobs? Can't you just buy them anywhere?"

She looked at him like he'd kicked her dog. "No, you can't. This one object establishes a kind of visual interest. It connects the past to the present. This simple crystal doorknob," she turned it over in her hand slowly and reverently, "will bring sparkle and add interest to a shadowed and overlooked door. It's important how you place a piece like this. You don't want it to end up looking like somebody's roadside cast-off."

A laugh escaped him. "Well, now that I see how it is, why don't we get all of them?"

She placed the screwdriver in his hand. "I'm glad I've helped you see the light. Too many people don't know the value of what they have."

"Obviously," he said bluntly, and his meaning was not lost on her.

She noticed a certain look in his eyes as he watched her, and it made her shiver with delight.

Chapter 28

The moon broke from behind a thick cloud and illuminated Jake's bedroom, spilling pale light across the floor. The next minute, his eyes came open, and he was suddenly alert. He heard a clink, then a thump. Easing out of bed, he reached behind the headboard and pulled out a pistol. Aiming it toward the ceiling, he stepped cautiously to the door and yanked it open, drawing the gun down on two very startled gray eyes.

"What are you doing? You could've been shot!" Jake lowered the weapon.

"Oh, you wouldn't shoot me. Who would you fuss with if I was gone?" she turned her attention back to the carved wooden box in her lap. "I found this in the attic. I was sound asleep, and the thought came out of nowhere. *Look under the window seat.* And, sure enough, I found this."

Jake glanced down at the gun in his hand, turned, and went to his room, carefully placing it back behind the headboard. A strange expression crossed his face as he stepped back to the doorway. "Whatever it is, couldn't it have waited until morning?" He was still a little shaken from drawing a gun on Lannie.

"No. Sit," she commanded, patting the step next to her.

He drew in a heavy, frustrated breath and plopped down next to her. He watched with mild interest as Lannie flipped through the contents of the box too rapidly for her to see anything. He recognized the workmanship of the wooden box as his father's. Then her fingers stilled. She stared down at an envelope and gently slid the letter from the box.

Lannie smoothed the letter in her lap and began reading. Tears filled her eyes, falling on the page as Jake looked on with growing concern. Coming to the end of it, she lifted the letter and handed it to Jake, wiping away her tears with her palms and sniffing softly.

More than a little baffled, he took the letter and began to read.

I trust God that whoever finds this letter was meant to. This is my confession. Many years ago, I found myself in a desperate state of being. My beloved husband, Daniel, died after a long eight-month illness. I was weak and tired and pregnant. As if that was not enough, I'd been diagnosed with breast cancer a few months earlier but had to postpone treatment because of the baby.

I was in a dark place. My "late in life" baby concerned me no small degree. Never had I been in such a frightening place. I sought the council of my dear friend and priest, Ignatius. Right or wrong, we devised a plan to save my baby and give him a life as my life was quickly draining away.

The baby boy was born during a hurricane on September 23rd. I named him Daniel Jake Chamberlain, giving him my maiden name to help with the transition. His birth certificate would read "Mother: Elizabeth M. Chamberlain." My brother, Saul, agreed to take the boy and raise him as his own. He promised me that he would see to it that my son would have every chance at a good life.

As the years passed, I grew stronger. So strong, in fact, that I became healthy once again and the cancer all but disappeared.

The boy grew into a fine young man under the care and watchful eye of my brother. I kept up with him and all of his accomplishments. I sent money for his education. I desperately wanted to be part of his life, but I knew it was too late. That door was shut, and as it shut, a window opened and a summer breeze blew in. That breeze was Lannie McPherson. I could not love her more if she was my very own flesh and blood.

So, you see, my home and all that I have in this world will one day belong to them, my children. I pray they come to love each other just as I love them.

While talking to Saul one Saturday evening, as was our habit, he informed me that Jake had been assigned to his first vessel, the Silver Leaf, *out of Norfolk, Virginia. God does move in mysterious ways.*

Elizabeth Matilda Wheeler

Jake folded the letter and sat there, staring straight ahead and not saying a word.

Biting a trembling lip, Lannie slipped her warm hand into his, covering it a moment before giving it a gentle, reassuring squeeze.

He grasped her hand, and they sat there, silently absorbing all that had been revealed. Then Jake spoke, his voice barely over a whisper. "I never imagined this. And to think, I was in the same room with my own mother and didn't even know it."

"I know," Lannie said, taking her hand and brushing back the hair from his forehead. The simple gesture touched something deep inside Jake. He put his arm around her, pulling her close, and whispered, "Thank you for telling me. It's hard to take, but even so, in my heart I know everything happened as it should."

Lannie's eyes flickered with concern, like a mother for a child. "Are you going to be...I mean, if you want me to..." She didn't know how to help or what to say. Feeling suddenly lost and helpless, she asked, "You want to watch a movie or something?"

Jake raised his eyebrows, "Sure."

The thought of Jake being by himself after receiving such news worried Lannie. She wasn't quite sure what she'd do, but she was determined not to leave him alone. "I'll make a snack."

"*You* have a TV?" he asked, unable to resist the temptation to tease.

"Of course, what do you take me for, Amish?" Standing, she crossed the hall and motioned for him to follow. "I even have a DVD player. I have a weakness for..."

"Don't tell me, love stories."

"Action movies like *Braveheart, The Patriot,* and a few others."

"Perfect."

Filling two tall, white glasses with Coke, Lannie handed one to Jake with a smile. "Here, take this and I'll get the popcorn."

"Whoa now," he said, throwing his hands up.

She followed his eyes to the white glass in her hands, then said, "Oh relax, Captain, I use these all the time."

He paused before taking the glass. "I think I may need to sign some kind of waiver or release before I take that glass."

"Oh hush," she teased, happy to see the smile on his face.

Taking a sip, he asked, "Did you put cherry juice in my Coke?"

She blushed slightly and looked away. "I got used to making what you like on board ship. Cornelius tacked a list on the refrigerator of the things you enjoy. Cherry Coke was one of them."

"How extensive was that list?"

The gray eyes moved slowly to meet his. "There wasn't room enough on the refrigerator to list *all* of your likes, Captain, so we stuck with food and drink only."

"I'm finding that my tastes are running more to a single serving of my favorite flavor these days, and not the flavor of the month."

She stared at him, not sure what to say to that, so she just smiled. After a moment, she said, "It's always good to know what you enjoy. That way you don't waste a lot of time spitting things out."

"Very true. So, are you and Jess Ray seeing each other?" Jake sat back on the couch and took a swig of his drink, trying hard to appear mildly interested.

"I like Jess Ray, and I respect him. He's a trustworthy officer and a good man, but I'm just not attracted to him."

Jake's brows lifted sharply. "Hmm, well tell me about your trip to South Carolina." She stepped into the kitchen to retrieve the bowl of popcorn and then sat down next to him on the couch. "I met a man, and I think we're going to be close friends."

"Oh?" Jake half turned to look at her but said none of the things that came to mind. His throat thickened and he swallowed hard.

"Uh-huh, his name is Mathias Williams, and he's an architect there in Charleston. He's a friend of Samuel's. As a matter of fact, Samuel introduced us." She sipped her Coke, unaware of Jake's growing discomfort. "Just when you think you're the only one in the world with certain…passions… along comes someone who feels the exact same way about the things you do." Lannie noticed that Jake was quiet. She turned to glance at him as she took a bite of popcorn and saw a strange look on his face. "What are you thinking about?"

"Nothing."

"Oh, I'm sorry, I forgot about the movie." She got up and slid a disc into the DVD player.

He was jealous, no doubt about it, but there was no way he was going to admit that to her. He could kick himself for taking that job and leaving her behind. If she'd fallen for some guy, he'd never forgive himself.

She paused, scanning the room. "Do you like to watch movies in the dark or with lights on?"

"It doesn't matter."

Lannie glanced briefly toward Jake, whose sudden sullen attitude confused her. Worry crossed her brow as she wondered at the change. Then, a thought hit her. "Yes, Mathias is a very distinguished gentleman. The city of Charleston even did a piece on him for black history month, and that piece hit every newspaper in the state! He told me that since he's semi-retired, he and his wife enjoy traveling around the countryside looking for interesting old places. I'd love to have the time and money to do that one day."

"I'll take you wherever you want to go. Just say when," Jake blurted out.

She waved her hand at him, as if to dismiss his comment, thinking he was teasing.

He caught her hand and held it tightly. "Lannie, I need to tell you something." A knock sounded at the door, interrupting him.

Glancing at the clock, Lannie noted the time, 12:28 AM. "Who could that be at this hour?"

"Stay here, I'll answer it." Jake got up and eased the door open. He stared down into the face of a young woman holding Sadie on her hip.

Upon seeing Jake, Sadie lifted her head from her mother's shoulder and stretched out her arms.

Jake gently lifted Sadie into his arms and said, "You must be Mindy."

Chapter 29

"Mindy! What's wrong?" Lannie shot up from the couch, putting the bowl of popcorn on the table with a bang. She hurried across the room to her sister.

Mindy began to cry. "Oh, I don't want Sadie to see me like this."

Lannie took control of the situation just like she'd always done when it came to Mindy. "Jake, can you take Sadie to her room and settle her into bed?" She led Mindy to the couch and sat her down.

Holding her face in her hands, Mindy cried, "I don't know what to do."

"What is it, Mindy?" Lannie asked directly. "Tell me."

"It's Dawson," she cried. "He's threatened to harm Sadie if I don't go back to him."

Jake stepped into the room, hearing the threat. "When did he tell you this?"

"Last week." Mindy's voice cracked as she held back tears. "I haven't told Joe. I'm just so embarrassed that I ever got mixed up with the likes of Dawson in the first place. Joe and I are supposed to get married on Saturday in Gatlinburg, but I can't leave Sadie! Not after this threat!"

Jake's calm, reassuring voice filled the room. "Yes, you can. We'll take care of Sadie. I promise you. Dawson won't get anywhere near her. I give you my word."

Lannie looked at Jake with new admiration and relief. It felt good to rely on someone else for strength in a crisis, and there was no better man than Jake Chamberlain to handle whatever happened to get tossed into your lap.

Moving to a chair, he plopped down, running a hand through his hair as he continued, "You have to tell Joe. He loves you and Sadie, and it's his responsibility to take care of you. You've got to trust him. Dawson is a coward; I sized him up the last time he was here. If he has the nerve to come around here, I'll handle it. And don't let Joe's easy-going manner fool you. He can take care of business, and he won't hesitate in defending you and Sadie."

Mindy's voice lowered. "I'm just so afraid. I've done too many stupid things in my life, and I'm afraid I'm about to do another one. I'd die if something happened to Sadie while I'm off on a honeymoon. I mean, I can't believe I've been so selfish all of my life, and now this is just another opportunity to abandon my child for my own interests. It just seems like a selfish act to me."

Lannie cleared her throat. "Mindy, everyone makes mistakes in life. If you've confessed it and asked God for forgiveness, then you need to receive His forgiveness and forgive yourself." Suddenly, Lannie understood her sister's fear with crystal clarity: she was afraid that she'd revert back to her old ways and that Sadie would suffer again because of her. "Put Sadie in God's hands, and in our hands, and trust. Go and marry the man you love, and when you get back,

Sadie will be here waiting for you to begin a new life. We'll always be here for you, and we'll help you in any way that we can. We love Sadie and want her to be in our life." *Did I just speak for Jake?* Without turning to see his expression, she felt his eyes on her.

"Oh, Lannie, I know God forgives me, but do you?"

"I forgave you a long time ago, you *and* Cade. But, that doesn't mean you get off scot-free. I insist that I have the same rights as I would if my husband were still alive. I want weekend visitations with Sadie at least once a month, maybe even twice a month. And Wren and I want to keep her down at the shop during the day while you work. We'll work out some sort of financial support, too."

"Deal," Mindy said, with tears streaming down her face. Reaching across the couch, she hugged her sister. "I've got Sadie's clothes in the car; I'll go get them."

"Just don't sling them all over the yard like you did the last time, would you?" The smile on Lannie's lips caused Mindy to chuckle.

"No more temper tantrums, promise. And, I know it will take time, but I'm going to prove to you that I'm a fit mother. I love Sadie and only want what is best for her, and I just happen to believe that she needs the two of you in her life." She smiled up at Jake, hesitating a moment before leaving the room.

Jake's presence lulled Lannie into a deep and restful sleep on the nights he was home. Sometimes she would wake to find a long shadow across the floor beside her bed. The moonlight outlined his form as he walked the porches at night as if he was on watch aboard ship. The feeling of security Jake brought to her was both strange and new, and she welcomed it.

Lannie relaxed thinking of Sadie sleeping peacefully in the house. An overriding sense of contentment seeped into her soul as she listened to the sounds of the night. The realization that her peace of mind was due largely to Jake's nearness didn't bother her. She liked it. In fact, she was growing to more than like it.

The sun touched the corners of the clothesline as an easy breeze lifted the white sheets, filling them with sweet air.

"Where'd you get that pretty colored skin?" a voice, honey warm and smooth, called from nearby.

Turning suddenly, Lannie spied her neighbor, Theda, standing with her hands balled into her apron pockets, her buttery skin gleaming in the sun.

"Good morning, Theda. I didn't hear you pull up."

Not one to be sidetracked from her original thought, Theda continued, "It's a soft gold, like my Lilly's skin."

Lannie smiled tenderly at Theda, watching her sparkling eyes shift to take in the tiny form of Sadie napping on a quilt. She thought back on Theda's life and how she'd lost her baby over thirty years ago, a baby conceived by force with the wealthiest businessman around those parts, Tom Bennett. After Tom's recent passing, many stories came to light, including the revelation that Tom was actually Michael Christenberry's biological father. As specified in Tom's will, all of his children were to receive an equal share in Bennett Shipbuilding Company. Under those conditions, Theda was now the recipient of her daughter's share of the business.

Reaching down into the laundry basket, Lannie pulled out a damp sheet and snapped it in the air. "As far as I know, Theda, I'm kind of a mixture of many cultures. French, Spanish, European, and who knows what else. I think they call us 'Creoles of Color.'"

"Well, child, we're all colored. Some are colored light, some are colored dark, but we're all colored." She shuffled her feet forward and sat down on a metal glider placed near the back porch. "Yes sir, the Lord sure does love to stir up His paint pots. Now you take my girl Telie, she's warm like sunshine, but you, you're moonlight, all glowin' like the moonflowers."

"You want a Coke, Theda? I'm going to have one."

"Oh that sounds nice."

"Well you just wait right here. I'll go get us one, and we can talk."

Theda waved her hand in the air as Lannie passed. "You go get that drink, and then we're gonna talk about that good lookin' man who lives here."

"Theda! You ought to be ashamed of yourself!" Lannie scolded her with her eyes. "Jake is my neighbor. Don't let your imagination run away with you." She looked at the woman and, seeing the mischief in her eyes, continued, "You need to lay off the soap operas."

"I may be old, girl, but I ain't dead." A hoot came from Theda's lips. "Go on now so you can get back and we can talk some about it."

Looking around, Lannie didn't see Theda's car. "Where is your car?" she asked, turning her attention back toward Theda.

"I walked down here."

"You did what? You walked?"

"Oh, quit your fussin'. You sound just like my niece. She's a lawyer, you know. All that fancy education put notions in her head. Look here," Theda lifted a lanyard from around her neck. "This thing is what calls for help if I was to fall. But my niece said it don't work if I leave the yard. Now, shouldn't you be able to leave your own yard if you have a mind too?"

"Theda, you must listen to your niece. She's only trying to protect you. What if you fall? With that little button you can press it and someone will come to help." Her eyes widened slightly, then her brow furrowed in worry as she stepped up on the back porch. "We'll have a Coke, and then I'm driving you home after our visit."

"No, thank you, I can walk."

Before Lannie could protest, she heard Jake's truck coming down the road. From a distance, she watched as a cloud of white dust rose from behind the wheels. "What if I ask Jake to take you home?"

"I should've put on some lipstick if that man's gonna take me home. I think I'm gonna limp just so he'll put his big strong arm around me." Theda's shoulders shook with a chuckle.

Shaking her head, Lannie said with affection, "Theda, you're a mess. Will you please watch Sadie for a minute?"

As Jake rounded the corner of the house, Theda demurely folded her hands in her lap and stared down at them. She'd been talking to Telie, and they'd figured out the man with the little bit of information Lannie had shared about him. Her voice was soft on the air, but her words found their mark.

"People give pain, make you cry, make you want to stop livin', but God and place heals hurt. Find your place, a place to sooth what hurts you in this hard world. And, when you find it, don't ever let it go."

Jake reached into his pocket for his pipe. From the looks of it, this was going to evolve into a long conversation. "Samuel Johnson said it best when he said, 'When men come to like a sea-life, they are not fit to live on land.' Based on my experience, I would tend to agree with the man."

Theda could hardly contain her words. She leaned closer to Jake, who had taken a seat next to her and was about to touch the flame to his pipe. "Oh, we've had our share of hardship, me and you, don't I know it. But, we're stronger for them troubles...better people, too. Yes, better people and have a heap more love in our hearts for others than before all them hurts came to us. I don't want no part of a life without me lovin' somebody, and I ain't talkin' 'bout no boat or no water neither, but a real live human being—somethin' that can love you back."

Lannie caught the slightest scent of vanilla tobacco on the air as it fluttered the kitchen curtains. She knew Jake was near. Grabbing an extra Coke from the refrigerator, she placed it on a tray and, with a bounce of her hip on the screen door, walked out into the yard.

At the sound of the slap of the screen door, Jake turned his thoughts onto a fresh track, considering the girl that approached him in a fresh light. "Someone once told me that there was nothing in this world like sleeping between sun-dried sheets," he remarked casually. "I must admit, I've never had the pleasure."

Something about the way he said that made her shiver. Or, was it the look in his eyes? "Here, have a drink to cool down." Lannie presented the tray with three ice-filled glasses and a plate of brownies.

He eyed the glasses suspiciously. "Are these safe?" he questioned, the meaning of his comment was not lost on Lannie.

"They're safe, just plain old Tupperware tumblers. No history, none that I'm aware of anyway."

With a hint of a wink in his eyes, he took the glass and gulped down his drink, wiping the corner of his mouth with the back of his hand. He scanned the girl, taking in her fresh, natural look, a look he was still trying to reconcile with the one of L. B., assistant to the chief steward, on board his vessel. He found himself fascinated with the woman who had come into his life with her unquenchable spirit. She was unlike all the other women he'd ever known. Other than her disguise on ship, with Lannie, everything was out in the open. There wasn't a pretentious bone in her body, but an easy, natural thing that Jake was finding hard to resist. She did something to him, and he knew it. He drank her in like a thirsty man in front of a fresh spring.

Theda idly traced the rim of her tumbler with her finger and then spoke up. "I'm just a small pea in this big ol' garden, but I do know this: love always finds a way. Now I need you to carry me home, Jake. I got to watch my program." She released a long sigh as she scooted to the edge of her seat.

"Here, let me help you." Jake handed the empty glass back to Lannie and in one smooth movement, reached around Theda and gently lifted her to her feet.

As Theda stood, she took one more sip of her Coke before handing the glass back to Lannie and winked at her with a mischievous grin on her face. "Nice talkin' to you, girl. You come see me, now." And with that, Jake took her arm and led her to his truck.

Chapter 30

A late evening thunderstorm dissipated over the coastal landscape. In the aftermath of the storm, a hush fell over everything as steam rose from the surrounding grounds and rooftops of the sea cottage and the main house.

After a light supper of cream cheese and crumbled bacon sandwiches, Lannie scooped up Sadie and headed for the bathtub. After giving her a bath, she rubbed her dry with a big, fluffy towel, slathered her pink skin with baby lotion, and dressed her in pajamas. They snuggled together in Sadie's tiny bed, and Lannie whispered low, "What story would you like to read tonight? *Good Night Moon*?" Inhaling the sweet fragrance of her skin, she tugged at a white curl of downy hair, watching it spring back into form.

Sadie pulled out another book, *There's a Fly in my Ear*, and began tracing the page looking for the hidden bug.

"Oh look, you found the dragonfly! You are *so* smart. Can you say dragonfly?"

Sadie shook her head.

"Well, dragonfly is a hard one. Can you say dog?"

A soft, kittenish sound came from Sadie's parted lips as she formed the word. "Dog."

Grabbing the little girl in a tight hug, Lannie squealed with delight. "You did it, you did it! Come on, let's go tell Jake."

Rapping on Jake's door, Lannie held Sadie on her hip as she waited impatiently to tell him the news. As the door opened, Lannie blurted out in a rush of words, "Sadie said dog!"

River faced them with a smirk on her face. "Oh my, why that's just wonderful," she exclaimed, her voice full of sarcasm. "You have a real genius on your hands."

Lannie cleared her throat, fighting the conflict raging within her. She smiled lamely at her cousin and forced herself to respond politely. "May I speak with Jake, please?"

"He's...uh, not available," she said with a sly smile. "But I'll tell him you dropped by."

The door shut in Lannie's face as she stood there, fighting the urge to kick it in and demand to see Jake. Just then, she heard the water pipe whistle and bang and knew he was probably in the shower. "Jake's taking a shower, Sadie. We'll come back tomorrow to tell him how smart you are."

The gritty sound of a shovel came through the kitchen window as Lannie swiped back the curtain. Jake was digging a hole, a deep hole. *What is he doing?* she wondered as she slowly wiped down a plate. She continued to observe him through the parted curtains, watching him as he unloaded beams from the bed of his truck. Just then, River pulled up, got out of her car, and slammed the door, mouthing words all the way over to Jake.

Jake's shovel slammed deep in the rich soil. He turned and faced River squarely, saying something to her. After saying his piece, he turned again to the task of digging, effectively dismissing her.

Lannie lowered her feet to the kitchen floor, unaware that she'd been standing on her tiptoes as she watched the exchange. A movement caught her attention through the screen door, and she glanced over at Cornelius. He also had witnessed the exchange, only he was within earshot. He was looking at Lannie, blowing a tuneless whistle through his teeth as he raised his eyebrows. Whatever was said, it was enough to cause River to leave in a huff.

Lannie watched Jake work in the fading light until she began to recognize a sturdy, wooden swing set take shape. He had stepped into the barn, so she had a chance to observe his handiwork. Cornelius had helped Jake set the beams before he'd driven off toward town. As she was looking over the swing set, she heard the shrill and alarming squawk of the guinea fowl, sounding out a warning.

Jake tightened his grip on his rifle, stepping from the barn as Dawson's car came into view. The slap of a screen door caught his attention, and he saw Lannie come out, armed with his pistol; he was beginning to have second thoughts about giving her the gun. From the determined look on her face and the way she bit her tongue, she was bent on shooting the man. Dawson got out of the car, started for the porch, and then froze when he saw Lannie.

Jake took a deep breath and stepped near the man, holding the barrel of his rifle squarely at Dawson's chest. "You need something, Dawson?" Jake asked, as he observed the man who was standing there in startled silence.

Lannie yelled across the yard, "Step back Jake, I'm going to shoot him, but don't go too far. I'll need your help to drag him in the house." Her finger squeezed the trigger several times, but the gun didn't fire. "What is wrong with this gun?"

Jake spoke low and matter-of-factly to Dawson, "If she ever finds the safety, you're a dead man."

With slack-jawed surprise, Dawson threw up his hands and slowly backed away, glancing toward Jake. "Is she serious?"

Jake's eyes never wavered. "Never more. Are you that big of a fool to come between a mama grizzly and her cub?"

"That ain't even her child!"

"Tell that to the grizzly."

Without hesitation, Dawson turned on the heel of his boot, jumped into his car, and took off, never looking back.

Jake casually stepped up on the porch, propped his rifle against the wall, and removed the pistol from her hand. "Lucky for him you didn't find the safety."

After placing the pistol on the table, he turned and flashed a smile so brilliant that Lannie felt its impact all the way to her toes. He leaned a shoulder against the door frame as he looked at her. She felt the air charge between them. It was a full moment before Lannie released her breath.

Jake eased closer. "The way I look at it, God spared that man today. Guess His mercy extends to even the likes of someone like Dawson. He just received a second chance. I hope he makes the best of it."

Lannie's jaw firmed. "He'd best stay away from here if he knows what's good for him."

He chuckled and pushed off the door frame before stepping into the house. "Lannie, you certainly know how to keep things interesting around here. But, next time," he warned softly, "wait until someone poses a real threat first. That way you'll stay out of jail and an innocent man stays alive a little longer. I hear those orange jumpsuits the inmates wear are kind of scratchy." Grabbing his rifle, he reached down and collected the pistol from the table. "As long as I am around, I'll keep these with me...for safe keeping."

It was nearly a month after the incident with Dawson. Lannie had heard that a few of the townspeople reported seeing him as he flew into town on the afternoon of their confrontation. They watched him pack in a hurry and leave without so much as a word to anyone.

Joe and Mindy returned from their honeymoon more starry-eyed than ever. They'd vowed to God and each other to build the best life possible for their little family. With the help of their loved ones, they felt sure they would make it.

Jake found himself alone in the barn, sharpening a blade on the lawn mower. He was glad to have some menial task to keep his attention. Lately, he was having difficulty concentrating on even the smallest chore, and it aggravated him.

The barn was quiet, except for an occasional giggle drifting on the early autumn air and the rhythmic sound of a squeaky swing. He paused by the barn door and watched as Lannie pushed Sadie into the air in the swing.

Every now and then, everything seems just right, the way it should be, and this was one of those times. Jake leaned against the barn door and took in the sight. Cocking his head to one side, he carefully studied them. A light shone from his eyes. They were his girls, whether they knew it or not. *Maybe Theda is right. Shouldn't a man love something that can love him back? Maybe we're not fit to bear the burden of life alone. Maybe, just maybe, we're meant to give love and receive love and enjoy the simple pleasures of life scattered all around us. Things like swing sets and lightning bugs and fresh, sun-dried sheets...simple pleasures to be claimed by those with the eyes to see them. Lannie has those eyes,* he thought. Suddenly, he knew exactly what he needed to do.

Mindy and Joe had arrived to pick up Sadie, taking her home. The blue feeling Lannie sometimes felt when Sadie left was quickly replaced by gratitude when she really thought about it. It was evident that Sadie was happy. She could see it in the little girl's eyes. But most importantly, Sadie had a mother's love; something she knew had tremendous value.

Stepping down the back porch steps with a laundry basket full of sheets, Lannie sensed a change in the air. Autumn had always held the feeling of melancholy for her, but this was something different, and she couldn't quite put a finger on it.

Rounding the corner of the house, Jake caught sight of Lannie near the clothesline and stopped. As he looked at her, hanging out sheets with the late afternoon sun shining in her hair, he was astonished. A new awareness had begun to open to him, one of home and place and loved ones. He stared as if seeing a vision, afraid that if he blinked it would vanish from sight.

Lannie glanced over her shoulder, arms held high with a clothespin between her fingers, and she froze, feeling like the breath had been knocked out of her. At the same time everything became so clear; she realized in the depths of her spirit that he was her one living and breathing necessity. She dropped her hands and faced him, looking at him straight on.

And so they stood there, looking at each other until they grew restless and began moving toward one another. It was as if keeping their lives separate for so long had finally given way to the invisible pull of the current.

"I've got a proposition for you," Jake said, his eyes taking in the flush of her face.

"Oh? Let's hear it?"

He cleared his throat. "I'd like to see you, Lannie, and *only* you. Will you consider it?"

She tried to pull her reeling thoughts into some kind of order. But as she looked at him, she knew what her answer would be.

"Now, listen to me," he supplied, in a low and husky voice. "I'll wait for you no matter how long it takes. And, when you feel it's an acceptable time, I want to take you out and get to know *all* the many sides of Lannie McPherson. Because wherever you are is the place I most want to be."

Smiling into his eyes, she lightly traced the outline of his rough jaw and knew without a single doubt in her mind that Tilda Wheeler had somehow arranged the whole affair. And for that, she would be eternally grateful. She stood on tiptoes and slipped her arms around his neck, giving him his answer.

His mouth lowered to take hers as if sealing the matter for good. A sense of perfect peace enveloped her as he wrapped his strong arms around her. Lannie pulled her head back and smiled, catching sight of a gleam of silver against his chest. A sudden breeze blew up. This time, when he lowered his lips to deepen the kiss, she was sure that she heard a long-held sigh escape from the depths of the silver leaf tree.

CPSIA information can be obtained at www.ICGtesting.com
Printed in the USA
BVOW021411020613

322143BV00010B/187/P

9 780741 477262